MANY DIMENSIONS

D0974451

by the same author

★

ALL HALLOWS' EVE
DESCENT INTO HELL
THE PLACE OF THE LION
WAR IN HEAVEN
THE GREATER TRUMPS

MANY DIMENSIONS

by

CHARLES WILLIAMS

WILLIAM B. EERDMANS PUBLISHING COMPANY
GRAND RAPIDS, MICHIGAN

© 1937 Charles Williams
© 1949 Pelligrini & Cudahy
All rights reserved

This edition first published in 1970 by
Wm. B. Eerdmans Publishing Co.
2140 Oak Industrial Drive N.E., Grand Rapids, Michigan 49505 /
P.O. Box 163, Cambridge CB3 9PU U.K.

Printed in the United States of America

20 19 18 17 16 15   20 19 18 17 16 15

ISBN 978-0-8028-1221-6

www.eerdmans.com

CONTENTS

Chapter One

THE STONE

"Do you mean," Sir Giles said, "that the thing never gets smaller?"

"Never," the Prince answered. "So much of its virtue has entered into its outward form that whatever may happen to it there is no change. From the beginning it was as it is now."

"Then by God, sir," Reginald Montague exclaimed, "you've got the transport of the world in your hands."

Neither of the two men made any answer. The Persian, sitting back in his chair, and Sir Giles, sitting forward on the edge of his, were both gazing at the thing which lay on the table. It was a circlet of old, tarnished, and twisted gold, in the centre of which was set a cubical stone measuring about half an inch every way, and having apparently engraved on it certain Hebrew letters. Sir Giles picked it up, rather cautiously, and concentrated his gaze on them. The motion awoke a doubt in Montague's mind.

"But supposing you chipped one of the letters off?" he asked. "Aren't they awfully important? Wouldn't that destroy the—the effect?"

"They are the letters of the Tetragrammaton," the Persian said drily, "if you call that important. But they are not engraved on the Stone; they are in the centre—they are, in fact, the Stone."

"O!" Mr. Montague said vaguely, and looked at his uncle Sir Giles, who said nothing at all. This, after a few minutes, seemed to compel Montague to a fresh attempt.

"You see, sir?" he said, leaning forward almost excitedly. "If what the Prince says is true, and we've proved that it is, a child could use it."

"You are not, I suppose," the Persian asked, "proposing to limit it to children? A child could use it, but in adult hands it may be more dangerous."

"Dangerous be damned," Montague said more excitedly than before, "It's a marvellous chance—it's . . . it's a miracle. The thing's as simple as pie. Circlets like this with the smallest fraction of the Stone in each. We could ask what we liked for them—thousands of pounds each, if we like. No trains, no tubes, no aeroplanes. Just the thing on your forehead, a minute's concentration, and whoosh!"

The Prince made a sudden violent movement, and then again a silence fell.

It was late at night. The three were sitting in Sir Giles Tumulty's house at Ealing—Sir Giles himself, the traveller and archaeologist; Reginald Montague, his nephew and a stockbroker; and the Prince Ali Mirza Khan, First Secretary to the Persian Ambassador at the court of St. James. At the gate of the house stood the Prince's car; Montague was playing with a fountain-pen; all the useful tricks of modern civilization were at hand. And on the table, as Sir Giles put it slowly down, lay all that was left of the Crown of Suleiman ben Daood, King in Jerusalem.

Sir Giles looked across at the Prince. "Can you move other people with it, or is it like season-tickets?"

"I do not know," the Persian said gravely. "Since the time of Suleiman (may the Peace be upon him!) no one has sought to make profit from it."

"Ha!" said Mr. Montague, surprised. "O come now, Prince!"

"Or if they have," the Prince went on, "they and their names and all that they did have utterly perished from the earth."

8

The Stone

"Ha!" said Mr. Montague again, a little blankly. "O well, we can see. But you take my advice and get out of Rails. Look here, uncle, we want to keep this thing quiet."

"Eh?" Sir Giles said. "Quiet? No, I don't particularly want to keep it quiet. I want to talk to Palliser about it—after me he knows more about these things than anyone. And I want to see Van Eilendorf—and perhaps Cobham, though his nonsense about the double pillars at Baghdad was the kind of tripe that nobody but a broken-down Houndsditch sewer-rat would talk."

The Prince stood up. "I have shown you and told you these things," he said, "because you knew too much already, and that you may see how very precious is the Holy Thing which you have there. I ask you again to restore it to the guardians from whom you stole it. I warn you that if you do not——"

"I didn't steal it," Sir Giles broke in. "I bought it. Go and ask the fellow who sold it to me."

"Whether you stole by bribery or by force is no matter," the Prince went on. "You very well know that he who betrayed it to you broke the trust of generations. I do not know what pleasure you find in it or for what you mean to use it, unless indeed you will make it a talisman for travel. But however that may be, I warn you that it is dangerous to all men and especially dangerous to such unbelievers as you. There are dangers within the Stone, and other dangers from those who were sworn to guard the Stone. I offer you again as much money as you can desire if you will return it."

"O well, as to money," Reginald Montague said, "of course my uncle will have a royalty—a considerable royalty—on all sales and that'll be a nice little bit in a few months. Yours isn't a rich Government anyhow, is it? How many millions do you owe us?"

The Prince took no notice. He was staring fiercely and eagerly at Sir Giles, who put out his hand again and picked up the circlet.

9

"No," he said, "no, I shan't part with it. I want to experiment a bit. The bastard asylum attendant who sold it to me——"

The Prince interrupted in a shaking voice. "Take care of your words," he said. "Outcast and accursed as that man now is, he comes of a great and royal family. He shall writhe in hell for ever, but even there you shall not be worthy to see his torment."

"—said there was hardly anything it wouldn't do," Sir Giles finished. "No, I shan't ask Cobham. Palliser and I will try it first. It was all perfectly legal, Prince, and all the Governments in the world can't make it anything else."

"I do not think Governments will recover it," the Prince said. "But death is not a monopoly of Governments. If I had not sworn to my uncle——"

"O it was your uncle, was it?" Sir Giles asked. "I wondered what it was that made you coo so gently. I rather expected you to be more active about it to-night."

"You try me very hard," the Prince uttered. "But I know the Stone will destroy you at last."

"Quite, quite," Sir Giles said, standing up. "Well, thank you for coming. If I could have pleased you, of course. . . . But I want to know all about it first."

The Prince looked at the letters in the Stone. "I think you will know a great deal then," he said, salaamed deeply to it, and without bowing to the men turned and left the house.

Sir Giles went after him to the front door, though they exchanged no more words, and, having watched him drive away returned to find his nephew making hasty notes.

"I don't see why we need a company," he said. "Just you and I, eh?"

"Why you?" Sir Giles asked. "What makes you think you're going to have anything to do with it?"

"Why, you told me," Montague exclaimed. "You offered me a hand in the game if I'd be about to-night when the Prince came in case he turned nasty."

"So I did," his uncle answered. "Yes—well, on conditions. If there is any money in it, I shall want some of it. Not as much as you do, but some. It's always useful, and I had to pay pretty high to get the Stone. And I don't want a fuss made about it—not yet."

"That's all right," Montague said. "I was thinking it might be just as well to have Uncle Christopher in with us."

"Whatever for?" Sir Giles asked.

"Well . . . if there's any legal trouble, you know," Montague said vaguely. "I mean—if it came to the Courts we might be glad—of course, I don't know if they could—but anyhow he'd probably notice it if I began to live on a million—and some of these swine will do anything if their pockets are touched—all sorts of tricks they have—but a Chief Justice *is* a Chief Justice—that is, if you didn't mind——"

"I don't mind," Sir Giles said. "Arglay's got a flat-footed kind of intellect; that's why he's Chief Justice, I expect. But for what it's worth, and if they did try any international law business. But they can't; there was nothing to prevent that fellow selling it to me if he chose, nor me buying. I'll get Palliser here as soon as I can."

"I wonder how many we ought to make," Montague said. "Shall we say a dozen to start with? It can't cost much to make a dozen bits of gold—need it be gold? Better, better. Better keep it in the same stuff—and it looks more for the money. The money—why, we can ask a million for each—for what'll only cost a guinea or two. . . ." He stopped, appalled by the stupendous vision, then he went on anxiously, "The Prince did say a bit any size would do, didn't he? and that this fellow"—he pointed a finger at the Stone—"would keep the same size? It means a patent, of course; so if anybody else ever did get hold of the original they couldn't use it. Millions . . . millions. . . ."

"Blast your filthy gasbag of a mouth!" Sir Giles said. "You've made me forget to ask one thing. Does it work in time as well as space? We must try, we must try." He sat down, picked up the Crown, and sat frowning at the Divine Letters.

"I don't see what you mean," Reginald said, arrested in his note-taking. "Time? Go back, do you mean?" He considered, then, "I shouldn't think anyone would want to go back," he said.

"Forward then," Sir Giles answered. "Wouldn't you like to go forward to the time when you've got your millions?"

Reginald gaped at him. "But . . . I shouldn't have them," he began slowly, "unless . . . eh? O if I'm going to . . . then I should be able to jump to when . . . but . . . I don't see how I could get at them unless I knew what account they were in. I shouldn't be that me, should I . . . or should I?"

As his brain gave way, Sir Giles grinned. "No," he said almost cheerfully, "you'd have the money but with your present mind. At least I suppose so. We don't know how it affects consciousness. It might be an easy way to suicide—ten minutes after death."

Reginald looked apprehensively at the Crown. "I suppose it wouldn't go wrong?" he ventured.

"That we don't know," Sir Giles answered cheerfully. "I daresay your first millionaire will hit the wrong spot, and be trampled underfoot by wild elephants in Africa. However, no one will know for a good while."

Reginald went back to his notes.

Meanwhile the Prince Ali drove through the London streets till he reached the Embassy, steering the car almost mechanically while he surveyed in his mind the position in which he found himself. He foresaw some difficulty in persuading his chief, who concealed under a sedate rationalism an almost intense scepticism, of the disastrous chance which, it appeared to the Prince, had befallen the august Relic. Yet not to attempt to enlist on the side of the Faith such prestige and power as lay in the Embassy would be to abandon it to the ungodly uses of Western financiers. Ali himself had been trained through his childhood in the Koran and the traditions, and, though the shifting policies of Persia had flung him for awhile into the army and afterwards into the diplomatic service his mind moved with most ease in the romantic regions of myth. Suleiman ben Daood, he knew, was a historic figure—the ruler of a small nation which, in the momentary decrease of its two neighbours, Egypt and Assyria, had attained an unstable pre-eminence. But Suleiman was also one of the four great world-shakers before the Prophet, a commander of the Faithful, peculiarly favoured by Allah. He had been a Jew, but the Jews in those days were the only witnesses to the Unity. "There is no God but God," he murmured to himself, and cast a hostile glance at a crucifix which stood as a war memorial in the grounds of a church near the Embassy. " 'Say: for those who believe not is the torment of hell: an evil journey shall it be.' " With which quotation he delivered the car to a servant and went in to find the Ambassador, whom he discovered half-asleep over the latest volume of Memoirs. He bowed and waited in silence.

"My dear Ali," the Ambassador said, rousing himself. "Did you have a good evening?"

"No," the young man answered coldly.

"I didn't expect you would," his chief said. "You orthodox young water-drinkers can hardly expect to enjoy a dinner. Was it, so to speak, a dinner?"

"I was concerned, sir," the Prince said, "with the Crown of Suleiman, on whom be the Peace."

"Really," the Ambassador asked. "You really saw it? And is it authentic?"

"It is without doubt the Crown and the Stone," Ali answered. The Ambassador stared, but Ali went on. "And it is in the hands of the infidel. I have seen one of these dogs——"

His chief frowned a little. "I have asked you," he said, "—even when we are alone—to speak of these people without such phrases."

"I beg your Excellency's pardon," the Prince said. "I have seen one of them use it—by the Permission: and return unharmed. It is undoubtedly the Crown."

"The Crown of a Jew?" the Ambassador murmured. "My friend, I do not say I disbelieve you, but—have you told your uncle?"

"I reported first to you, sir," the Prince answered. "If you wish my uncle——" He paused.

"O by all means, by all means," the Ambassador said, getting up. "Ask him to come here." He stood stroking his beard while a servant was dispatched on the errand, and until a very old man, with white hair, bent and wrinkled, came into the room.

"The Peace be upon you, Hajji Ibrahim," he said in Persian, while the Prince kissed his uncle's hand. "Do me the honour to be seated. I desire you to know that your nephew is convinced of the authenticity of that which Sir Giles Tumulty holds." He eyed the old man for a moment. "But I do not clearly know," he ended, "what you now wish me to do."

Hajji Ibrahim looked at his nephew. "And what will this Sir Giles Tumulty do with the sacred Crown?" he asked.

"He himself," the Prince said carefully, "will examine it and experiment with it, may the dogs of the street devour him! But there was also present a young man, his relation, who desires to make other crowns from it and sell them for money. For he sees that by the least of the graces of the divine Stone those who wear it may pass at once from place to place, and there are many who would buy such power at a great price." The formal phrases with which he controlled his rage broke suddenly and he closed in colloquial excitement, "He will form a company and put it on the market."

The old man nodded. "And even though Iblis destroy him ——" he began.

"I implore you, my uncle," the young Prince broke in, "to urge upon his Excellency the horrible sacrilege involved. It is a very dreadful thing for us that by the fault of our house this thing should come into the possession of the infidels. It is not to be borne that they should put it to these uses; it is against the interests of our country and the sanctity of our Faith."

The Ambassador, his head on one side, was staring at his shoes. "It might perhaps be held that the Christians derive as much from Judah as we," he said.

"It will not so be held in Tehran and in Delhi and in Cairo and in Beyrout and in Mecca," the Prince answered. "I will raise the East against them before this thing shall be done."

"I direct your attention," the Ambassador said stiffly, "to the fact that it is for me only to talk of what shall or shall not be done, under the sanction of Reza Shah who governs Persia to-day."

"Sir," the Prince said, "in this case it is a crown greater than the diadem of Reza Shah that is at stake."

"With submission," the old man broke in, "will not your Excellency make representations to the English Government? This is not a matter which any Government can consider without alarm."

"That is no doubt so," the Ambassador allowed. "But, Hajji Ibrahim, if I go to the English Government and say that one of their nationals, by bribing a member of your house, has come into the possession of a very sacred relic they will not be in the mind to take it from him; and if I add that this gives men power to jump about like grasshoppers they will ask me for proof." He paused. "And if you could give them proof, or if this Sir Giles would let them have it, do you think they would restore it to us?"

"Will you at least try, sir?" Ali asked.

"Why, no," the Ambassador answered. "No, I do not think I will even try. It is but the word of Hajji Ibrahim here. Had he not known of the treachery of his kinsmen and come to England by the same boat as Giles Tumulty we should have known very little of what had happened, and that vaguely.

But as it is, we were warned of what you call the sacrilege, and now you have talked to him, and you are convinced. But what shall I say to the Foreign Minister? No; I do not think I will try."

"You do not believe it," the Hajji said. "You do not believe that this is the Crown of Suleiman or that Allah put a mystery into it when His Permission bestowed it on the King?"

The Ambassador considered. "I have known you a long while," he said thoughtfully, "and I will tell you what I believe. I know that your family, which has always been known for a very holy house, has held for centuries certain relics, and has preserved them in great secrecy and remoteness. I know that among them tradition has said that there is the Crown of the King, and that, but a few weeks since, one of the keepers was bribed to part with this Crown—if such it be—to an Englishman. I believe that many curious powers exist in such things, lasting for a longer or shorter time. And—because I believe Ali—I believe that it has seemed to him that a man has been here and there in a moment. But how, or whether indeed, this has been I do not know, and I do not desire to argue upon it with the English ministers." He shook his head. "I risked too much even when I permitted you semi-officially to try and buy it back from Sir Giles."

"But he would not sell it," the Prince cried.

"A very natural feeling," the Ambassador said, and added rather incautiously, "if I had it myself I don't suppose I should sell it."

"Then," the Prince insisted, "if your Excellency will do nothing, it is for me to act. There is a sin upon my house till I recover the Crown."

"And what will you do, my friend?" the Ambassador asked.

"I shall cause all my relatives and my acquaintances in Persia to know of it, and I will take such an oath that they will certainly believe," the Prince answered. "I will send the news of it through all the palaces and bazaars. I will cause

16

this sacrilege to be known in every mosque, and the cry against the English shall go from Adrianople to Hong Kong. I will see if I can do a little in all the places of Islam."

"You will make the English Government curious, I believe," the Ambassador said, "and you may kill a few soldiers. But I do not think you will recover the Crown. Also you will do these things against my will."

Hajji Ibrahim said suddenly, "By the Permission it was taken; by the Permission it will return. When the Unity deigned to bestow the Stone upon the King it was not that he might go swiftly from place to place. I think it shall return to the Keepers only when one shall use it for the journey that is without space, and I do not think that shall be you, my nephew, nor any of us. Let spies be set upon the infidels and let us know what they do. But do not let us wake the bazaars. I do not think that will help you at all."

"And the English Government?" the Ambassador asked.

"A soft word in the ear of a friend," the Hajji said. "Be very friendly with them—and that your Excellency may well do, for you are almost as one of them. But speak only of a relic and not of the virtues of the relic; seek peace and ensue it, as their scriptures say. The English will not have war for the sake of Giles Tumulty, unless their pride is touched." He rose to his feet. "The Peace be upon you," he said and went to the door.

Chapter Two

THE PUPIL OF ORGANIC LAW

"You ought to know by now," Lord Arglay said into the telephone, "that I can't possibly put any money into your companies. . . . Caesar's wife. . . . No, I am. . . . O never mind . . . Yes. . . . Certainly. . . . As much as you like. . . . Lunch then." He put the receiver back. "It's an extraordinary thing," he went on to Chloe Burnett, as she lifted her hands again to the typewriter, "that Reginald won't realize how careful I have to be of what my money is in. It's a wonder I have any private income at all. As it is, whenever I give a decision in a financial case I expect to be left comparatively penniless in a month or two."

"Does Mr. Montague want you to invest?" Miss Burnett asked.

"He wants me to give him five hundred, so far as I can understand," Lord Arglay said, "to put in the best thing that ever was. What is the best thing that ever was?"

Miss Burnett looked at her typewriter and offered no opinion.

"I suppose that I ought to think the Twelve Tables were," the Chief Justice went on, "officially—or the Code Napoléon —but they're rather specialist. And anyhow when you say 'that ever was,' do you mean that it's stopped being? Or can it still be? . . . Miss Burnett," he added after a pause, "I was asking you a question."

"I don't know, Lord Arglay," Chloe said patiently. "I never can answer that sort of question. I suppose it depends on what you mean by 'was.' But oughtn't we to get on with the rest of the chapter before lunch?"

The Pupil of Organic Law

Lord Arglay sighed and looked at his notes. "I suppose so, but I'd much rather talk. *Was* there ever a best thing that ever was? Never mind; you're right as usual. Where were we? The judgement of Lord Mansfield——" He began dictating.

There was, in fact, time for an hour's work before Mr. Montague arrived for lunch. Chloe Burnett had been engaged six months before by Lord Arglay as general intellectual factotum when he had determined to begin work on his *Survey of Organic Law*. When the Chief Justice was at the Courts she spent her time reducing to typed order whatever material Lord Arglay left ready for her the night before. But during the vacation, since he had remained in town, it had become a habit for them to lunch together, and neither Chloe's intention of withdrawing or Mr. Montague's obvious uneasiness caused Lord Arglay to break it.

"Of course you'll lunch here," he said to Chloe, and to Mr. Montague's private explanations that the matter in hand was very secret, "That's all right; two can spoil a secret but three make a conspiracy, which is much safer."

"And now," he said to his nephew after they were settled, "what is it? What do you want me to put my money in this time? I shan't, of course, but what's it all about?"

"Well, it's a kind of *transport*," Reginald said. "It came to me through Uncle Giles, who wanted me to help him in an experiment."

"Was it a dangerous experiment?" Lord Arglay asked.

"O I don't think *dangerous*," Montague answered. "Unusual perhaps, but not dangerous. When he came back from Baghdad this time he brought with him a funny kind of a thing, something . . . well, something like a crown and something . . . something . . ."

"Something not," said Lord Arglay. "Quite. Well?"

"Made of gold," Reginald went on, "with a stone—*that* size . . . in the middle. Well, so he asked me over to help him experiment, and there was a man from the Persian Embassy there too, who said it was what Sir Giles thought it was—at least, he'd bought it as being—but that doesn't matter. Well now, this thing—I know you won't believe it—it sounds so silly; only you know I did it. Not Sir Giles—he said he wanted to observe, but I did. The Persian fellow was rather upset about it, at least not upset, but a bit high in the air, you know. Rather frosty. But I'm bound to say he met us quite fairly, said he was perfectly willing to admit that we had it, and to make it clear to us what it was; only he must have it back. But that would have been too silly.''

As Mr. Montague paused for a moment Lord Arglay looked at Chloe. "It's a fact I've continually observed in the witness box," he said abstractedly, "that nine people out of ten, off their own subject, are incapable of lucidity, whereas on their own subject they can be as direct as a straight line before Einstein. I had a fellow once who couldn't put three words together sanely; we were all hopeless, till counsel got him on his own business—which happened to be statistics of the development of industry in the Central American Republics; and then for about five minutes I understood exactly what had been happening there for the last seventy years. Curious. You and I are either silent or lucid. Yes, Reginald? Never mind me, I've often been meaning to tell Miss Burnett that, and it just came into my mind. Yes?"

"O he was lucid enough," Reginald said. "Well it seems this thing was supposed to be the crown of King Suleiman, but of course as to that I can't say. But I can tell you this." He pointed a fork at the Chief Justice. "I put that thing on my head—" Chloe gave a small gasp—"and I willed myself to be back in my rooms in Rowland Street, and there I was." He stopped. Lord Arglay and Chloe were both staring at him. "There I was," he repeated. "And then I willed myself back at Ealing, and *there* I was."

Chloe went on staring. Lord Arglay frowned a little. "What

do you mean?" he said, with a sound of the Chief Justice in his voice.

"I mean that I just was," Reginald said victoriously. "I don't know how I got there. I felt a little dizzy at the time, and I had a headache of sorts afterwards. But without any kind of doubt I was one minute in Ealing and the next in Rowland Street, one minute in Rowland Street and the next in Ealing."

The two listeners looked at each other, and were silent for two or three minutes. Reginald leaned back and waited for more.

Lord Arglay said at last, "I won't ask you if you were drunk, Reginald, because I don't think you'd tell me this extraordinary story if you were drunk then unless you were drunk now, which you seem not to be. I wonder what exactly it was that Giles did. Sir Giles Tumulty, Miss Burnett, is one of the most cantankerously crooked birds I have ever known. He is, unfortunately, my remote brother-in-law; his brother was Reginald's mother's second husband—you know the kind of riddle-me-ree relationship. He's obscurely connected with diabolism in two continents; he has written a classic work on the ritual of Priapus; he is the first authority in the world on certain subjects, and the first authority in hell on one or two more. Yet he never seems to do anything himself; he's always in the background as an interested observer. I wonder what exactly it was that he did and still more I wonder why he did it."

"But he didn't do anything," Reginald said indignantly. "He just sat and watched."

"Of two explanations," Lord Arglay said, "other things being equal, one should prefer that most consonant with normal human experience. That Giles should play some sort of trick on you is consonant with human experience; that you should fly through the air in ten minutes is not—at least it doesn't seem so to me. What do you think, Miss Burnett?"

"I don't seem to believe it somehow," Chloe said. "Did you say it was the Crown of Suleiman, Mr. Montague? I thought he went on a carpet."

Lord Arglay stopped a cigarette half way to his lips. "Eh?" he said. "What a treasure you are as a secretary, Miss Burnett! So he did, I seem to remember. You're sure it wasn't a carpet, Reginald?"

"Of course I'm sure," Reginald said irritably. "Should I mistake a carpet for a crown? And I never knew that Suleiman had either particularly."

Lord Arglay, pursuing his own thoughts, shook his head. "It would be like Giles to have the details right, you know," he said. "If there was a king who travelled so, that would be the king Giles would bring out for whatever his wishes might be. Look here, Reginald, what did he want you to do?"

"Nothing," Reginald answered. "But the point is this." Confirming the Chief Justice's previous dictum he became suddenly lucid. "The Persian man told us that small fractions taken from the Stone—it's the Stone in the Crown that does it—have the same power. Now, if that's so, we can have circlets made—with a chip in each, and just think what any man with money would give to have a thing like that. Think of a fellow in Throgmorton Street being able to be in Wall Street in two seconds! Think of Foreign Secretaries! Think of the Secret Service! Think of war! Every Government will need them. *And we have the monopoly.* It means a colossal fortune— colossal. O uncle, you *must* come in. I want a thousand: I can get six hundred or so quietly—not a word must leak out or I could do more, of course. Give me five hundred and I'll get you fifty thousand times five hundred back."

Lord Arglay disregarded this appeal. "Did you say the other man belonged to the Persian Embassy?" he asked. "What did he want anyway?"

"He wanted it back," Reginald said. "Some sort of religious

idea, I fancy. But really Sir Giles only needed him in order to make sure it was authentic."

"If Giles thought it *was* authentic," Lord Arglay said, "I'd bet any money he wanted to tantalize him with it. If there was an *it*, which of course I don't believe."

"But I saw it, I touched it, I used it," Reginald cried out lyrically. "I tell you, I did it."

"I know you do," the Chief Justice answered. "And though I shan't give you the money I'm bound to say I feel extremely curious." He got up slowly. "I think," he said, "the telephone. Excuse me a few minutes. I want to try and catch Giles if he's in."

When he had gone out of the room a sudden consciousness of their respective positions fell on the other two. Reginald Montague became acutely aware that he had been revealing an immense and incredible secret to a girl in his uncle's employment. Chloe became angrily conscious that she could not interrogate this young man as she would have done her own friends. This annoyed her the more because, compared with Lord Arglay's learning and amused observation, she knew him to be trivial and greedy. But she, though certain of a greater affection for the Chief Justice than he had, was a servant and he a relation. She thought of the phrase again—"the Crown of Suleiman." The crown of Suleiman and Reginald Montague!

"Sounds awfully funny, doesn't it, Miss Burnett?" Mr. Montague asked, coming carefully down to her level.

"Lord Arglay seemed to think Sir Giles was having a joke with you," she answered coldly. "A kind of mesmerism, perhaps."

"O that's just my uncle's way," Reginald said sharply. "He likes to pull my leg a bit."

"So Lord Arglay seemed to think," Chloe said.

"No, I mean Lord Arglay," Reginald said more irritably than before.

The Pupil of Organic Law

"You mean Lord Arglay really believes it all?" Chloe said, surprised. "O do you think so, Mr. Montague?"

"Lord Arglay and I understand one another," Reginald threw over carelessly.

"One another?" Chloe said. "Both of you? But how splendid! He's such an able man, isn't he? It must be wonderful to understand him so well." She frowned thoughtfully. "Of course I don't know what to think."

"Ah well, that doesn't so much matter, does it? I mean——" He hesitated.

"O I know it isn't my money that comes in," Chloe hastened to say. "I do realize that, Mr. Montague."

"It isn't a question of money—not first of all," Reginald protested. "It's a matter of general interest."

Chloe said nothing, chiefly because she was a little ashamed of herself, but the result was almost worse than if she had made another effort. The commenting silence extended itself for some minutes and was broken at last by Lord Arglay's return.

"Well," he said, "I've been talking to Giles. I'm bound to say he swears it's quite right, and sticks to you in every particular, Reginald. However, he's asked us to go over to-night and see. Miss Burnett, can you come?"

"O but, Lord Arglay, ought I to . . ." Chloe said doubtfully; and "I don't suppose Miss Burnett would find it very interesting," Reginald hastily threw in.

"Civilized man," Lord Arglay said, "is known by the capacity of his intellect to produce convincing reasons for his emotions. *Convincing*, Reginald. Say anything you like, except to suggest that anyone wouldn't be interested in this new interstellar traffic of yours. Besides, I need my secretary. I shall be out this afternoon and I officially request her to spend her time looking up all the references to Suleiman the son of David that she can find. We will all dine here at seven and then go to Ealing. That suit you, Miss Burnett? You, Reginald? Right."

Reginald got up to go. "Well, you won't finally decide against coming in until to-night, will you, uncle?" he said. "Good-bye, Miss Burnett. Don't let my uncle persuade you to come if you don't want to."

"I won't," Chloe said politely, "as I shan't be able to have a financial interest. Good-bye, Mr. Montague."

When Reginald had gone—"And why the scratch, Miss Burnett?" Lord Arglay asked. "Quite right, of course, but why to-day especially? Generally you just let Reginald fleet by. Why this unwonted sharpness?"

"I beg your pardon," Chloe said. "I don't quite know. It was impertinent of me. I didn't mean to be rude to you."

"Not in the least impertinent," the Chief Justice answered. "Quite remarkably relevant. But why to-day?"

"I think it was his talk of the Crown of Suleiman," Chloe said reluctantly. "Somehow . . ."

Arglay shook his head. "I wouldn't pin much to that. My belief is still that Giles has been hocussing that young man. But I'm curious to know why; and anyhow it wouldn't do me any harm to know as much as you about the son of David. I can't think of another fact about him at present. So you dig out what you can and then clear off and be back by seven."

"Are you going out, Lord Arglay?" Chloe asked.

"Certainly not," the Chief Justice said. "I am going to lie in my deepest armchair and read *When Anarchy came to London*, which has an encouraging picture of the Law Courts being burnt on the cover. Till seven, then."

The dinner was largely occupied, much to Reginald's boredom, by Chloe's account of what she had discovered about King Suleiman and Lord Arglay's comments on it. It seemed she had been right in her remembrance that the Majesty of the King made its journeys accompanied by the Djinn, the doctors of the law, and the viziers, upon a carpet which accommodated its size to the King's needs. But there were also tales of the

Crown and the Stone in the Crown, and (more general) of the Ring by virtue of which the King understood all languages of men and beasts and Djinn and governed all created things, save only the great Archangels themselves who exist in immediate cognition of the Holy One. "For," said Chloe thrilling, "he was one of the four mighty ones—who were Nimrod and Sheddad the Son of Ad, and Suleiman and Alexander; the first two being infidels and the second two True Believers."

"Alexander?" Arglay said in surprise. "How jolly! Perhaps Giles will produce the helmet of the divine Alexander too. We shall have a regular archaeological evening, I expect. Well, come along, *Malbrouck s'en va t'en guerre.* . . ." He carried them off to the car.

Sir Giles received the party with an almost Christlike, "What went ye out for to see?" air, but he made no demur about producing the Crown for their examination. The Chief Justice, after examining it, showed it to Chloe.

"And the markings?" he asked her.

Chloe said nervously, "O you know them, Lord Arglay."

"I know they are Hebrew," the Chief Justice said, "and I know that Sir Giles is sneering at me in his heart. But I haven't an idea what they are."

"I suppose you've never had a Hebrew Rabbi before you?" Sir Giles said. "That's how you judges become educated men, isn't it? The letters———"

"I asked Miss Burnett, Giles," Lord Arglay interrupted, and Sir Giles with a shrug waited.

"They are the four letters of the Tetragrammaton, the Divine Name," Chloe said still more nervously. "Yod, He, Vau, He. I found it out this afternoon," she said suddenly to Sir Giles, "in an encyclopedia."

"Some of us write encyclopedias," Arglay said, "—that's you, Giles; some of us read them—that's you, Miss Burnett; some of us own them—that's me; and some of us despise them —that's you, Reginald."

"Encyclopedias are like slums," Giles said, "the rotten homes of diseased minds. But even Hoxton has to pretend to live, it thinks, and of course it doesn't know it stinks."

Arglay was looking at the letters. "The Divine Name," he said musingly. "Yod, He, Vau, He. Umph. Well. . . . We were going to experiment, weren't we?" he added, almost as if recovering himself. "Who begins? Reginald, suppose you show us."

"Certainly," Montague said. "Now look here, uncle, let's really show you. Tell me something I can bring you from your study."

"Bring me the pages of manuscript on the small table by the window," Arglay answered at once. "The top one is marked *Chapter IV.*"

Montague nodded and taking the Crown put it on his head; he settled it comfortably, then taking a step or two backwards sat down in the nearest convenient chair. Lord Arglay watched him attentively, occasionally darting his eyes sideways towards Sir Giles, who—as if bored with the repetition of a concluded experiment—had turned to the papers on which he had previously been working. Chloe suddenly caught Arglay's arm; he put up his other hand and pressed hers. At once they found themselves looking at an empty chair. Chloe cried out; Arglay took a step towards the chair. Sir Giles, looking round, said casually; "I shouldn't get in the way; he may be back at any moment, and you might get a nasty knock."

"Well, I'm damned," Lord Arglay said. "It's all——" he began, looking at Chloe, but, impressed by the vivid excitement that possessed her, ceased in the middle of the reassuring phrase he had begun. They waited in silence.

It was only about two or three minutes before, suddenly, they saw Reginald Montague again in front of them. He sat still for another minute or two, then he stepped forward and gave the Chief Justice several pages of manuscript. "Well, uncle?" he asked triumphantly.

Arglay took the papers and looked at them. They were those on which he had been making notes that afternoon, and he had, he knew, left them on his table. He turned them over in silence. Chloe released his arm suddenly and sat down. Sir Giles strolled back to them. "Interesting exhibit, what?" he said.

The Chief Justice's mind admitted the apparent fact. It was impossible, but it had happened. In less than five minutes these papers had been brought from Lancaster Gate to Ealing. He loosed the little sigh which always preceded his giving judgement and nodded. "I don't know whether it's the Crown of Suleiman, Giles," he said, "or some fantasia of your own. But it certainly seems to work."

"What about trying it, uncle?" Reginald said invitingly, removing the gold circlet from his head and holding it out. "It's quite simple. You just put it on and wish firmly to go— wherever you choose."

"Wishing firmly is a very difficult thing," Lord Arglay said. "But if you can I suppose I can." He took the Crown and looked at Chloe. "Where shall I go, Miss Burnett?" he asked.

"Somewhere quiet," Sir Giles interjected. "If you choose the House of Commons or London Bridge or anything like that you'll cause a sensation. Try your—" he paused a moment, "dining-room," he added.

"I'd rather go somewhere I didn't know," Arglay said.

"Go to my sitting-room, Lord Arglay," Chloe put in swiftly. "I don't suppose you even remember what the address is. On —let me think—on the table is last week's *New Statesman*."

"There isn't likely to be any other fellow there?" Sir Giles asked. "No? All right, Arglay. Better sit down; it's apt to jar you, they say. Now—will yourself there."

Lord Arglay took the Crown in both hands and set it on his head. Chloe involuntarily compared the motion with Montague's. Reginald had put it on with one hand as if he were settling a cap; against his thin form the Chief Justice's assured

28

maturity stood like a dark magnificence. He set on the Crown as if he were accepting a challenge, and sat down as if the Chief Justice of England were coming to some high trial, either of another or of himself. Chloe, used to seeing and hearing him when his mind played easily with his surroundings, used to the light courtesy with which he had always treated her, had rarely seen in him that rich plenitude of power which seemed to make his office right and natural to him. Once or twice, when, in dictating his book, he had framed slowly some difficult and significant paragraph, she had caught a hint of it, but her attention then had been on her work and his words rather than his person. She held her breath as she looked, and her eyes met his. They were fixed on her with a kind of abstract intimacy; she felt at once more individual to him than ever before and yet as if the individuality which he discerned was something of which she herself was not yet conscious. And while she looked back into them, thrilling to that remote concentration, she found she was looking only at the chair, and was brought back at once from that separate interaction to the remembrance of their business. She started with the shock, and both the men in the room looked at her.

"Don't be frightened," Sir Giles said, with an effort controlling his phrases, and "It's all right, you know," Montague added coldly.

"I'm not frightened, thank you," Chloe said, hating them both with a sudden intensity, but she knew she lied. She *was* frightened; she was frightened of them. The Crown of Suleiman, the strange happenings, Lord Arglay's movements—these were what had stirred her emotions and shaken her, and those shaken emotions were loosed within her in a sudden horror, yet of what she did not know. It seemed as if there were two combinations; one had vanished, and the other she loathed, but to that she was suddenly abandoned. It was ridiculous, it was insane. "What on earth are you afraid of?" she asked herself, "do you think either of them is going to

assault you?" And beyond and despite herself, and as if thinking of some assault she could not visualize or imagine she
answered, "Yes, I do."

Lord Arglay, as he sat down wearing the Crown, had directed his eyes and mind towards Chloe. For the first few moments
half a score of ordinary irrelevant thoughts leapt in his mind.

She was efficient, she was rather good-looking, she was,
under the detached patience with which she took his dictation,
avid of ideas and facts, she was desirous—but of what Lord
Arglay doubted if she knew and was quite certain he did not.
He put the irrelevancies aside, by mere habitual practice,
held his mind empty and prepared, as if to receive some
important answer which could then be directed to its proper
place in the particular order to which it belonged, allowed the
image of Chloe Burnett and the thought of her home to enter,
and shut his mind down on them. The Crown pressed on his
forehead; he involuntarily united the physical consciousness
and the mental; either received the other. His interior purpose
suddenly lost hold; a dizziness caught him, through which he
was aware only of a dominating attraction—his being yearned
to some power above, around, within him. The dizziness
increased and then was gone; his head ached; the Stone
pressed heavily on it, then more lightly. He found himself
opening his eyes.

He opened them on a strange room, and realized that he
was standing by the door. It was a not too well furnished room
—not, obviously, his own kind. There were two comfortable
armchairs; there was a bookcase; a table; another chair;
pictures; a little reproduction of the Victory of Samothrace, a
poor Buddha, a vase or two. On the table a box of cigarettes
and a matchbox; some sort of needlework; a book; the *New
Statesman*. Lord Arglay drew a deep breath. So it worked. He
walked to the table, then he went over to the window and
looked out. It was the ordinary suburban street, a few ordinary
people—three men, a woman, four children. He felt the

curtains—they seemed actual. He felt himself with the same result. He went back to the table and picked up the *New Statesman*, then he sat down in one of the comfortable chairs as if to consider. But as he leant back against the cushions he remembered that the experiment was only half done; he could consider afterwards. The immediate thing was to return with the paper; if that were done, all was done that could be at the moment. "I wish there were someone here to speak to," he thought. "I wonder—I suppose they would see me." He thought of going down into the street and asking his way to some imaginary road, but the difficulty in passing anyone outside Chloe Burnett's room occurred to him and he desisted. Return, then. He gripped the *New Statesman* tightly, and began to think of Sir Giles at Ealing. But the notion of introducing Sir Giles offended him; so, almost as much, did the thought of Reginald Montague, and he was content at last to make an image, as near as possible, of the room from which he had come, with the thought of his secretary attached to it. "My dear child," Lord Arglay said unconsciously, and shut his eyes.

When, after a similar play of feeling to that which he had experienced before, he opened them to see Reginald Montague in front of him there flashed across his mind the idea that the Crown had somehow muddled things. But it was gone as he came to himself and recognized that he had indeed returned. He looked at his watch; the whole episode had taken exactly five minutes. He sat for a minute, then he got up, walked across to Chloe and gave her the paper. "Yours, I think, Miss Burnett? I'm sorry to give you the trouble of carrying it back," he said, and wondered whether he had only imagined the look of relief in her eyes. "Well," he went on to the other two, "it seems you're quite right. I don't know what happens or how, but if this sort of thing can go on indefinitely, space doesn't exist—for purposes of travel."

"You see it?" Reginald cried out.

"Certainly I see it," Lord Arglay answered. "It's a little startling at first and I want to know several more things, but they can wait. At the moment I have enough to brood on. But we're forgetting our duty. Miss Burnett, wouldn't you like to try the . . . to put on the Crown of Suleiman?"

"No," said Chloe. "No, thank you, Lord Arglay. Thank you all very much, but I think I had better go."

"Go—at once?" Arglay asked, "But give me a few more minutes and we'll all go back together."

"I shouldn't press Miss Burnett to stop if she wants to go," Sir Giles said. "The station is about the fourth turning on the right."

"Thank you, Sir Giles," Chloe answered him. "Thank you for showing me the—the Crown. Good night, Mr. Montague. Good night, Lord Arglay."

"All right, Giles," Arglay stopped a movement Tumulty had not made. "I'll see Miss Burnett out." As the room door closed behind them he took her arm. "Why the rush?" he asked gently.

"I don't . . . I don't really know," Chloe said. "I'm being rather silly but I felt I couldn't stop there just now. It *is* rather upsetting, isn't it? And . . . O I don't know. I'm sorry to seem a fool."

"You are not in the least like a fool," the Chief Justice said equably. "And you will tell me to-morrow what the matter is. Are you sure you are all right now?"

"Quite all right," Chloe said as he opened the door for her. "Yes, really, Lord Arglay." She added with a sudden rush of temper, "I don't like Sir Giles."

"I couldn't," Arglay smiled at her, "have much use for a secretary who *did* like Sir Giles. Or Reginald either, for that matter. A vulture and a crow—but that's between ourselves. Well, if you will go, good night."

"Good night," Chloe said, took a step forward, and looked back suddenly. "You aren't going to try it again yourself?"

"Not I," Lord Arglay said. "I'm going to talk to them a little and then go. No more aerial flights to-day. Till to-morrow then." He watched her out of the gate and well along the street before he returned to the others.

He discovered then that Reginald had not been wasting his time.

Anxious to lay hands as soon as possible on some of the colossal fortune that seemed to be waiting, the young man had extracted permission from Sir Giles to make an effort to remove a small chip from the Stone, and had been away to bring a chisel and hammer from the tool-box. Arglay looked at Tumulty.

"You're sure it won't damage it?" he asked.

"They all say it won't," Sir Giles answered. "The fellow I had it from and Ali Khan who was here the other night and the manuscripts and all. The manuscripts are rather hush-hush about it—all damnably veiled and hinting. 'The division is accomplished yet the Stone is unchanged, and the virtues are neither here nor there but allwhere'—that kind of thing. They rather suggest that people who get the bits had better look out, but that's Reginald's business—and his covey of company-promoters. He'd better have a clause in the agreement about not being responsible for any damage to life or limb, but it's not my affair. *I* don't care what happens to them."

"Who is this Ali Khan?" Arglay asked, watching Reginald arrange the Stone conveniently.

"A fellow from the Persian Embassy," Sir Giles told him. "He was on to me almost as soon as I reached England, wanting to buy it back. So I had him out here to talk to him about it, but he couldn't tell me anything I didn't know or guess already."

Reginald struck the chisel with the hammer, and almost fell forward on to the table. For, unexpectedly, since the Stone had been hard enough to the touch, it yielded instantaneously to the blow, and, as Reginald straightened himself with an oath, they saw, lying on the table by the side of the Crown, a second Stone apparently the same in all respects as the first.

"Good God!" Lord Arglay exclaimed, while Reginald gazed open-mouthed at the result of his work, and Sir Giles broke into a cackle of high laughter. But they all gathered round the table to stare.

Except that one Stone was in the Crown and the other not they could not find any difference. There was the same milky colour, flaked here and there with gold, the same jet-black markings which might be letters and might be only accidental colouring, the same size, the same apparent hardness.

" 'The division is accomplished yet the Stone is unchanged' ", Lord Arglay quoted at last, looking at his brother-in-law. "It is, too. This is all very curious."

Tumulty had thrust Reginald aside and was peering at the two Stones. After a minute, "Try it again, Reginald," he said —"the new one, not the old. Come round here, Arglay." He caught the Chief Justice by the arm and brought him round the table. "There," he said, "now watch." He himself, while Lord Arglay leant forward over the table, moved a step or two off and squatted down on his heels, so that his eyes were on a level with the Stone. "Now slowly, Reginald, slowly."

Montague adjusted it, set the chisel on it, raised the hammer and struck, but this time with less force. The watchers saw the chisel move down through the Stone which seemed to divide easily before it and fall asunder on both sides. Sir Giles scrambled to his feet and he and Lord Arglay leaned breathlessly forward. There on the table, exactly alike, lay two Stones, each a faithful replica of its original in the Crown.

Montague put the chisel and hammer down and stepped back. "I say," he said, ."I don't like this. Stones don't grow out of one another in this way. It's . . . it's uncanny."

"Stones don't carry you five miles through the air and back usually," Arglay said drily. "I think you're straining at a gnat.

Still . . ." The perfect ease with which the Stone had recreated itself, a ghastly feeling of its capacity to go on producing copies of itself to infinity, the insane simplicity, the grotesque finality, of the result, weighed on his mind, and he fell silent.

Sir Giles, alert and eager, picked them up. "Just a moment," he said, "let me weigh them."

He went to a corner of the room where a small balance stood in a glass case, and put one of the Stones on the scales. For a minute he stared at it, then he looked over his shoulder at the Chief Justice.

"I say, Arglay," he cried, "it doesn't weigh anything."

"Doesn't weigh——" Lord Arglay went across to him. The Stone lay in the middle of the scale, which remained perfectly poised, balanced against its fellow, apparently unweighted by what it bore.

"But——" Arglay said, "but—— But it *does* weigh. . . . I mean I can feel its pressure if I hold it. Very light, but definite."

"Well, there you are," Giles said. "Look at it." With the tweezers he picked up a gramme weight and dropped it on the other scale, which immediately sank gently under it.

"There," he said, "the balances are all right. It just doesn't weigh." He took up the Stone and they returned to the table, where all three stood staring at the marvel, until Sir Giles grew impatient.

"We look like Hottentots staring at an aeroplane," he said. "Reginald, you baboon-headed cockatoo, show a little gratitude. Here instead of a mere chip you can give every one of your degenerate Jew millionaires a stone as big as the first one, and you stand gaping like a cow with the foot-and-mouth disease."

Reginald made an effort at recovery. "Yes," he answered rather quaveringly, "yes, of course I see that. It made me feel funny somehow. But—yes, of course. It'll save any difficulty about chipping the original, and they'll look much better—much. Can I leave them here to-night?"

"Why, you're scared out of what wits you've got," Sir Giles said. "What about you, Arglay? Will you have one?"

"No," Lord Arglay said soberly. "I think not; not to-night. I feel rather as if I'd been scared out of what wits I'd got, and was just getting over it. If I were you, Reginald, I should think a great many times before I started that transport scheme of yours."

"Eh?" said Reginald. "But surely Sir Giles is right? This'll make it even easier."

"Just as you like," Lord Arglay said. "I think I will go now, Tumulty. I should like to come and see it again soon, if I may."

Sir Giles nodded casually, and as casually bade his visitors good-night.

On the way back to town Lord Arglay said very little, and ignored Reginald's occasional outbreaks of mingled hope and nervousness. He found himself wishing Chloe Burnett had not gone; he would have liked to have his own silence buttressed by another instead of harassed by a futile and spasmodic volubility. His mind gazed blankly at the riddle of the three Stones in an awe which he usually kept for Organic Law. There must be some conclusion, he felt, but he couldn't think —not yet. "—pay even more," he heard at his side and drove faster. "Is there no intelligent creature about?" he thought. "I wish that girl hadn't—no, perhaps it's as well. Damn it, I'm muddled."

He reached his house almost at the same time that Chloe by a slower and longer method came to her own, full of similar half-conscious anxieties and alarms. She found, opened, and read a couple of letters that awaited her, and realized when she had finished that she knew nothing of their contents, and did not particularly want to know. She put down the *New Statesman* in its place on the table, took off her things, and looked vaguely round the room. It was here then that Lord Arglay had been during that unbelievable and terrifying disappearance; to this the Crown of Suleiman had transported

him. The Crown of Suleiman. . . . the Lord Chief Justice. . . .
Chloe Burnett. It might have happened but she didn't believe
it; at least, except that she couldn't disbelieve in that sharp
spasm of fear. She moved towards a chair and noticed, with a
slight annoyance, that she had forgotten to shake the cushions
up when she left the house that evening. Or had another
visitor——? Chloe dropped into the chair where Lord Arglay
had sat and burst into tears.

Chapter Three

THE TALE OF THE END OF DESIRE

When Miss Burnett arrived at the Chief Justice's house the next morning she found him reading his correspondence in a perfectly normal way. He looked up to welcome her and considered her carefully. "No worse?" he said. "Good night? Well, you missed something even more eerie."

"O Lord Arglay! Nothing happened?"

"Something happened all right," Arglay answered, and his face grew grave. "Up to last night," he went on, "I thought Giles was monkeying about with something, and playing tricks on Reginald for some infernal reason of his own. But I don't know now; I really don't. He didn't seem to expect what did happen."

"But, Lord Arglay! What did?"

The Chief Justice told her. Chloe sat gazing at him. "It multiplies itself?" she breathed. "But it must be something—magical, then. Something unnatural."

Arglay shook his head. "I wouldn't say that," he answered. "Atoms do it, or electrons, or something. But I admit to having a nasty jar when I saw the three things all exactly alike. Somehow the sight of Reginald producing stones of Suleiman ben Daood at the rate of two a minute with a chisel—it didn't seem decent."

"That," Chloe said with conviction, "is what I felt; that's why I ran away. Lord Arglay, could . . ." she hesitated, "could those letters be real?"

"If they are, if the Stone is," the Chief Justice said, "it looks as if it were real in another manner—more or less real than we are. No, that's absurd, of course. There can't be degrees in Reality. But we know that we can pass through space by its means—we both know that—and I have seen what was one become two, and then three, and lose nothing in the process. And now this morning . . ." He gave her a letter and she read—

"*Foreign Office*,
"10 *May*.

"MY DEAR CHIEF JUSTICE,

"I wonder if you could spare me a few minutes to-day, and if so whether you would mind ringing up and making an appointment. Nothing to do with you directly, but the fact is we have been approached—very tentatively—on a little matter relating to your brother-in-law Sir Giles Tumulty. And as, on the few occasions when I've met him, he always seemed to me rather a difficult man to deal with, I thought my way might be smoother if I could have a chat with you first. Pray forgive me for troubling you.

"Yours very truly,

"J. BRUCE CUMBERLAND."

Miss Burnett looked up. "You think it's the same thing?"

"I shouldn't wonder," Lord Arglay answered. "Of course it may not be. Giles always seems to be conducting several lines of research at once, some perfectly harmless and one or two perfectly loathsome. But the F.O. has had trouble with him once or twice before—obscure troubles no one seemed to know the rights of, except Giles who (it is said) was the proximate cause of one Secretary's resignation. I don't wonder Bruce Cumberland hesitates to tackle him."

"Who is Mr. Cumberland?" Chloe asked.

"One of the smaller great guns there," Arglay told her. "A Permanent Official in many impermanent offices. But I've rung up already and made an appointment for twelve. I want——"

39

The Tale of the End of Desire

There was a tap at the door and a maid came in. "Sir Giles Tumulty would like to see you, my lord," she said.

"Sir Giles——? O bring him in, bring him in," Arglay said and met the visitor at the door. "Hallo, Tumulty, what brings you here so early?" he asked.

Sir Giles came briskly in, threw Chloe a glance, and sat down. "Three things," he said. "My house was burgled last night, I'm going to Birmingham to-day, and I want to warn you, or rather other people through you."

"Burgled?" Arglay said. "Casually or deliberately? And by whom, or don't you know?"

"Of course I know," Sir Giles said. "It's the Embassy people; I shouldn't be a bit surprised to find Ali Khan did it himself. I'm only surprised they didn't try to tackle me. They did it pretty well on the whole, felt under my pillow while I was trying not to snigger, and went all over the study, got what safe there is open, and made very little noise. I dare say I shouldn't have heard them if I hadn't been awake."

"Did they get what they wanted?" Arglay asked.

"Get it?" Sir Giles almost shrieked. "Do you suppose, Arglay, that any set of half-caste earthworms would find anything I wanted to hide? No, they didn't. Suleiman and I are going off to see Palliser at Birmingham to-day. But I thought I'd leave one of those little fellows with you and one with Reginald. I've dropped his in on him and here's yours." He pulled one of the Stones from his pocket and threw it on to the table. "And now for the warning. You're mixed up with all this Whitehall crowd of simians, Arglay, and for all I know the Persians may be trying to pull the strings they dance to. Well, if you hear anything about it, tell them to be careful. For if they try to get the Crown out of me they'll get more than they want. Tell them if they give me any trouble I'll make enough Stones to build a wall round London. I'll sell them at two a penny to the children in the streets. I'll set up a Woolworth's to show nothing but Stones. The whole population of this blasted sink you call London shall be playing hop-scotch with them. I'll give them relics enough, and you tell them so. I've written to Ali Khan warning him and referring him to you for confirmation." He started to go, and stopped. "O and if they try and get me knocked on the head *that* won't help. For I'll leave it in proper keeping and I'll have a mausoleum of relics built over me. So they know."

With which Sir Giles flung out of the room, but he was back again before Lord Arglay could say more than "Cheery creature!"

"My own advice to both of you," he said, "is to say nothing at all whatever leprous hooligan from the Foreign Office or the Embassy you may be pestered with. You play your office, Arglay, and Miss Burnett can play her sex. Justice and innocence, that's your line, though I don't suppose either of you's either."

He was gone again, this time for good, and they heard the front door close.

"Giles always reminds me of the old riddle," Lord Arglay said in a moment. "Would you rather be more abominable than you sound or sound more abominable than you are? The answer is I would rather be neither but I am both. And now what do we do?" He looked at his watch. "I go to the Foreign Office," he said, and considered. "I think, Miss Burnett, if anyone comes from the Persian Embassy you had better see them. Don't know anything; just be obliging. I've asked you to take any message that comes, to interview any callers—that sort of thing. Lord Arglay was particularly anxious—you know. I'm not sure that I oughtn't to cut adrift altogether, but there's Bruce Cumberland, and, as a matter of fact, I'm horribly curious. Well, I'll go. I'll tell them to show anyone from the Embassy in to you. Good-bye, and good luck. I shall be back to lunch."

"They may want you to lunch at the Foreign Office," Chloe suggested.

The Tale of the End of Desire

"Then I shan't," Lord Arglay said firmly. "We must talk the whole thing over. O and this?" He picked up the Stone. "I think this shall go in my private safe upstairs. Good-bye. You might sort out the notes for the next chapter of *Organic Law*."

Chloe did her best, but even the thesis of law as a growing and developing habit of the human mind, with its corollary of the distinction between organic consciousness expressed in law and inorganic rules imposed from without, failed to hold her. It might be true that the whole body of criminal law was, by its nature, inorganic, which was the point the Chief Justice had reached, though whether in agreement or opposition she had no idea, but she could not keep her mind away from what seemed an organism of unexpected power. "It must be alive," she found herself saying, and went on to ask herself, "But then does it know? Does it know what it does and what we do to it? Who ever heard of a living stone?" She went on, nevertheless, thinking along that road. "Does it know what Mr. Montague is doing with it? What else can it do? and can it do anything to us?"

The maid came in. "A gentleman from the Embassy is downstairs, Miss Burnett," she said. "Lord Arglay told me to show him up. Will that be all right?"

"Certainly," Chloe said nervously, "yes, please bring him in."

In a minute the maid announced "Mr. Ibrahim", and vanished. A little old gentleman, in Western dress but for his green turban, walked placidly into the room.

"Do sit down," Chloe said, mastering her agitation. "Probably the maid told you that Lord Arglay was so sorry he had had to go out, but he hoped you would be good enough to leave any message with me. If possible."

Hajji Ibrahim bowed and sat down. "You know, I think, what I have come about?" he said.

"I'm sorry, but Lord Arglay didn't tell me—only that it might be rather important," Chloe answered.

The Tale of the End of Desire

The Hajji smiled slightly. "I believe that Lord Arglay did not tell you," he said, "but I think you must have seen something last night when you went with him to Sir Giles Tumulty's house."

"If you know that," Chloe answered, disagreeably surprised, "you will know that I left before Lord Arglay and wasn't with him there—not for long."

"Long enough," the Hajji nodded. "Do not let us dispute on that, Miss Burnett—it was Miss Burnett your servant said? —or we shall waste our time and our spirit. You know what it is we are seeking, though you may not know all that it means. It is the End of Desire."

"The end of desire?" Chloe repeated.

"It is called the White Stone and the Stone of Suleiman ben Daood (on whom be the Peace!)," the Hajji went on, "and it has other names also. But that is its best name, as that is its best work. Now that it is at large in the world it may bring much sorrow. I think Lord Arglay would be wise to do what he can to bring it back. No," he added as he saw Chloe about to make another effort at denial, "you are acting in good faith but it is quite useless. I can see that you know the thing if not the work."

"If you have any definite message," Chloe said, "I shall be most careful to give it to Lord Arglay."

"I think you have a premonition of the message," Hajji Ibrahim answered. "Tell me, have you not seen certain of the marvels of the Stone and are you not afraid in your heart? Else why should you be so shaken at speaking with me?"

"I am not shaken," Chloe said indignantly.

The other smiled. "Child," he said, "you have done what you can to be loyal, but you cannot control your eyes, and there is fear at the back of them now. Do not fear us who serve the Stone but fear those who attempt to rule it."

"What is this Stone?" Chloe asked, hoping rather vainly that the intensity of her feeling would sound like a mere business interest.

The Tale of the End of Desire

"I will tell you what is said of it," the Hajji said, "and you shall tell Lord Arglay when he returns. It is said that in the Crown of Suleiman ben Daood there was a strange and wonderful Stone, and it is said also that this Stone had belonged of old to the giants, to Nimrod the hunter and his children, and by its virtue Nimrod sought to build Babel which was to reach to heaven. And something of this kind is certainly possible to those who have the Stone. Before Nimrod, our father Adam (the Peace be upon him!) had it, and this only he brought with him out of Paradise when he fled before the swords of the great ones—Michael and Gabriel and Raphael (blessed be they!). And there are those who say that before then it was in the Crown of Iblis the Accursed when he fell from heaven, and that his fall was not assured until that Stone dropped from his head. For yet again it is told that, when the Merciful One made the worlds, first of all He created that Stone and gave it to the Divine One whom the Jews call Shekinah, and as she gazed upon it the universes arose and had being. But afterwards it passed from Iblis to Adam, and from Adam to Nimrod, and from Nimrod to Suleiman, and after Suleiman it came into the sceptre of Octavianus who was called Cæsar and Augustus and was lord of Rome. But from Rome it came with Constantine to New Rome, and thence eastward—only in hiding—till our lord Muhammed (blessed be he!) arose to proclaim the Unity. And after he was received into the Mercy it belonged to seven Khalifs, and was taken into Spain when the Faith entered there, and some say that in his wars Charlemagne the Emperor found it and set it under the hilt of his sword, which was called Joyeuse because of it, and from that the Franks made a war-shout and cried *Montjoy St. Denis*. And because of its virtue and his will the Emperor made himself lord of the world. After him the world became very evil, and the Stone made for itself a place of repose and remained therein until to-day. This is the tale of the Stone of Suleiman, but its meaning is in the mind of him who hears it."

44

The Tale of the End of Desire

Chloe Burnett said abruptly, "And they use it for——"

The Persian smiled. "They use it as they will," he said. "But there are those who know it by its name which I have told you."

"But can the end of desire be an evil?" Chloe said.

"If the End is reached too violently it may mean chaos and madness," Ibrahim told her. "Even in lesser things it is not everyone who can bear to be carried hither and thither, in time or place or thought, and so in the greater it is necessary to grow accustomed to the Repose of the End. I think if you were to set it on your head now and offer your soul to it, the strength of your nature would be overthrown and not transformed by its own strength, and you would be destroyed. There is measure and degree in all things, even upon the Way."

"The Way?" Chloe asked.

"The Way to the Stone, which is in the Stone," the old man said. "Yet you have a hint of the holy letters on your forehead, and Allah shall bring you to the Resignation. For you are of Islam at heart."

"I—of Islam?" Chloe cried. "Do you mean a Muhammedan?"

"There is no God but God and Muhammed is the Prophet of God," the old man intoned gravely. "Yet the Resignation is within. Say what you will of this to your master, but bid him if he is a wise judge assist us in the restoration of the Stone."

"But if Sir Giles bought it——" Chloe began.

"He that sold it and he that bought it alike sinned," the Hajji answered. "Tell your lord that at any time I will come to him to speak of it if he will. For I do not wish my nephew to let war loose on the world."

"War?" Chloe exclaimed.

"It is the least of the plagues, perhaps," Ibrahim said. "But tell your master and bid him think what he will do."

Gravely he took his leave, with a murmured benediction, and left Chloe in a state of entire upheaval to await Lord Arglay's return.

45

The Tale of the End of Desire

When he came she saw that he was himself perplexed and troubled. But with the exception of asking whether she had had a visitor he said nothing, either of information or inquiry, until after lunch. When they were back in his study he gave her cigarettes and sat down opposite her. "And now," he said; "let's talk. No—stop—let us have . . . what Giles left with us here too." He went for the Stone and set it, rather seriously, on the table by them. "Now for your visitor," he said.

Chloe went over the conversation as far as she could. When she had finished——

"You didn't tell him about the division of the Stone?" Lord Arglay asked.

"I didn't tell him anything at all," Chloe said. "I didn't have the chance. He did all the talking."

"Well, that was the idea, after all. I did exactly the same, only less tactfully," Arglay assured her. "Bruce Cumberland was in the extreme jumps, all nicely hidden of course, but there without a doubt. He was so sorry—not at all—yes, but he was, only I was the only respectable person in touch with Sir Giles. And they wanted, they very much wanted—well, in short they wanted to know what Sir Giles had been up to. Yesterday, it appears, at some conference on the finances of Baluchistan or the reform of the gendarmerie in the suburbs of Erzerum, the Persian Ambassador whispered in Birlesmere's ear—he's the Foreign Secretary, you know. There was a matter of a relic, feloniously abstracted, under cover of a payment which was really a bribe, by one of our nationals. The Ambassador himself had no use for it, nor, he thought, had Riza Khan—but the populace, the fanatical Muhammedan populace . . . his lordship the Secretary would understand. Well, Birlesmere's used to these unofficial hints, only it seems for the last month things *have* been a bit more restive than usual all over the Near East, in expanding circles. So he began to sit up. Could his Excellency tell him at all . . .? His Excellency, *most* unofficially, had heard rumours of Suleiman, and

46

a crown, and even—without any sort of accusation—of Sir Giles Tumulty. He didn't press, he didn't even ask, for anything; he only remarked that rumours were about. Pure friendship. Of course if his Britannic Majesty's Government could reassure him, just in case the Imams (or whatever) went to Riza Khan. There was even a young fellow at the Embassy inclined to make trouble; he would be exchanged certainly—Moscow perhaps. Still. . . . Birlesmere was pushed; he had to go off to Sandringham last night, so he switched Cumberland on to it. Who did me the honour to remember that I was Sir Giles's brother-in-law, and begged me to sound him. Had I heard? Could I think? Would I investigate—delicately? I promised I would, told him nothing, and came away. So there we are."

They sat and looked at each other. Then Lord Arglay said, "I can only think of one thing to be done at once, and that's to stop Reginald. He won't want to run risks with the Government, at least I shouldn't think so, though he's thinking in millions. But he *must* keep quiet anyhow till I can see Giles again. City five seven three eight," he added into the telephone.

"You'll see Sir Giles when he comes back?" Chloe asked.

"I shall see *everybody*," Lord Arglay said. "Giles and the Ambassador and your Hajji and Cumberland again and so on. If I'm in the centre of it I'm going to enjoy it. Is that Mr. Montague's? Is Mr. Montague in? . . . Lord Arglay. . . . That you, Reginald? . . . Look here, I've just been in touch with the Foreign Office and I'm rather anxious about you. It's most important you should do and say nothing, absolutely *nothing*, about the Stone at present. You've got one, haven't you? Sir Giles left one with you? . . . Yes, well you mustn't even *look* at it yet. I'll tell you . . . what?"

Chloe watched anxiously. In a minute, "O my dear God in heaven!" Lord Arglay said. "No . . . O yes, keep it quiet *now*. . . . Who is Angus M. Sheldrake? . . . yes, *who*? Who? *I* don't know his name. . . . Oh. Can we get at him? . . . No, I don't think you'd better; perhaps I will. . . . Good-bye."

He looked round. "Reginald has sold a Stone to a fellow who has made a fortune in gallipots and other pottery ware and is called Angus M. Sheldrake. He is an American and may have left London by now."

"But," Chloe cried, "do you mean he's sold his one Stone already?"

"No," Lord Arglay said. "He has divided it and sold the new one."

"But he was going to have it set!" Chloe said.

"But he had a chance of meeting Angus M. Sheldrake, who is the richest man that ever motored across Idaho, and as Angus was leaving London, Reginald scrapped the setting, took an hour to convince him, and did it. While Bruce Cumberland was talking to me about the necessity of caution. Caution! With Reginald being creative. Do you know I entirely forgot he could do that? Ring up the Savoy and see if the unmentionable Sheldrake is still there."

Chloe leapt to the telephone. After a few minutes—"He's left London till Monday," she said.

"And to-day's Friday," Lord Arglay said. "I wish I had Reginald in the dock on an embezzlement charge. Well—I don't want to see the Ambassador till I've seen Giles; not after this morning. You know I'm terrified in case he *does* start multiplying—either he or Reginald. But I can't bring him back quicker; if I try he'll just stop away. I really don't see what else we can do—till Monday. I can talk to Reginald of course, and I will."

"Do you believe in it?" Chloe asked.

"In the Stone?" Arglay said. "I suppose I do—in a sense. I don't know what your friend means by calling it the end of desire."

"What do you think he meant by saying that the way to the Stone was in the Stone?" Chloe asked again. "And what is the way?"

"I do not know what he meant," Arglay answered, "though certainly the way to any end is in that end itself. For as you cannot know any study but by learning it, or gain any virtue but by practising it, so you cannot be anything but by becoming it. And that sounds obvious enough, doesn't it? And yet," he went on as if to himself, "by becoming one thing a man ceases to be that which he was, and no one but he can tell how tragic that change may be. What do you want to be, Chloe?"

The use of her name was natural enough to pass outwardly unheeded, if not unnoticed by some small function of her mind which made a sudden movement of affection towards him.

"I do not know," she said.

"Nor I," he said, "for myself any more than for you. I am what I am, but it is not enough."

"You—the Chief Justice," she said.

"I am the Chief Justice," he answered, "but the way is in the end, and how far have I become justice? Still"—he recovered lightness and pointed to the typescript of *Organic Law* —"still we do what we can. Well—— Look here now, you can't do anything till Monday. If there are any developments I will let you know."

"Are you sure I can't do anything?" she said doubtfully.

"Neither of us can," Arglay answered. "You may as well clear off now. Would you like to use the Stone to go home by?"

"No, thank you," she said. "I think I'm afraid of the Stone."

"Don't think of it more than you can help between now and Monday," Arglay advised her. "Go to the theatre to-night if you can. If anything happens messenger boys in a procession such as preceded the queen of Sheba when *she* came to Suleiman shall be poured out to tell you all."

"I *was* going to the theatre," she said, "but I thought of postponing it."

"Nonsense," said the Chief Justice. "Come on Monday and we'll tackle Sir Giles and the Ambassador and Angus M.

49

Sheldrake and Reginald and the Hajji and Bruce Cumberland—and if there are any more we will deal with them also. Run along."

By midnight however Chloe almost wished she had not followed Lord Arglay's advice. For she was conscious that the evening had not been a success, and that the young man who accompanied her was conscious of it too. This annoyed her, for in matters of pleasure she had a high sense of duty, and not to cause gaiety appeared to her as a failure in morals. Besides, Frank Lindsay was working very hard—for some examination in surveying and estate agency—working in an office all day and then at home in the evening, and he ought to be made as happy as possible. But all her efforts and permissions and responses had been vain; she had said good night to her companion with an irritable sense of futility which she just prevented herself expressing. He had, as a matter of fact, been vainly contending all the evening, without knowing it, against two preoccupations in Chloe's mind—the Stone and Lord Arglay. Not only did the Stone lie there, a palpitating centre of wonder and terror, but against the striving endeavour of Frank Lindsay's rather pathetic culture moved the assured placidity of Lord Arglay's. It did not make Frank less delightful in the exchanges discoverable by him and her together, but it threw into high relief the insufficiency of those exchanges as more than an occupation and a means of oblivion; it managed to spoil them while providing no substitute and no answer for the desires that thrilled her.

It seemed to her that all things did just so much and no more. As, lying awake that night, she reviewed her activities and preoccupations, there appeared nothing that consumed more than a little part of her being, or brought her, by physical excitement or mental concentration, more than forgetfulness. Nothing justified her existence. The immortal sadness of youth possessed her, and a sorrow of which youth is not always conscious, the lucid knowledge of her unsatisfied desires. There was nothing, she thought, that could be trusted; the dearest delight might betray, the gayest friendship open upon a treachery and a martyrdom. Of her friends, of her young male friends especially, pleasant as they were, there was not one, she thought, who held that friendship important for her sake rather than for his own enjoyment. Even that again was but her own selfishness; what right had she to the devotion of any other? And was there any devotion beyond the sudden overwhelming madness of sex? And in that hot airless tunnel of emotion what pleasure was there and what joy? Laughter died there, and lucidity, and the clear intelligence she loved, and there was nothing of the peace for which she hungered.

Her thought went off at a tangent to Reginald Montague's preoccupation with the Stone. If there could be an end to desire, was it thus that it should be used? Was it only that men might hurry the more and hurl themselves about as if the speed of Chloe Burnett or Reginald Montague were of moment to the universe? She hated Montague, she hated Sir Giles, she hated Frank Lindsay—poor dear!—she hated—no, she did not hate Lord Arglay, but she hated the old man who had come to her and talked of kings and prophets and heroes till she was dizzy with happiness and dread. Most of all she hated herself. The dark mystery of being that possessed her held no promise of light, but she turned to it and sank into it, content so to avoid the world.

Chapter Four

VISION IN THE STONE

Lord Arglay spent some part of the same evening in trying to define the process of his thought on organic law and a still larger part in contemplation of the Stone in his possession. The phrase that had most struck him in Chloe's account of her conversation with Hajji Ibrahim was not, as with her, "the Way to the Stone which is in the Stone," but the more definite "movement in time and place and thought." The same question that had struck Sir Giles inevitably occurred to him; if in place, then why not in time? He wondered whether Sir Giles and Palliser, whoever Palliser might be, were making experiments with it that very evening at Birmingham. The difficulty, he thought, was absurdly simple, and consisted merely in the fact of the Stone itself. Supposing you willed to return a year, and to be again in those exact conditions, interior and exterior, in which you had been a year ago—why then, either you would have the Stone with you or you would not. If you had, you were not the same: if you had not, then how did you return, short of living through the intervening period all over again? Lord Arglay shuddered at the possibility. It would be delightful, he thought, to know again the thrill which had gone through him when he had heard of his appointment to the office he held. But to have to go again through all those years of painful appeals, difficult judgements, distressing decisions, which so often meant unhappiness to the innocent—no. Besides—supposing you did. When you reached again this moment you would again return by virtue of the Stone—and so for ever. An infinite series of repetitions of those same few years, a being compelled to grow no older, a consciousness forbidden to expand or to die. So far as Lord Arglay could see five minutes' return would be fatal; if, now, he willed himself back at the beginning of his meditations necessity would keep him thinking precisely those thoughts through an everlasting sequence. For if you willed yourself back you willed yourself precisely to be without the Stone; otherwise you were not back in the past as the past had truly been. And Lord Arglay had a suspicion that the Stone would be purely logical.

Yes, he thought, but what, in that sense, were the rules of its pure logic? How could you exist in that past *again* except by virtue of the Stone? if that were not there you yourself could not be there. The thing was a contradiction in terms; you could not be in the past without the Stone yet with the Stone you could not be in the past. Then the Stone could not act in time. But Chloe's visitor had said it could. And a Stone that could create itself out of itself and could deal as it had dealt with space ought to be able to deal in some way or other with time. For time was the same thing as space, or rather duration was a method of extension—that was elementary. "Extension," he thought, "I extend myself into—into what? Nothingness; the past is not; it doesn't exist." He shook his head; so simple a solution had never appealed to him. Every infinitesimal fraction of a second the whole universe peeled off, so to speak, and passed out of consciousness, except for the extremely blurred pictures of memory, whatever memory might be. Out of existence? that was his difficulty; was it out of existence? He remembered having read somewhere once a fantastic theory that whenever a man made a choice, a real choice—whenever he definitely did one of two things he also did at the same moment the other and brought an entire new universe into being that he might do so. For otherwise an infinite number of potentialities would exist for ever unfulfilled—which, the writer had said, though Lord Arglay had forgotten his reasons, was absurd. It had occasionally consoled him, or at least had appeared

to him as a not disagreeable hope, when the Court had rejected an appeal from a sentence of death, to think that at the
same time, in a new universe parting from this one as the Stone
before him had parted from its original, they had allowed it.
In which case a number of Christopher Arglays must exist; the
thought almost reduced him to idiocy. But in the same way the
past might, even materially, exist; only man was not aware of
it, time being, whatever else it was, a necessity of his consciousness. "But because I can only be sequentially conscious," he
argued, "must I hold that what is not communicated to consciousness does not exist? I think in a line—but there is the
potentiality of the plane." This perhaps was what great art
was—a momentary apprehension of the plane at a point in the
line. The Demeter of Cnidos, the Praying Hands of Dürer, the
Ode to a Nightingale, the Ninth Symphony—the sense of vastness
in those small things was the vastness of all that had been felt
in the present. Would one dare wish to *be* the Demeter? to be
—what? Stone? yes, presumably stone. But stone of an intense
significance—to others; but to itself? Agnosticism checked him;
no one knew. No one knew whether the Demeter had consciousness, or if so of what kind. Lord Arglay abandoned art
and returned to the question of time.

Frankly he was not going to risk perpetual recurrence. He
had no intention—his mind chilled suddenly within him as he
thought of Giles Tumulty. Would that insane scientist mind
risking recurrence—for someone else? If he could find someone
who didn't see the catch, he would risk it quite happily, the
Chief Justice thought, and stood up in agitation. Some wretched laboratory assistant, some curator, some charwoman even,
anyone who would put that bit of gold on their heads and try
to will themselves back ten minutes. If his own thought was
right . . . Giles would watch the fellow thinking, doing, being,
the same thing for ever. But no—that would involve Sir Giles
being there to give him, whoever it might be, the Stone. Only
a past Giles though, not the present. The Giles whom the

victim knew—there needn't be a real Giles at all. But then the victim would just disappear—he wouldn't be there at all. Well, Giles, he knew, would sacrifice anyone in creation just to prove that. And would look, with a grin of pleasure, at the placards announcing a sensational disappearance. In the horror of approaching a conception of real hell Lord Arglay for the first time since his childhood found himself almost believing in God from sheer fright.

He walked about the room. He had meant to try and think out the future but this agony was too much for him. Who was the Palliser Giles was working with? He flung himself at such works of reference as he possessed—a *Whitaker*, a *Who's Who*—and found him. Abel Timothy Palliser, Professor of Relative Psychology at the University of Birmingham, born 1872, educated—and so on, unmarried. Career—and so on. Author of *Studies in Hypnotic Consciousness; The Mind as a Function of Approach; the Discontinuous Integer*. The titles, in his present state, seemed to Lord Arglay merely sinister. He had a moment's vision of two men playing with victim after victim. Well, they wouldn't succeed with him—they didn't know of Sheldrake—they might trick Reginald, and though Reginald was a besotted idiot, still even Reginald—"Ass," Lord Arglay said, "they're in Birmingham," and immediately went on, "How do I know they're in Birmingham? They may have taken a late train—but they needn't take a train! Fool that I am, this thrice infernal Stone will do it for them! O damn the day when that accursed Giles——"

In the middle of the imprecation he stopped and made himself sit down. A small voice within him said "Something must be done about this." After all, he might be wrong; the Stone might act, in time, in ways he could not foresee. Or Chloe might have got Hajji Ibrahim's words wrong. His first impulse was to go to Sir Giles and stop whatever devilry might be taking place. But, short of violence, it would be difficult to stop Tumulty doing whatever he wanted. An alternative was to find out, if he could, exactly what the powers of the Stone were, and the only person who could tell him, so far as he could see, was Hajji Ibrahim. At the moment, Lord Arglay realized, he himself was the passive centre of the whole affair; the Government, the Embassy, Sir Giles, Reginald, all their activities were communicated to him. It might be possible to lay Sir Giles out; on the other hand, Giles was an awkward enemy and might lay him out, and then the confusion would, he thought more or less impartially, be worse. It looked like the Embassy first, and in something under five minutes he was speaking to Hajji Ibrahim on the telephone.

"I am Lord Arglay," he said. "I wonder, Hajji, if you could spare me ten minutes."

"I will come at once," the answer reached him. "You are willing to help us, yes?"

"I am willing to talk to you," the Chief Justice answered. "You will be round here immediately? Good."

It took him, however, when the Hajji arrived, more than ten minutes to reach tactfully the two questions he was anxious to have answered. What *was* the Stone? and what could it do?

"What is it in itself, I mean?" he urged. "Yes, Miss Burnett told me its history—but what is it? Is it a new element?"

"I think it is the First Matter," the Hajji told him, "from which all things are made—spirits and material things."

"Spirits?" Arglay said. "But this is matter"; he pressed a finger on the Stone.

"Matter to matter," Ibrahim answered, "but perhaps mind to mind, and soul to soul. That is why it will do anything you ask it—with all your heart. But you must will truly and sincerely."

"In the matter of time," Arglay, after a moment's meditation, went on, "can it transfer a man from one point to another?"

"Assuredly," the Hajji said. "But you must remember that the Keepers of the Stone have not for centuries of generations

56

laid hands on it, far less used it for such things. It has been kept in profound seclusion, and now that it is loose I fear greatly for the world. I think this Giles Tumulty has little reverence and few scruples."

"So do I," Lord Arglay said grimly. "He has told you that he will multiply it?"

"He has threatened us with the most awful and obscene sacrilege," the Hajji answered, trying to keep his voice calm. "He has sworn that he will divide the Indivisible for his own ends."

"But *time*——" Arglay, returning to his point, laid the problem before the Persian but he got no satisfaction.

"I tell you since the Shah Ismail laid hands on it five hundred years ago no one has desecrated it so," Ibrahim insisted. "For he perished miserably with all his house. How should I know in what manner the Holy Thing permits itself to be used? Give me the Stone which you have and let us seek the other."

"Others," Lord Arglay said. "The affair's gone farther than you think, Hajji. And it won't be an easy thing to get it back from Giles without worse trouble."

"Cannot your Government seize it?" the other asked, but Arglay shook his head.

"To be perfectly frank," he answered, "I doubt if the Government would go to extremes unless they realized something of its value. And then—I hope for the best—but it's no use blinking the possibility—then, if they knew its value, they mightn't very much want to give it back."

"Ali Khan will raise all the deserts and bazaars against them," Ibrahim said—"Egypt and Arabia, Africa and Syria and Iraq and Iran and India and beyond."

"I dare say," Arglay answered gloomily. "But Ali Khan won't have the Stone. And if it comes to raising the Government can do a little. Besides, what do you suppose the other Powers would be doing—if the whole of Islam was at war? No,

Hajji, I wouldn't trust the Government so far as to tell them what it can do."

"I know," the Hajji answered. "I did but seek for your thought. I have told Ali Khan we shall never recover it by war."

"What is worrying *me*," the Chief Justice went on, "is what devil's tricks Giles may be playing all this while and what I ought to be doing to stop them."

"Ask it if you will," Ibrahim said.

"Eh?" Lord Arglay stared.

"Ask it to illuminate your mind and show you what your brother is doing at this moment. The manuscripts tell us that it moves in the world of thought as in the world of action. Only take care that you are not snared in his thought so that your mind cannot return to itself."

"If it can do all this," Arglay said, "cannot it reunite itself and return of its own virtue, if you will it so?"

"No," the Hajji answered, "for it will do nothing for itself of itself, neither divide nor reunite. One Stone has no power upon its Type unless they are under the will of a single mind. Unless indeed——" He paused.

"Unless——?" Lord Arglay asked.

"Unless anyone should will that it and he should be with the Transcendence," Ibrahim said in a very low voice. "But I do not know who would dare that; and if he presumed and failed he would be destroyed and the Stone he held would be left in the world where he failed. For the Stone is he, and will go where he goes and no farther. But if he came to the End . . . . I do not know; these are very terrible things."

"And can none of the house of the Keepers," the Chief Justice asked, "dare to will this thing to save the Stone from its enemies?"

"I have asked that," Ibrahim answered, "but we know too little and too much. We know we are not worthy, and we do not know what is its will. Ali Khan desires to redeem the Stone for the sake of his Faith and I for the honour of my house, and my brothers in Persia for their glory or their peace, but we dare not bring these things into the Transcendence."

Lord Arglay was silent again. His mind told him the Persian's meaning but his being did not respond to it. Long since he had left these questions aside, unless—as in rare moments he sometimes fantastically hoped—the nature of law was also the nature of God. But if so it was not in the Transcendence but in the order of created things. In a minute or two he brought the talk back to the immediate necessities.

"Do you tell me," he said, "that I can know what Giles is doing or purposing?"

"The Traditions say so," Ibrahim answered. "But it is a perilous thing to undertake; for you must sink into the life of thought and you may not easily return."

"I am a worm and no man," Lord Arglay said, "but if Giles can catch *me* in his mental perversities——"

"Take care," the Hajji interrupted him. "I think it is not your strength that shall save you."

The Chief Justice suppressed his words but he was conscious that a very strong sense of pride was on tip-toe within him, anxious to defy Giles and all his works. He waited till it had sunk down a little, and said: "What shall I do then? For if any wretched charwoman is being trapped to-night . . ." It was ridiculous, he thought at the same moment, how his mind kept running on charwomen. But he had a vision of some thin, rather harassed, grey-haired female being persuaded to take the Stone and being caught in an everlasting cleaning of some stone corridor. All wrong metaphysically, no doubt, he protested—but possible—no, not possible: no more than sudden passage from place to place or a Stone that divided itself and was yet unchanged.

Ibrahim answered, "You need but take it into your hand and will."

"And you?" Arglay said. "Will you do it with me?"

Vision in the Stone

The Hajji hesitated. "It is almost sacrilege," he murmured, "yet it is with a right desire. I dare not use my will, but I may sit by you while you use your own. So much is perhaps not against my oath. . . . Under the Protection." He stretched out his hand. "Take the Stone and let it lay in your palm, and I will put my hand over it, and set your desire to know what Giles Tumulty does and purposes."

"And for the return?" Arglay asked.

"That is with Allah," Ibrahim said. "Will you dare it now?"

For all answer the Chief Justice pulled an armchair near and parallel to his visitor's; then he sat down in it and laid his arm on the arm of the chair. On his palm the Stone rested. Ibrahim laid his own hand lightly over it and so they remained.

Arglay, as he leaned back, formed in his mind, out of the impulse of distaste which grew in it, the image of Giles Tumulty. He suppressed, as quickly as he could, the criticisms of his brother-in-law which he was tempted to make to himself; he compelled them to define the central idea more exactly. Then he released upon that image the anxiety which had possessed him; he made a demand of it and sent it out to compel an answer. The antipathy he always felt grew stronger but it was controlled and directed by his intention; Giles's mind should lie open to his, he was determined. He felt, but without attending to it, Ibrahim's hand quiver upon his, as he was still vaguely aware of the chair on which he was sitting. Slowly those details of sensation vanished, and instead he became aware that he was holding, or seemed to be holding, a living thing, a moving, pulsating something which he hated. It was approaching him; he drove his detestation forward to meet it. The sensation of enclosing it in his hand disappeared; physical connection ceased, and he seemed to know as a mental experience alone. Only that experience now existed; he was repelled, yet since nothing but repulsion was to be felt it was that which passionately concerned his whole being. He allowed that repulsion to enter him, but as his spirit seemed to retire before it, so at the same time it overcame and dominated it. There ensued a moment's balance between those contending forces; they swung equal and then the effort ceased. His mind was aware of an ordered arrangement, as if in the outer world it had been considering the plan of a great city; he concentrated his attention even more strongly, and found himself conscious of an overpowering desire.

But it was a consciousness purely intellectual; the normal confusion of the mind by the emotions was absent. He was not concerned to excuse, justify, or condemn the desire he felt existing; rather he observed it merely. Nor indeed was he at first clear what he was considering, until there shaped itself against the darkness a face, a large, youthful, eager face which was gazing at him with a docile attention. It had red hair, a rather squab nose, a high colour, a weak mouth slightly open, brown and expectant eyes. His mind remarked that it was a face hitherto unseen; it reported at the same time a hatred of the face, combined with a desire to see it hurt and damaged —yet not in mere uselessness but in the process of extracting some personal profit out of its existence and its pain. The face removed itself to a little distance and developed into the whole figure of a young man, a lower middle-class young man, who was speaking. A small, very distant voice floated into his mind. "Yes," it was saying, "yes, sir; and then?" He heard another strange voice—an older, sharper voice—say, "That's the whole thing; you understand?" and the rest of his being underwent a sudden spasm of delight.

"Christ Almighty," Lord Arglay thought suddenly, "this is happening," and with the momentary distraction the form flickered and seemed to fade. But he made a desperate effort to hold it, and at once a strength flowed out from him. The young man's figure no longer appeared alone; it was in a room, a long room, with windows, instruments, books, and there was another figure by it. A tall, lean, oldish man, with

61

a sharp anxious face, was standing there, playing with something in his hand. It was one of the Stones—no, it was the Crown itself, and with the sight his mind realized what and where it was. It was looking out, his mind, through Giles Tumulty's eyes; it was Giles Tumulty's desire that it knew; it was Giles Tumulty's experiment that was beginning—and Christopher Arglay's mind that watched it.

But that mind was so detached that it seemed incapable of staying or hastening the intention that flowed around it; as often as it turned inwards to realize its own separate existence the appearances which it beheld mingled and faded. It was suspended and observant.

Yet, as if on the outskirts of its own nature, it presently found itself observing other thoughts. Much the same argument that Arglay had already gone over flashed through it; scattered phrases—"if he just disappears"—"time and place" —"I wonder what Arglay would say to this"—struck it and passed. The figure of the young man put out its hand and received something from the tall man. Lord Arglay's mind made an effort forward. "Stop, you fool," it knew itself thinking, and heard Giles's voice say, close and loud, "Calm now, quite calm. Just make as near an image of what you were doing as you can."

The alien mind that received those words shuddered with the horror. But the mental habits of so many years befriended it then; it realized, as it felt the pang, that it could do nothing then and there. It must act in its own medium; on the crowd of diabolic curiosities that surged around it, it could produce no effect. "I am here," Lord Arglay's mind said to itself, "by my will and the virtue of the Stone. I can do nothing here— nothing. I must return by virtue of the Stone." It sought to shut out the vision in front of it; it sought to concentrate on itself and to will to know again the vehicle that was natural to it. And even as it did so Lord Arglay heard a voice saying to him: "Have you seen? have you seen?"

Vision in the Stone

He was lying back in his own chair. Beside him Hajji Ibrahim was looking anxiously at him. The Stone? yes, the Stone still lay quietly enough on his palm. Lord Arglay stared at it as if his eyes would never shift. Then very slowly he got to his feet and laid it carefully on the table. As he did so Ibrahim repeated: "Have you seen?"

"Yes," Lord Arglay said, again slowly. "Yes, I have seen. And if what I have seen is true, and if it is as I fear it may be, I will choke Giles Tumulty's life out of him myself. Have *you* seen?"

"I think I slept and dreamed. And in my dream——" the Hajji said, and described the room and the two forms. But he went on—"Also I saw a little brownish man standing by a table, and his eyes were all alight with curiosity and desire. Also I saw," and he began to tremble, "that they had again divided the Stone; for they did not give the Crown to the youth, but only a Stone. I think they are very evil men."

"I believe you care more about the division of the Stone than about the harm they may do with it," Arglay dispassionately said.

"Certainly I do," the Hajji answered, "for the one is an offence against the Holy One, but the other only against man. He who divides the Unity is a greater sinner than he who makes a mock of his brother."

"You may be right," Lord Arglay said, "but of the Unity I know nothing, and of man I know something." He stamped suddenly with sheer rage. "Why did I return?" he cried out.

"You did wisely," the Hajji said, "for you had not gone to fight his will but to observe it. You will not find it easy, I know now, to break Giles Tumulty's will, and you could not have done it in that way. Consider that, if what you fear has happened, this young man's mind will not perhaps suffer so much, for in the very nature of things he will not know that he is living but that one period of past time over and over again, until the day when the End of Desire shall come indeed; nay, for all we know, he may be saved from many evils so."

"He may be saved from what you will," Lord Arglay said, and his face set as he spoke, "but no human being shall be turned into an automaton at the will of Giles Tumulty while I am living and sane."

There was a short silence, then Arglay went on. "But you are so far right that we do not know what arrangements Giles has made, nor what the end of this experiment of his may be. And till we know where the Types of the Stone all are—if that is what you call them—we must move slowly. To-morrow I will go to the Foreign Office again, and after that we will talk with one another further."

The Hajji stood up. "The Peace be upon you," he said.

"It will be a peace that passeth all understanding then," the Chief Justice answered, and took him to the door.

Chapter Five

THE LOSS OF A TYPE

Nor was Lord Arglay any nearer to an apprehension of that mystical Peace when he discovered on the next morning, that everybody had taken advantage of the week-end to vanish from London. Mr. Bruce Cumberland was expected back on Monday; so was Mr. Reginald Montague; so was Mr. Angus M. Sheldrake. As for Sir Giles he might be back any moment, but so far as he was expected at all it was on Monday. The Persian Ambassador even (not that he was wanted) had gone to Sandringham,—so *The Times* said— where presumably he and Lord Birlesmere were being diplomatic. London—to the Chief Justice's irritation—consisted of himself, the Hajji, and Chloe, neither of whom seemed at the moment to be much good to him. He thought of confronting Sir Giles, wherever he might be, but he was unwilling to give his brother-in-law that advantage of circumstances which he would then undeniably possess, and at last he resigned himself to spending a day of enmity deferred which, if it did not make his heart sick, made it at least extremely and unusually sullen.

He would not have been any happier if he had known what was happening, on that same Saturday morning, at a country house some fifty miles out of London, the property of Mr. Sheldrake and his occasional retreat from high finance and the complications of industry when he was in England. The Chief Justice had done him some wrong in limiting him to gallipots; actually there were few branches of production and distribution in which he had not, somehow or other, a share. These had mostly come to him from his father, as Rivington Court had

come to him from his mother, and Sheldrake's own additions
had consisted of several large motor factories and the establish-
ment of an Atlantic Airways Company to the first, and an
entirely unnecessary though quite beautiful wing to the second.
Neither it nor the Atlantic Airways would probably have come
into existence but for Cecilia Sheldrake, who, having been
forestalled in her desire to be the first woman to fly the Atlantic, had determined that at least most of the others who did
so should do it by her permission. Her husband had founded
the company, as he had built the wing, in order that she might
have everything she wanted to play with, and when he had
bought the Stone from Reginald Montague he had done it
with a similar intention in his mind.

In actual fact it had taken a longer time to persuade Sheldrake to buy than Reginald had admitted to his uncle. But
the surprising chances of that Friday—the coming of Sir Giles
with the Stone, the meeting with Sheldrake at an unexpected
conference on the same morning, the discovery that the richest
man of Idaho, of the States, of the world (report varied) was
a young fellow not quite so old as he himself was—all these
had convinced Reginald that what, at a pinch, he would have
been driven to call Providence was on his side,, and had given
him an increased audacity. He had caught Sheldrake by men-
tioning, almost in one breath, transport, the Lord Chief
Justice, and a rare stone, thus attacking at once through the
American's sense of business, security, and romance. Certainly
there had been a few minutes' danger when the Stone was discovered to be no jewel, as jewels are ordinarily known; indeed,
Reginald had been driven to a rather hasty demonstration,
which, in its turn, startled Sheldrake so greatly as seriously to
endanger the negotiations. Two ideas, however, occurred to
the financier, though he spoke of neither to Reginald; one was
motor-cars and airways, the other was his wife. To protect the
one and delight the other made it the aim of his morning to
procure the Stone, and the eventual seventy-three thousand

guineas at which it changed hands was a lesser matter. Neither of them were ever quite clear how that particular sum was reached; though Reginald flattered himself that the guineas made it a far more reputable transaction than if it had been merely pounds. He had pressed on Sheldrake the advisability of secrecy, but he had been compelled to admit that a few other Stones of the kind were in existence—not more than half a dozen. The American had displayed some curiosity as to their owners, but here the mere facts enabled Montague to be firm. He admitted that Sir Giles Tumulty had one; he thought the Chief Justice had; and he himself—well, of course, he had kept one, that was reasonable. But he said nothing of his intention to spend the afternoon creating a few more Stones nor of the names of buyers which were already floating in his mind. On his side Sheldrake said nothing of his intention to communicate the mystery at least to his wife, nor of his anxiety to procure, if he anyhow could, the other existing examples of it. Equally satisfied, equally unsatisfied, they parted, and while Reginald went first to his office and then to Brighton, Sheldrake went straight by car to Rivington Court.

He waited however till the next day, and till he had, rather nervously, at a very early hour the next morning, tried a few more minor experiments, before he spoke of the new treasure. The experiments were tried cautiously, in a small wood near the house, and were limited to the crossing of a brook, the passage of a field, and so on, concluding with the grand finale of a return to his own room, where he contentedly locked the Stone away and went to breakfast. It was some time later, not very long before lunch, while Lord Arglay raged in London, that he took his wife across the terraces and lawns to a hidden summer-house and revealed the secret to her.

Cecilia took it with surprising calm—took, indeed, both the secret and the Stone with a similar calm. She was delighted, she was thrilled, but with an obscure and egoistical acceptance of things she was not wildly surprised. If such treasures existed, they did so, both she and her husband felt, chiefly for Cecilia Sheldrake. Her life had refused her only one thing—to be the first woman to fly the Atlantic, and Cecilia, like everyone else, felt that life owed her every sort of gratification in return for that disappointment. Not that anything could really make up for it, but other tributes might help her to forget. Even miracles were reasonable since they happened for her, and Angus, in the depths of his nature, though his brain moved more slowly, felt that a world whose chief miracles were the existence of Cecilia and her existence as his wife might easily throw in a few more to make things pleasant for her. She did indeed open her eyes a little at the price, but that also seemed reasonable since it was for her, and she was more ready to risk extended experiments than her husband had been. Indeed it was she who made what must up to then have been the longest journey yet taken by those high means—at least for some centuries— in going direct to her bedroom in London and returning with a dress she had left behind and had changed her mind about on the way down the day before. When she had safely returned——

"Darling, how sweet of you!" she cried to Angus. "I never had anything like it before."

"I don't suppose many people have, or will have," Angus said, with justice. "Not many will have the chance."

"But will *anybody*?" Cecilia said, a little shocked. "Are there more of them?"

"Only about half a dozen, I gathered," Angus told her. "And I don't know who's going to buy them."

Cecilia looked depressed. "Where did they come from?" she asked in a moment.

"Sir Giles Tumulty brought them from the East, Montague said," Angus answered. "He's a traveller and explorer."

His wife looked at him meditatively. "You don't think he'd sell them *all*?" she asked. "O Angus, if somebody else got hold of them."

"Well, Sir Giles has," Sheldrake pointed out.

"O him!" Cecilia said. "I mean somebody else like us." She sat up suddenly. "Angus! What about Airways?"

"I know," Angus said, "I thought the same thing. It might be awkward. Of course, it's not so bad because you'd want to be pretty sure of anyone before you lent them the Stone."

Cecilia shook her head. "We mayn't know everything," she said. "They may have cheated you. This Mr. Montague didn't *say* it was the only one?"

"Sweetheart, he said it *wasn't*," Angus pointed out.

"Then he *has* cheated you," Cecilia said impatiently. "O Angus, we *must* put it right. After all, the Airways ought to have control, oughtn't they?"

"It may be a little awkward," Angus answered. "I think one of them is with the Lord Chief Justice."

Cecilia opened her eyes. "But I thought judges weren't supposed to have financial interests," she exclaimed. "Isn't it corruption? . . . Angus, they can't *make* them, can they?"

"What!" said her husband, startled. "Make them? O no—at least I suppose not. They came from the East."

"Yes, but do they *make* them in the East, or dig them up, or magnetize them, or something?" Cecilia persisted. "Angus dear, you must see what I mean. If there was a mine now, how dreadful it would be."

"Darling, I think you're getting unnecessarily alarmed," Sheldrake protested. "There can't be a mine—not possibly—not of stones that do this."

"Why not?" Cecilia asked.

"Well, could there? It isn't reasonable," her husband urged. "Stones like this *must* be rare." But he looked uneasily at it as he spoke.

"Anyhow—it's near lunchtime—anyhow I think you ought to do something. Get it forbidden by law or something."

"But then what about us?" Sheldrake asked.

Cecilia took his arm. "Darling," she said, "you're awfully slow. There could always be a special licence to the Airways."

"It'd be very difficult to explain to the Home Secretary without telling him everything, and I don't know that I want to tell him everything," Angus murmured. "Besides, if one licence is granted others could be, and suppose you got a Labour Government in again?"

Cecilia almost stamped. "I suppose you could buy a monopoly or a charter or something of that sort for twenty-one years or so?" she asked plaintively. "Darling Angus, we do want to stop it going further, don't we?"

"O rather, yes," Angus agreed. "It's the explaining that will be difficult."

"It won't be any more difficult for you than for me to explain to Elsie how this frock came down here," his wife said. "Dearest, it's a lovely present and I do thank you *enormously*. But if you could just prevent anyone else having one, it would be too perfectly sweet! You will try, won't you?"

"O I'll try," Angus answered, kissing her. "But it'll take some doing. There'd have to be an Act, I'm afraid—and if the Lord Chief Justice was nasty——"

"He wouldn't have anything to do with politics though, would he?" Cecilia asked. "And as a matter of fact he might, if you put it to him nicely, be willing to sell."

They returned to the house to lunch.

About the same time a less elaborate lunch was being served in the inn of the village close by to Chloe Burnett and Frank Lindsay. Chloe had been half-unwilling to leave London, for fear the Chief Justice should want her, but a sense of duty, a necessity to recompense Frank for the unsatisfactory result of the Friday evening, had compelled her to accept his suggestion; though, for some undefined reason, she had caused him to take Lancaster Gate on the way. Lord Arglay's house had offered no more information than she expected, but the sight of it enabled her more freely to devote all her energies to making the day's amusement a success. She had received with interest and encouragement Frank's serious efforts towards culture, although a part of her mind remotely insisted on comparing his careful answers with Lord Arglay's casual completeness. Sir Giles's epigram on encyclopedias—"'the slums of the mind" —recurred to her, and she went so far to meet it as to admit that Frank's information was rather like a block of model dwellings compared with the tumultuous carelessness of a country house. The contrast had been suddenly provoked by Frank's short lecture in answer to her question—"O by the way, what is a Sufi?"

"It is a Muhammedan sect," he had answered. "Muhammed, you know, who was a fanatical monotheist, wrote the Koran, or rather claimed that the Koran had been delivered to him by Gabriel." He had gone on, with what seemed a good many references to Muhammed. Chloe's intelligence reminded her that by the phrase "Muhammed was a fanatical monotheist"—he meant what Lord Arglay—or was it the Hajji?—had meant by saying "Our lord the Prophet arose to proclaim the Unity," but she found the one phrase unusually trying after the other. As penance and compensation she allowed her hand, which lay lightly in Frank's, to give it a small squeeze of thanks, and diverted his attention by saying, "O what a jolly house!"

The lecture had taken place soon after lunch while they were wandering in the lanes round the village. There was in fact very little of the house to be seen—it was too far off and hidden by trees, but perhaps sufficient to justify Chloe in saying, "Let's go through that gate and get a bit nearer."

"You'll be trespassing," Frank said, looking at the obviously private road on the other side.

Chloe laid her hand on the latch and gazed along the empty road. "Frank, in two minutes," she said, "there will rush round that corner a herd of maddened cows—look, there they are. I shall take refuge behind this gate, and I pull you in too." She did, and shut it after them. "Being here, don't you think we might just go as far as that bend and see if we can see the house better?"

"Certainly," Frank said obligingly. "As a matter of fact, according to English law, trespassers——"

"O don't talk about the law," Chloe said very hastily. "I don't want anyone but Lord—the Chief Justice to talk to me about that."

"Poor dear, you must get enough of it. I forgot you live with it perpetually," Lindsay answered. "You must be jolly glad to get away from it a bit."

Chloe, with a certain throb of conscience, attended to the house, of which a great deal more became visible as they reached the bend. The private road ran on towards it, but both the trespassers lingered.

"It is rather jolly, isn't it?" Frank said, and stopped dead. Chloe gave a cry of fear. For before the words had been well spoken or heard the air in front of them seemed suddenly to quiver, a quick brightness shone within it, and they found standing in front of them, where no one had been, whither no one had come, a well-dressed young lady. She seemed to be equally startled, and her gurgling cry caught up Chloe's shriek. There was a minute's silence while they all gazed, then——

"The Stone," Chloe cried out. "You've got the Stone."

Rather shaken still, the stranger looked at her, but hostilely.

"What do you mean? what stone?" she asked.

"You must have it," Chloe said breathlessly. "I know—I've seen. It was exactly that; the wind, the light, the—you. You *have* got the Stone."

Her words sounded almost accusingly. Mrs. Sheldrake unconsciously clenched her hand a little more tightly round what was, surely, her property, and said: "I suppose you know you're trespassing?"

Frank re-acted to the commonplace remark, feeling that he

must have been day-dreaming a few moments. The new arrival had, of course, walked up the road.

"We're so sorry," he said. "As a matter of fact we came in to shelter——" He paused in a confused realization that he had been on the point of repeating Chloe's preposterous tale about the cows.

"To shelter!" the lady said.

"Well, no, not to shelter," Frank stammered, feeling suddenly angry with Chloe, who was still staring, almost combatively. "I'm so sorry—I mean—we just came a step or two in to look at the house. From here, I mean. We weren't going nearer. I do apologize, I—I——"

Cecilia looked at Chloe. "What did you mean by the Stone?" she asked again.

"I mean the Stone," Chloe said with a clear vigour. "Is there another then, or have you bought one?"

Cecilia came a step nearer. "What do you mean about the Stone?" she asked, and made a mistake which in a less startled moment she would not have made. "You had better tell me," she added.

Chloe flushed a little. "I shall certainly not——" she began, and stopped as a confused dream of Lord Arglay, Charlemagne, Gabriel, the Tetragrammaton, and the End of Desire swept across her. "I beg your pardon," she went on. "It was only that I was so surprised."

"Is this Mr. Montague?" Cecilia asked, abruptly shifting her attack to Frank, who was too taken aback to do more than begin a hasty denial before Chloe interrupted him.

"No," she said, "he has nothing to do with it. Are you Mrs. Sheldrake?"

"I am Mrs. Sheldrake," the other said, "but what do you know?"

Chloe hesitated. "I know that you have one of the Stones," she said, "but it ought not to have been bought or sold. It wasn't Mr. Montague's and it can't be yours."

"Don't be absurd," Cecilia said sharply. "How many of these Stones are there then?"

"I don't know," Chloe answered truthfully. "There was only one at first, but that can't be yours for that was in the Crown."

"The Crown? what Crown?" Cecilia asked again, feeling that this was intolerable. There were, it seemed, goodness knows how many of those Stones—and now there was more talk of a Crown—as if seventy-three thousand guineas oughtn't to have bought the whole thing. She was half-inclined to throw the Stone in the girl's face—only that would be silly; as a mere precaution she ought to keep it.

Chloe said anxiously, "You ought to see Lord Arglay; the Chief Justice, I mean. He could tell you better than I can. He's Mr. Montague's uncle and he warned him not to sell it."

"Is it Lord Arglay's property then?" Cecilia answered.

"I don't know whose property it is," Chloe admitted rather helplessly. "But you ought to be very careful what you do with it."

"I should like very much to see Lord Arglay," Mrs. Sheldrake said, "if he could make things any clearer." She lifted the hand that held the Stone. "Can we reach him by this?"

"Certainly not," Chloe said, with a return of firmness. "We can't use the Stone of Suleiman for that."

"My good girl," Cecilia said contemptuously, "that's what it's for."

"It isn't," Chloe cried out, "and if you use it for that you've got no business with it. Any more than Mr. Montague. It's for getting somewhere."

"Well," said Mrs. Sheldrake, "I want to get to Lord Arglay. Will you tell me how and where I can find him? Or must I do it myself?"

"O don't," Chloe said. "He's in London, I think." She gave the address. "But he won't be pleased if you use the Stone."

"I shall go," Mrs. Sheldrake announced, "by car. And now don't you think you'd better get out of these grounds?"

Mr. Lindsay, who had been anxious to do so for the last five minutes, flung her a vicious glance and started. Chloe, who wanted to say a good deal without saying anything, gave her intelligence the victory and accompanied him. But over at the gate she seized his hand and forced him to run with her. "Quick," she said, "quick. We must get back to London."

"London?" Frank protested. "Why on earth——? Why, it's not three yet. Surely——"

"O we *must*," Chloe exclaimed. "I must see Lord Arglay. I must find out if I've done right. I must see what he says to her."

"But surely he can manage her *without* you," Frank said. "It can't be so absolutely vital to you to be there. If she's got something that doesn't belong to her, I shouldn't think she really does want to see him—— I should think it was all bluff. If," he added, "you'd tell me what it's all about I should know better what we ought to do."

What they ought to do was not Chloe's concern; what she was going to do she knew perfectly well. She was going straight back to Lancaster Gate; so straight that the idea of telephoning occurred to her only to be dismissed. Nor had she any intention of explaining to Frank; she had been agreeable to him all day, it was now his turn to start being agreeable. She kept up a steady speed towards the inn.

"I can't explain now," she said after a moment or two. "If I possibly can I'll tell you some other time. The Foreign Office comes into it," she added, as an exciting suggestion. "But don't talk now—run."

It appeared to Frank the most curious day in the country with a girl friend that he had ever spent. Short of Bolsheviks—in whom he was reluctant to believe, being a typical Liberal in politics, though he professed a cynical independence—he couldn't imagine why the Foreign Office should come in. But he was genuinely anxious to please Chloe, and though he offered one or two more disjointed protests he headed the car for London as soon as possible, once they had reached the inn; warning Chloe, however, that this little two-seater was unlikely to be able to arrive before whatever kind of magnificent car the Sheldrakes owned.

"O but we *must*," she said. "Try, Frank, try. I *must* be there when she gets there. I must know what's happening."

"But what *is* this blessed Stone?" Frank asked.

"Darling, don't worry now," Chloe urged him. "Just see to getting on. Lancaster Gate, you know. As quick as ever."

"I might be a taximan," Frank let out. "All right."

They fled through various lanes and emerged on a more important side road which would take them on to the main road for London. As soon as they did so however Frank began to slow down. A short distance in front of them, halfway up the steep bank, was another car, and out of it Mrs. Sheldrake was scrambling.

"O don't stop," Chloe cried, but Cecilia had recognized them and run into the middle of the road.

"Stop," she said, and Frank was compelled to obey. She came up and addressed Chloe.

"A most annoying thing has happened," she said, "and perhaps you'll help us. The Stone's somewhere over there." She pointed to the bank and the hedge. "I was looking at it in the car and Angus—Mr. Sheldrake—had to swerve suddenly and it flew out of my hand, and now he can't find it."

"What!" Chloe exclaimed.

"It must be there," Cecilia went on sharply. "I was just holding it up to the sun, to get the colour in the light, and the car jerked, and it had gone. But it's only just over there, it must be, and I thought you wouldn't mind helping us look."

Chloe was out of the car in a moment. "You've lost it," she said. "O Mrs. Sheldrake!"

"It can't possibly be *lost*," Cecilia assured, rather annoyed. "And please—I'm afraid I don't know your name—remember that it's my property."

"We can settle that after," Chloe said, beginning to mount the bank. "We can't possibly leave it lying about for someone to pick up. We can ask Lord Arglay whom it ought to belong to."

"This," Frank put in before Mrs. Sheldrake could speak, "is Miss Burnett. She is the Chief Justice's secretary," he added as impressively as possible, as Chloe caught the hedge at the top of the bank, pulled herself up, and wriggled and pushed through. "My name is Lindsay."

Cecilia eyed the bank. "Well, Angus?" she called.

A rather strained voice answered her from above—"No, no luck. O—er—are you helping? Somewhere about here, we thought."

"Will you help me too, Mr. Lindsay?" Cecilia asked. "So tiresome, all this business. But one can't afford to throw away seventy thousand guineas." Some reason, after all, had to be given to this young man who was obviously in a state of mere bewilderment, and perhaps the price——

So far she was right. He gaped at her. "A stone," he said. "But what kind of a stone then?"

"O about *so* large," Cecilia told him. "A kind of cream colour, with gold flakings, and funny black marks. *Will* you? It would be so good of you. Miss Burnett's too kind. All four of us ought to find it, oughtn't we? Thank you."

He began to help her to climb. Why Chloe, who had been so intent on rushing to London—but of course if the stone was really worth seventy thousand—seventy thousand, it would be rather fascinating even to see a stone worth that.

But half an hour's search, though they all tramped round, parted the thick grass, bent and grovelled and peered, brought them no nearer success. Cecilia, Angus felt, could hardly have chosen a worse place to look at the Stone; nor could Angus, his wife felt in turn, have chosen a worse place to swerve. For besides the bank and hedge by the road, at this particular point two fields were divided by another thorny hedge, at the base of which the grass on each side grew long. There were nettles and thistles and much larger stones on which the men seemed to be continually kneeling, and they all had a feeling that any one of the others might be trampling it into the ground at any moment. And Cecilia distrusted Chloe and Frank, and Chloe distrusted Cecilia and Angus, and Frank was wondering what the whole business meant, and Angus was wondering who the strangers were, and as they searched this wonder, suspicion, and irritation grew every moment more violent. But the End of Desire remained hidden.

At last, as they met in their circumambulations, Frank murmured to Chloe, "Is this really our business? Is it your Stone or theirs?"

"It isn't mine," Chloe said, trying not to sound irritable but conscious she was looking hot and dirty and anxious, "but it isn't really theirs. They bought it all right, but they oughtn't to have it."

"Are you tired out, Mr. Lindsay?" Cecilia called impatiently. "It *must* be somewhere here."

"Yes, Mrs. Sheldrake," Frank rebelled suddenly, "but Miss Burnett wanted to get to London, and really we seem to be going over the same ground again and again."

"Please don't stop then," Cecilia said. "I'm sorry to have kept you."

"O nonsense," Chloe broke in. "Of course we must stop. We *must* find it. We can't let a thing like that be about loose. If *someone's* got it at least we shall know where it is, if not whose."

"There's no question of that," Cecilia threw at her, "since we paid for it. As it is, I think your friend Mr. Montague has cheated us."

"He is *not*——" Chloe began and then remembered she was looking for the End of Desire. With a muddled prayer to the

78

The Loss of a Type

Stone—since, being a modern normally emotional girl she was, quite naturally, an idolater—she stopped and, to her own astonishment, experienced a sudden flicker of amused peace, accompanied by a clearer intellectual survey.

"But we are getting confused, I think," she said.

At this moment Angus, having stung himself again, swore violently and got up, kneeling on something sharp as he did so. Moved by this exactly as by unexpected opposition at a board meeting he began to decide things at once. "We can't go on like this," he said. "After all, so long as things are left undisturbed here we're damn well certain to find it if I have every blade of grass pulled up separately. The point is—do you want to go to London now, Cecilia, or back to the Court?"

His wife looked at Chloe, who knew the Chief Justice. Let her talk to him while she sat ignorant? Never. If they couldn't find this stone they could anyhow get on the track of the others.

"London," she said. "But you had better stop here, Angus, and perhaps Mr. Lindsay will go back to the Court and send someone to you."

Chloe felt clear that this would do what she wanted with Frank without her interfering. She went on moving the grass with her foot and looking at the ground, as did everyone else except Frank who glanced back towards the road and said coldly, "I'm afraid that's impossible. Miss Burnett wants to go to London too."

There was a short silence. Then Angus, still murmuring curses, said abruptly to his wife, "Then you'd better take the car and get on to London with Miss Burnett. And I'll stop here, and then perhaps Mr. Lindsay won't mind going back to the Court."

"I shall very much mind," Lindsay answered. "I am going to take Miss Burnett to London at once—myself. I daresay someone will pass pretty soon who'll take a message for you."

Chloe's hand on his arm distracted him. "Frank dear," she said, *"would* you go? I know it sounds beastly, but if you would . . ."

Frank stared at her. "Do you want me to?" he asked stupidly.

"I don't—I don't—want you to," Chloe in confusion murmured. "But I think it would be—O sporting—of you. It's not a bit nice, but I think we ought."

"I think it's perfectly insane," Frank answered in a low voice. "Do you want them to have their own way altogether?"

"Not altogether," Chloe protested, also speaking softly, "but it seems as if we ought," she ended again lamely.

Frank, in a very bad temper, gave way. "O anything you like, of course," he said coldly. "I go back to this Court then, and after that I can come to London by myself, I suppose?"

"I know it's beastly, Frank," Chloe answered appealingly. "I'd go myself or I'd come with you—I'd love to come with you—but I must get to Lord Arglay as soon as Mrs. Sheldrake." She was not quite clear why, since she realized even then that two sentences of Cecilia's conversation would let the Chief Justice know everything. But she could not yet face that abolition of her own secret desires which the abandonment of any attempt to witness their meeting would involve. Besides, Frank would be bound to want to know—still, it was hard on him and it was quite natural he should turn away and say to Sheldrake very politely, "Miss Burnett thinks your suggestion a very good one, and so do I. Will Mrs. Sheldrake take her on to London then?"

Cecilia with a cold grudge assented. But Chloe said suddenly to Angus—"O but, Mr. Sheldrake, if you *do* find it, you'll tell us, won't you? That would be only fair." Angus agreed. "If I find it I'll let you know at once," he said. "At Lord Arglay's?"

"Please," Chloe said gratefully, and tried to catch Frank's eye. She failed, and went sadly to the bank. She was always doing the selfish thing, she felt. But after all Lord Arglay might

—might very easily—want several things done at once when he knew the situation. She wished she wanted to be with Frank a little more strongly. Duty with a strong inclination looked so dreadfully selfish beside duty with a mild inclination. She sat down gloomily in the Sheldrakes' car and it moved off.

The two men looked at each other. "I don't understand what all this is about," Frank said, "or whose this precious stone is. But I have your word that if you find it while I'm gone, or at all for that matter, you'll let us know."

"I don't mind telling you what *I* know," Angus answered. "I bought, from a fellow named Montague, who seems to be a nephew of this Lord Arglay your friend's so keen on, a rather valuable stone for my wife. She understood that it was—well, practically, unique—and now there seems to be some question on our side of misrepresentation, and on yours—theirs, I mean, —of other rights in the property. I daresay it can all be settled by a few minutes chat between me and Lord Arglay or whoever knows, but till then, since I've parted with my money, I consider I've a right to hold the stone. But I'm anxious to be quite fair and I'll certainly let you or Miss Burnett know if it's found. I shall have a very careful search made, and if it's necessary I shall buy both these fields."

"I see," Frank said, a little impressed by this method of dealing with difficulties. "And you want me to go and let your people know where you are."

"If you will," Angus assented. "It's very good of you, but you'll agree that Miss Burnett seemed almost as keen as my wife."

"O yes," Frank answered gloomily. "What's the best way to your place from here?"

Sheldrake told him and he departed, car and all. Angus, allowing about an hour before he was relieved, lit a cigarette and sat down under the hedge to wait. He was too tired to do any more searching; indeed, when the cigarette was finished, he found himself disinclined to move in order to reach another, but, stretching himself out, lay half-asleep and half-brooding.

He was only partly conscious of feet that sounded on the other side of the hedge, though a certain subconscious knowledge told him that someone was coming along a footpath that ran alongside the hedge, a couple of feet away. As they came nearer however he moved so as to be just in time to see a tall figure take a short stride up to the hedge, reach up and pick something from the top of the intertwining twigs. A sudden fear assailed him. The stranger was back on the footpath before Angus could scramble to his feet, and was beginning to move away by the time he reached the hedge.

"Hi!" Angus cried out, seriously alarmed. "Hi, you!"

The stranger paused and looked back. He was a tall, rather dark young man, of about thirty, carrying sketching materials, and he looked at Angus with a certain hard surprise.

"Hi!" said Angus again. "Is that mine?"

The young man looked at him, took a step or two farther on, and said over his shoulder, "Is what yours?"

Angus ran a few feet along his side of the hedge and said, "What you've just picked up. If it's a funny looking stone, it's mine."

"Is it really?" the stranger said. "And why did you put it there?"

"Never mind about all that," Sheldrake said impatiently. "Just hand it over, will you?"

The young man began to walk slowly on, and Angus, tripping over roots and stones every other second, kept pace with him, cursing aloud.

"I ask you," the stranger said to the sky, "what would *you* think? I pick a—something—from a hedge and am vociferously told that it belongs to *him*"—he threw a disagreeable glance at Sheldrake. "And you, I suppose," he said bitterly, "were looking for it?"

"I had been," Angus said, almost falling once more. "I had only just sat down."

"Well, if you will take a rest in the middle of pitch and toss—" the young man flung over. "If it's yours how did it get to the top of the hedge?"

"My wife threw it there from a car," Sheldrake answered incoherently as they reached the bank of the high road.

"And then went away, car and all," the stranger said looking at the empty road. "Family happiness. Is marriage a success?"

"Don't be a damned idiot," Angus snapped. "Give me that stone at once."

The stranger pondered. "I half-believe you," he said, "but only half. And anyhow I may tell you I dislike nothing so much as to be called Hi. I don't mind calling myself I, though of course—yes, I know what you're going to say—there's no proof of it. It's a convenience elevated into a philosophy—yes, I agree. But even so I don't like strangers using what is, so to speak, my own pet name for myself. And still more do I dislike their aspirating it. An aspirate so generously bestowed is almost snobbish. I don't say——"

"Will you give me that stone?" Sheldrake shouted.

"If you had asked me politely," the young man went on gravely, "I probably should—more out of surprise than conviction. Holy awe and so on. But as it is—no. However, if it's yours, you shall have it. My name is Oliver Doncaster, and I am staying for a few weeks at Mrs. Pentridge's in the village over there. I am now going there to tea. *After* tea"—he looked at his watch—"a quarter to five say, about six, if you will call and convince me you shall have your stone. What is your name—besides Hi, which is, I suppose, generic?"

Angus tried to pull himself together; he felt such a fool wrangling through a hedge. Besides he was not finally certain that this fellow had the stone. "I beg your pardon if I was rude," he said, "but it was all so sudden. . . ."

The Loss of a Type

"Very sudden," Doncaster agreed politely.

". . . and I was so anxious to stop you, that I just called out . . . If you would let me see what it was you took out of the hedge. . . ."

"It was," the other allowed, "a stone. It just happened to catch my eye. After six I shall be delighted to let it catch yours. Never mind about your name if you'd rather keep it dark. In about an hour or so then? So pleased to have—well, this is hardly a meeting, is it?—heard from you. Good-bye, good-bye." He waved his hand gracefully and went off along the footpath which here turned to the left and took him to a gate half-way along the field. By the time Angus had got to the bottom of the bank he had come into the road, passed across it, and disappeared down a side lane.

At tea he examined his find. It seemed dull enough indoors, though the colour was pure and the markings curious, but it lacked something of the golden light with which it had seemed to shine in the afternoon sun. A little disappointed he went up to his bedroom and paused on the way at another door.

"Hallo," he said, "may I come in?"

In the bed in this room lay Mrs. Pentridge's mother, Mrs. Ferguson, who had been paralyzed from the waist downward for the last year. Opinion in the house was silently divided whether it would have been better for her to be taken altogether or not. Mr. Pentridge thought it would be a merciful release for her. Mrs. Pentridge thought it was a merciful blessing that she had been so far spared. Mrs. Ferguson disguised her own opinion, if she had one, and concentrated her energies on making the most of what visitors and what talk she could still have. Doncaster had fallen into what he felt to be a ridiculous habit of showing her his day's work after tea, and was even, half-seriously, trying to teach her his own prejudices about art; not that he allowed himself to call them that. Mrs. Pentridge, who was also in the room, examining pillow-cases, welcomed him as warmly as her mother.

"Did you get a nice view, Mr. Doncaster?" she asked.

He sat down smiling. "A very pretty bit of work," he said. "No, Mrs. Ferguson, I don't mean mine—I mean the thing I was trying to do. But I had to alter one branch. I couldn't somehow find out exactly what spot nature meant me to stand at. Now look there——" He held out the sketch and Mrs. Ferguson stared at it while he expatiated. Mrs. Pentridge went on with her pillow-cases. When at last he rose—"O by the way," he said, "I'm expecting a man in a few minutes, to talk about something I found. Look, did you ever see a stone like that?" He passed it over to Mrs. Ferguson. "Look at the colour, isn't it exquisite?"

"What is it?" the old lady asked.

"Lord knows," said Oliver. "I should like it to be chrysoprase, but I don't suppose it is. The Urim and Thummim perhaps."

"That was what the high priest had on his breastplate," Mrs. Ferguson said, looking at the Bible that lay by her bedside. "I remember that well enough."

"I'm sure you do," Oliver said smiling.

"I was little enough when I heard about them," Mrs. Ferguson went on. "At the Sunday school it was. I remember it because I learned them the Sunday before I went to the treat for the first time. Urim and Thummim, that was it. I remember Susie Bright pretending to look for them all the way home in the ditch. O I do wish I could run now as well as I could then."

Mr. Sheldrake's knock at the door below passed unnoticed. For Mrs. Pentridge had dropped her pillow-cases, and with staring eyes was watching her mother struggling up in bed. She sat up, she gasped and gazed, her hands drooped and waved in front of her. She began to shift round; oblivious of Oliver's presence she felt for the side of the bed and began to slip her feet over it. "Mother," shrieked Mrs. Pentridge and flew to one side as Oliver leapt to the other. Mrs. Ferguson, panting with surprise and exertion, came slowly to her feet, and holding on to her two supporters, took a step or two forward.

"I'm all right," she gasped, released Oliver, took another step, "quite all right," and let go of her daughter. "I think," she added, "I must be feeling a bit better to-day."

There was a stupendous silence. Mr. Sheldrake knocked again at the front door.

Chapter Six

THE PROBLEM OF TIME

Sir Giles lay back in a chair and grinned at Professor Palliser. "Well," he said, "we've spent twenty-four hours on it and here's the result." He read from a paper.

"1. It is of no known substance.

2. It answers to no re-agents.

3. It can be multiplied by division without diminution of the original.

4. It can move and cause movement from point to point, without leaving any consciousness of passage through intervening space.

5. It can cause disappearance—possibly in time."

"Certainly in time," Palliser said, but Sir Giles shook his head.

"Only possibly," he answered, "we don't know that your bright young pathological specimen has gone back in time; we only know he isn't here and the Stone is. I thought you told a very good story this morning to that mother of his."

"I don't like it," Palliser answered seriously. "It's all very disturbing. I suppose the police will be coming here soon."

"I should think certainly," Sir Giles agreed. "But I heard him say good night. And there's no reason why you should murder him—I suppose there isn't?—and no way for you to do it. So I can't see that you're likely to be troubled seriously. And anyhow they haven't got a body nor any trace of one. Let's get on with the inquiry."

The Problem of Time

"I expect you're right," the Professor said. "What do you think we ought to do next?"

Sir Giles leaned forward. "If this assistant of yours has moved in time," he said, "if he has gone back, wherever he's gone to, I suppose he might have gone forward instead?"

"I suppose so," Palliser assented slowly.

"Then that seems to be the next thing," Sir Giles said. "But that I think we shall have to do ourselves. We can't run any risk of giving too much away. And, I don't see any chance of being permanently lost there because the future must be the present some time."

"All the same, I shouldn't go too far at first," Palliser suggested. "A quarter of an hour, say."

Sir Giles took a Stone from the table, and was about to speak when Palliser suddenly went on. "Look here, Tumulty, if it worked that way, it wouldn't be a certainty, would it? Supposing I project myself an hour forward and find I'm sitting in this room—and then suppose I return to the present and go to my bedroom and have myself locked in for two hours, say, how can I be doing what I saw myself doing? And the shorter the time the more chance of proving it wrong. In six days anything might happen, but in six minutes. . . ."

Sir Giles brooded. "You probably wouldn't remember," he pointed out. "But I like the idea of your defying the future, Palliser. Try it and see." Palliser's tall lean form quivered with excitement. "It would snap the chain," he said. "We should know we weren't the mere mechanisms of Fate. We should be free."

"I sometimes think," Sir Giles answered reflectively, "that I'm the only real scientist in this whole crawling hotbed of vermin called England. There isn't one of all of you that doesn't cuddle some fantastic desire in his heart, and snivel over every chance of letting it out for an hour's toddle. Do be intelligent, Palliser. How can any damned happening break the chain of happenings? Why do you want to be free? What good could you do if you were free?"

88

The Problem of Time

"If a man can defeat the result of all the past," the Professor said, "if he can know what is to be and cause that it shall not be——"

"O you're drunk," said Sir Giles frankly. "You're drunk with your own romantic gin-and-bitters. If you're going to be sitting here in an hour's time you're going to be, even if this bit of prehistoric slime has to bump you on your crazy noddle and shove you into a chair all on its own. But try it, try it and see."

"Well, you try it too," Palliser said sullenly. "I'm going to keep you under my eye, Tumulty. None of your kidnapping games for me."

"You romantics are always so suspicious," Sir Giles said. "But for once I don't mind. Let's try it together. Where's the Crown?"

Palliser took it out of the old safe in which it had rested all night, and sat down beside Tumulty. "How long do we make it?" he asked. "Half an hour?"

"Good enough," Sir Giles answered ."You locked the door? Right. Now—where's the clock? Half-past eleven. Wait. Let me write it on a bit of paper—so, and put that on the table. What's the formula?"

"To be as we shall be at twelve o'clock, I suppose," Palliser said, and the two—Palliser wearing the Crown, Sir Giles clutching the Stone—framed the wish in their minds.

". . . though I don't suppose I can tell you anything new," Palliser ended, looking at the police inspector.

Sir Giles looked round over his shoulder—he was standing by the window—but he was only half-attending. Had or had not the experiment succeeded? He couldn't remember a thing out of the ordinary. He had sat with Palliser for what seemed a long time—but which the clock had shown to be only ten minutes, and had been vaguely conscious of a rather sick feeling somewhere. And then they had looked at one another and Palliser had abruptly said, "Well?" He had stirred and stood up, looked at the slip of paper with "11.30" written on it, looked at the clock which marked twenty to twelve, looked back at Palliser, and said with some irritation, "God blast the whole damned thing to hell, I don't know."

"What do you mean?" or something like it, Palliser had asked. The picture was becoming fainter, but roughly he could still fill it in. Every minute made all that had happened in that half hour more of a memory; but had it happened at all or was it memory to begin with? And was what was happening now actually happening or was it merely foresight?

Sir Giles in a burst of anger and something remarkably like alarm, realized that he didn't know.

He remembered the knocking, the caretaker, the entrance of the inspector to whom Palliser was talking—very well the Professor was doing, Sir Giles thought, only he probably hadn't realized the difficulty; he wouldn't, not with that kind of cancer-eaten sponge he called an intellect. "But I *remember*," Tumulty thought impatiently. "How the hell could I remember if it hadn't happened? There'd be nothing to remember." He plunged deeper. "But at twelve I should remember. Then if it's come off—I remember what hasn't happened. I'm in a delusion. I'm mad. Nonsense. I'm in the twelve state of consciousness. But the twelve state couldn't be unless the eleven to twelve state had been. Am I here or am I sitting in that blasted chair of Palliser's knowing it from outside time?"

He had a feeling that there was another corollary just round the corner of his mind and strained to find it. But it avoided him for the moment. He looked over his shoulder to find that the inspector was going, and as soon as the departure was achieved rushed across the room to Palliser. "Now," he said, "what *has* happened? O never mind about your fly-blown policeman. *What has happened?*"

"Nothing has happened," Palliser said staring. "It evidently doesn't work in the future."

"You seem jolly sure about it," Sir Giles said. "How do you *know*? You wanted to be as you would be at twelve, didn't you? Well, how do you know you're not? You seem to remember, I know; so do I."

"Well then," Palliser argued—"Yes, I see what you mean. This is merely knowledge—premature knowledge? Umph. Well, let's return to eleven-thirty." He took a step towards the safe, but Sir Giles caught him by the wrist. "Don't do that, you fool," he said. "Why the hell didn't I see it before? If you once go back, you'll bind yourself to go on doing the same thing—you *must*."

Palliser sat down abruptly and the two looked at each other. "But you said the present would be bound to become the future," he objected.

"I know I did," Sir Giles almost howled at him. "But don't you see, you fool, that the action of return must be made at the starting-point? That's why your oyster-stomached helot vanished; that's the trick that's caught you now. I won't be caught; there must be a way out and I'll find it."

"Look here, Tumulty," Palliser said, "let's keep calm and think it out. What do you mean by the action of return being made at the starting-point?"

"O God," Sir Giles moaned, "to be fastened to a man who doesn't know how to ask his mother for milk! I mean that you must condition your experiment from without and not from within; you must define your movement before you make it or your definition will be controlled by it. You can say *I will go and return in such and such a manner*, but if you only say *I will go* your return is ruled by sequence. Can't you think, Palliser?"

"Then we *are* in the future?" Palliser said, "and we can't go back to live that half-hour? Well, does it very much matter?"

"If we are," Sir Giles said, "we—O it's no good trying to explain to you." He began to walk about and then went back to the chair in which he had been sitting originally and stared at it. "Now am I there?" he asked grimly, "or am I here?"

The Problem of Time

There was a silence of some minutes. Then Palliser said again, "I still can't see why you're so excited. That half-hour wasn't of any importance, surely?"

Sir Giles, having reached his limit of exasperation, became unexpectedly gentle. He went back to Palliser and said almost sweetly, "Well, don't worry over it, don't hurt your brain, but just try and follow. If this is a forecast in consciousness, that consciousness is, so to speak, housed somewhere. And it's housed in your body. And where's your body? And how do you get your mind-time and your body-time to agree?"

"My body is here," Palliser said, patting it.

"O no," Sir Giles said, still sweetly. "At least perhaps it is and perhaps it isn't. Perhaps all this is occupying a millionth part of a second and we're still sitting there."

"But Pondon disappeared?" Palliser objected, "into his past, I suppose? Mayn't we have disappeared into our future?"

"I hope we have," Sir Giles assented. "But we seem to remember—or to know—what happened, don't we? We seem to know that we talked and the police came and so on? Did it happen or has it got to happen or hasn't it happened and will it never happen? If we will to return we seem to me—but of course I'm a little child crooning on your knee—to be in a constant succession of the same period. And if we don't?"

"Well, we go on," the Professor said.

"Till we become conscious of death?" Sir Giles asked. "And then what happens? Till these apparent bodies die and corrupt and our minds return to our real bodies and live it again—is that the truth? Years and years and years and all in less than a second and all to be repeated—do you like it, Palliser?"

"But Pondon disappeared," the Professor said again.

"You keep on repeating that," Sir Giles told him. "Don't you see, you cow, that the conditions may be different? Whatever the past is, it has been in everyone's knowledge; whatever the future is it hasn't."

The Problem of Time

"What do you propose to do about it, anyhow?" the Professor asked.

Sir Giles considered. "I propose to think over it for a few days," he said, "and see if I can think of any formula to find out, first where that assistant of yours is and secondly where we are. Also to see if Whitehall is doing anything, because I'm not going to be taken by surprise by *them*, not under present conditions. So I shall go back to London this afternoon."

All the way to Euston—he didn't want to use the Stone again at the moment—Tumulty brooded over the problem that confronted him. He devised several formulæ for getting into touch with the unfortunate Mr. Pondon; the most obvious experiment—that of willing him back—had been tried by himself and the Professor on the previous evening without success. It seemed that the Stone could not be used to control others; its action was effective only over the action of whoever held it. Sir Giles regretted this rather keenly; the possibility of disarranging other people's lives had appeared to him a desirable means of experiment, since he was on the whole reluctant to conduct experiments on himself. That state of being which lies between mysticism, madness, and romanticism, had always been his chosen field, but it was a field in which few suitable subjects grew. He found it impossible not to desire to be able to dispose of objectionable people by removing them to some past state of being, and he almost sent a telegram to Palliser urging him to acquaint Mrs. Pondon and the police with the facts of the case and to inquire whether the police "in the execution of their duty," would be bound to follow the vanished assistant to the day before yesterday. Pondon had certainly gone of his own free will, even if his superior had refrained from explaining the possibilities clearly enough. However, Pondon could wait a few days. That morning, Sir Giles had noticed in their short interview, he had cut himself while shaving; it afforded Tumulty a certain pleasure to think of that small cut being repeated again and again until he himself had time, inclination, and knowledge to interfere. But the other problem worried him more considerably. That missing half hour haunted him; had he lived through it or had he not, and if he had not could even the Stone release him from the necessity of doing so?

He began to wonder if the Stone could help him, but he didn't see how, unless it could present thoughts to his mind—or to other people's. If there was someone he could trust to tell him what could be learnt from such a trial of the Stone? He thought of Lord Arglay, a trained and detached, and not unsympathetic, mind. Palliser was no good because Palliser was mixed up with it. And you couldn't go to everyone asking them to help you look for half an hour you had mislaid. Also Arglay would know if Whitehall were moving—not that he minded very much if it were.

At Euston he took a taxi to the Chief Justice's.

Lord Arglay's Saturday afternoon therefore broke suddenly into activity. Some time after tea, while he was playing with the idea of bringing *Organic Law* into the Stone's sphere of activity, though he felt certain the Hajji would disapprove of any such use, he was startled by the announcement that Mrs. Sheldrake had called. "Miss Burnett is with her, sir," the maid added.

"Now what on earth," Lord Arglay said as he went to the drawing-room, "is Chloe doing with Mrs. Sheldrake? How did she get hold of her, I wonder? and has she brought her here to be instructed or to be frightened?"

It soon appeared however that if anyone were frightened it was Chloe herself. Mrs. Sheldrake took the conversation into her own hands, with a brief explanation of her connection with the Stone, and a light reference to the fact that it had been, for the moment, mislaid. She wanted to know, since Miss Burnett had mentioned Lord Arglay several times, whether he claimed any rights in the Stone.

"Not in that particular Type," Lord Arglay said.

The Problem of Time

"Type, Lord Arglay?" Cecilia asked. "How do you mean—Type?"

"The position is a little obscure," the Chief Justice said, considering rapidly Mrs. Sheldrake's appearance and manner, Mr. Sheldrake's riches and position (which he had looked up), and the desirability of subduing them both without antagonism. "I say Type because the Stones which exist—and there are several—are apparently derivations from one Original, though (and perhaps therefore) possessed of the same powers. But how far they are to be regarded as being identical with it, for proprietary reasons, I cannot at the moment say. Nor in whom the title to the property inheres. I may add that certain foreign representatives are deeply interested, and the Government is observing matters. I think that in the present situation your husband should preserve the utmost secrecy and caution. His title appears to me uncertain, both so far as the acquisition of his Type is concerned and in the relation of that Type to the Original."

He delivered this with occasional pauses for meditation and with a slight pomposity which he put on at necessary moments. Mrs. Sheldrake, a little impressed, nevertheless appeared to receive it with frigidity.

"But, Lord Arglay," she said, "we can't be expected to sit quiet while other people use our property in order to ruin our companies. I am thinking of the effect it may have on Atlantic Airways. What is this original you are talking about?"

"It is the centre of the derivations," Lord Arglay said at random, but ridiculously enough the phrase in Chloe's mind suddenly connected itself with "the End of Desire." The chance and romantic words came to her like a gospel, none the less emotionally powerful that at the moment she didn't understand it. What were the derivations? She had a vague feeling that the sentence suggested Lord Arglay himself as the centre though she knew he would have been the first to mock at the ascription. But there was certainly something in them that referred if not to him, then to something connected with him. He was walking on some firm pavement, where she wanted to be walking too.

She came back to hear Mrs. Sheldrake end a sentence—"opinion on it."

"Madam," Lord Arglay said, "it must be clear to you that I can give no opinion until a case is before the Court. I am not a solicitor or a barrister. I am the Chief Justice."

"But we must know what to *do*," Mrs. Sheldrake said. "Don't you even know where the original, whatever it is, came from?"

Lord Arglay suppressed a desire to offer her a précis of the Hajji's history of the Stone of Suleiman, and leaned forward.

"Mrs. Sheldrake," he said, "by the folly of my nephew you have come into actual—if not legal—possession of a Type of Stone which is said to be regarded by millions as a very holy relic, and the ownership of which may have the most important repercussions. I beg you to act with great care. I venture to suggest that you should at least consider the propriety of giving it into my care until more is known and decided. It is, I know, an audacious proposal, but the seeming audacity is due to the anxiety with which I regard the situation. I am not speaking casually. I do not think it likely, but in certain remote yet not impossible circumstances I can believe that even your life and your husband's might be in danger. Consult with him and believe me that this warning is meant very, very seriously."

"That," he thought, "ought to worry her." She was staring at the ground now, and he threw a side glance at Chloe, whose face reinforced his words.

Cecilia felt baffled. She saw nothing to do at the moment but to talk to Angus and take other ways of finding out the mystery. As she began to shape a phrase of dubious farewell the door was thrown open and Sir Giles Tumulty came in. He nodded to Arglay and stared at the visitors.

"Busy, Arglay?" he asked. "I want to talk to you."

"I want to talk to *you*," the Chief Justice said, with something in his voice that made Chloe look up suddenly and even distracted Cecilia, to whom he turned. "I can do no more for you now, Mrs. Sheldrake," he ended.

"It's very unsatisfactory," she complained. "I almost think I had better go to the Ambassador. You see, we don't come under your jurisdiction, if that's what you call it. We belong to the States."

"Quite," Lord Arglay said, waiting for her to go.

"After all, someone must know to whom the Stone belongs, and who can or can't sell it," Cecilia went on.

"Hallo," Sir Giles said, "have you got one too? Is this yours, Arglay, or is it Reginald's? I hope you didn't overcharge for it."

Cecilia almost leaped at him. "O," she said, "I'm afraid I don't know your name but can you tell me anything about this Stone? It's all so very mysterious. We—my husband and I—bought it from a Mr. Montague, and now we are told it's very doubtful whether he had the right to sell it."

"Of course he had the right," Sir Giles said. "I gave him one yesterday morning."

"Was it yours then to begin with?" Cecilia asked.

"Certainly," Sir Giles said. "Does anyone deny it?"

"Yes," Lord Arglay said, "and you know they do."

"O a set of religious maniacs," Sir Giles tossed them aside. "Do you, Arglay?"

The Chief Justice paused for a half second, then his training won.

"No," he said, "I don't deny it for I don't know. But I want to talk to you about it, Tumulty, after this lady has gone." He felt it was rude but he couldn't help it. A more urgent matter than Mrs. Sheldrake's trouble was obsessing him. That she had actually lost the Stone he had not understood; her references to that part of the adventure had been so general as to leave the impression that her husband was finding it just as she set off with Chloe.

Now she retaliated by turning her back full on him and saying to Tumulty: "I should like to talk with you, Sir Giles. Could you spare me half an hour at Grosvenor Square?"

Sir Giles's first impulse was to tell her to go to hell. But he felt that Lord Arglay had changed in something; his previous good temper had gone. Tumulty had been through too many dangerous experiences in remote parts of the world not to recognize hostility when he met it, and he knew that Arglay was hostile now. Why he couldn't imagine but that was the fact. If Arglay was going to turn nasty it might be as well to be in with this woman, whoever she was. If she had bought the Stone there must be money and therefore power and probably position, and perhaps a counterweight to the Chief Justice's enmity. Not that it mattered very much; he wasn't going to spend any time shooting at Arglay with any possible kind of inconvenient elephant rifle. But obviously these two weren't on the best of terms, and Sir Giles's generally diffused contempt suddenly crystallized in a definite hatred of this large man looming in front of him. He accepted a card, refused to make a definite promise; he wasn't going to be rung up as if he were her chauffeur—but said something about ringing up, and with a malicious benevolence got rid of her. She departed, her mind stabilized by his brusque assurance that she had an entire right to her Stone. Chloe half rose; Lord Arglay waved her back. Sir Giles flung himself into a chair. "Now," he said, "what's *your* trouble, Arglay—that is, if it's fit for your . . . secretary . . . to hear." It was the minutest pause before "secretary"; both his hearers remarked it, and neither of them took any notice of it.

"I want to know," Arglay said, "what you've been doing at Birmingham."

Genuinely surprised, Sir Giles stared at him. "But that's exactly what I want to tell you," he said. "I want you to find out, one way or another, what *has* happened."

"I promise you I will do that," Arglay answered. "But you shall tell me first what you have done."

"Don't talk to me like that," Sir Giles snapped back. "You're not in your bestial Law Courts now. Palliser and I made an experiment this morning, and I'm not at all clear——"

"I want to know" Arglay interrupted "about your experiment last night."

More and more astonished, Sir Giles sat up. "Last night?" he said, "what do you know about last night? Not that there's anything particular to know. You're not interested in Palliser's kindergarten school, are you?"

"Who was the man you gave the Stone to?" the Chief Justice insisted, "and what happened to him?"

"Now how do you know all that?" Sir Giles said meditatively. "God strike you dead, Arglay, have you been spying on me with that blasted bit of dried dung? You have, have-you? So it does do something with knowledge. Good, that's what I wanted to know. Now listen. This morning Palliser and I——"

"What happened to the man last night?" Lord Arglay said again.

"O how the hell do I know?" Sir Giles said fretfully. "That's part of the whole thing. You can have him—I don't want him. He's probably messing round last week—no, we said twelve hours so he won't be. As a matter of fact I thought he might come back in another twelve but we were there—at least, Palliser was—by nine this morning and he hadn't. But you can go and look for him. Only I want you to tell me first whether I'm here or not." He succeeded in outlining his problem.

In spite of himself Lord Arglay was held by it.

"But so far as I'm concerned, it's certainly you—the normal corporeal sequential you I'm talking to," he said. "I've not missed half an hour."

"I know *that*," Sir Giles moaned. "I know that what's happening now is happening to you. But I don't know whether

99

I'm knowing it all first of all. It's this damned silly business of only actually experiencing the smallest minimum of time and all the rest being memory that does me in. I know it was memory at twelve o'clock but if I'd lived through it all it would still be memory. O for God's sake, Arglay, don't be as big a fool as Palliser. I suppose you've got *some* brains; after all they made you Chief Justice. And if you can see what happened in Birmingham last night you can see what happened there this morning. You needn't be afraid; we can define the whole thing first of all, so you're bound to come back all right."

"I will do nothing at all," Lord Arglay said, "until I have done what I can for your——" he paused on the word " victim " which sounded theatrical. "And even then," he said, slurring it, "I do not know what I can do, for I do not think this Stone was meant to be used to save such men as you from the consequences of their actions."

"What *do* you think it was meant for?" Sir Giles said. "And not so much of this infant school Scripture lesson. I'd see your inside torn out, Arglay, before I asked you to save me. I want to know what *does* happen and if you won't tell me the nearest warder in the Zoological Gardens will do as well."

"Then you can go and ask him," Lord Arglay said, recovering something of his good temper, partly because he began to discern that, somehow or other, the unfortunate assistant might be given a chance of return, and partly because he did not dislike seeing Sir Giles really thwarted. "I'm not going to do a thing without very great care. And you'd better take care what you do because, if you're right, you'll have to do it all again."

"O my lord God Almighty," Sir Giles said, "can't you see that, *if* I'm right, I can't choose till next time? You are a louse-brained catalept, Arglay." His interest in pure thought vanished and his personal concern returned. "So you're not going to do anything, aren't you?" he said.

"Not for a day or two," Lord Arglay said. "It'll do you all

the good in the world, Giles, to be a little uncertain of yourself. Well, you can't object to that way of putting it, surely; you are exactly a little uncertain of yourself, aren't you?"

Sir Giles said nothing. He sat for a minute or two gazing at the Chief Justice, then he got up, and with a conversational, "Well, well, well," walked straight out of the room. Lord Arglay looked at Chloe.

"I refrain from saying 'Curiouser and curiouser,' " he said, "but I can't think of anything else to say. The efficient Giles has been caught. How just a compensation! The Stone is a very marvellous thing." His voice, even on the words, changed into gravity. "And now," he went on, "suppose you tell me what did happen this afternoon."

When she had done so—"Then for all we know one of them is lying about the English countryside?" the Chief Justice said. "Pleasant hearing for our friend the Hajji. And now for my experiments." He went over his experiences of the previous evening.

"So," he ended, "we know it moves in time and space and thought. And in what else?"

"But what else is there?" Chloe said.

"The Hajji talked of the Transcendence," Lord Arglay answered. "But who knows what he meant or if what he meant is so?"

Chloe said, almost with pain, "But what do *you* think he meant?"

"Child," Lord Arglay said, "I am an old man and I have known nothing all my life farther or greater than the work I have taken to do. I have never seen a base for any temple nor found an excuse to believe in the myths that are told there. I will not say *believe* or *do not believe*. But there is one thing only at which I have wondered at times, and yet it seemed foolish to think of it. It will happen sometimes when one has worked hard and done all that one can for the purpose before one—it has happened then that I have stood up and been content with the world of things and with what has been done there through me. And this may be pride, or it may be the full stress of the whole being and delight in labour—there are a hundred explanations. But I have wondered whether that profound repose was not communicated from some far source and whether the life that is in it was altogether governed by time. And I am sure that state never comes while I am concerned with myself, and I have thought to-day that in some strange way that state was itself the Stone. But if so then assuredly none of these men shall find its secret."

"Is that the end of desire?" Chloe said.

"I have no desire left at all," Lord Arglay said, "but I think that other is the better ending of desire. And though I cannot tell how you should seek for it, I think it waits for everyone who will have it. Also I think that perhaps the Stone chooses more than we know; and yet that is a fantasy, is it not?"

"*Was* there a stone in the Crown of Suleiman?" she said, "and was Suleiman the wisest of men?"

"So they say," Lord Arglay answered. "And will you seek for wisdom in the Stone?"

"What is wisdom?" Chloe said.

"And that, child," Lord Arglay answered again, "though I am an interpreter of all the laws of England, I do not know."

Chapter Seven

THE MIRACLES AT RICH

Half-way down the stairs Mrs. Pentridge and Oliver Doncaster began to realize that someone was knocking, loudly and continuously, at the door. But the spectacle of Mrs. Ferguson in front of them, progressing, in the dressing gown which she had put on, from stair to stair with an alertness which her age, to say nothing of her paralysis, would have seemed to forbid, so occupied and distracted them that it was with reluctance that Mrs. Pentridge at last rushed to open, and with delight that she said, hastily returning, "It's for you, sir."

"Eh?" said Oliver, "me? O nonsense! O damn!" He remembered the lunatic who wanted the stone, and strode across. "Hallo," he said, "O it *is* you! Well, yes; yes, I'm sorry, but we're in a bit of a confusion just now owing to a paralyzed old lady suddenly skipping like the high hills. Could you wait a few minutes or go and have a drink or something?"

"No, I couldn't," Sheldrake said. "You've made me come all this way and given me all this trouble, and now you talk to me about an old woman. An old woman won't stop you giving me my stone."

"By the way, what did I do with it?" Doncaster asked vaguely. "I know I had it a few minutes ago. Now what—I remember, I was showing it to Mrs. Ferguson when she began to curvet. I wonder if she dropped it somewhere."

Sheldrake swore under his breath, then ceased as an incredible idea came into his mind. "Who's Mrs. Ferguson?" he asked.

"Mrs. Ferguson is my landlady's mother," Doncaster said. "Who having been in bed to my knowledge since just before

I came last year is now jazzing like a two-year-old. Peep round the door. Well, you don't suppose I'm going to interrupt her by asking for my—I mean your—at least I mean you said your—pebble, do you? Bless her, she's like a child at a Sunday school treat."

Sheldrake became more and more uneasy. If this infernal old woman—if the Stone could cure—if it got about——

"Look here," he said quite untruly to Oliver, "I've got to get on to London and I want to take my property with me. A joke's a joke, but——"

"And a jubilee's a jubilee," Oliver said. "Still, I see your point. Well, wait a minute—— Good heavens, she's going out."

Mrs. Ferguson indeed was coming straight to the door. When she reached it Oliver pulled Sheldrake aside. "Still feeling better, Mrs. Ferguson?" he asked.

"Much better, thank you, sir," the old lady said. "But I feel as if I could do with a little fresh air, and if it looked a nice evening I was thinking I'd just pop along and see my sister Annie. I haven't seen much of her this year owing to her asthma and my not being able to get out. Mary, my dear," she added to Mrs. Pentridge, "I think I'll dress."

"O mother," said Mrs. Pentridge, "do you think you ought to go out? Suppose you were taken bad again?"

Mrs. Ferguson smiled serenely. "I shan't be taken bad," she said, "I never felt better in all my life. And I owe it all to you, Mr. Doncaster," she added.

"Me?" said the surprised Oliver.

"I felt the strength just pouring into me from that stone you gave me, sir," Mrs. Ferguson assured him. "I've got it tight. You don't want it back this minute, do you, sir?"

"Certainly not, Mrs. Ferguson," Doncaster said promptly. "Keep it an hour or two and see how you feel."

"O nonsense," Sheldrake broke in,—"look here, Mrs.——"

"Shut up," said Oliver. "That's all right, Mrs. Ferguson. Carry on."

"I won't shut up," Sheldrake shouted. "What the hell do you think you're doing, throwing other people's property about?"

"How do I know it's your property?" Oliver shouted back. "I pick a bit of stone out of a hedge and you pop up out of a sound sleep and say your wife threw it there and will I give it back? Who are you, anyhow?"

"My name is Sheldrake, Angus M. Sheldrake," the other answered. "I'm the chairman of Atlantic Airways and half a dozen other things. I gave seventy thousand pounds for that stone and I want it back at once."

"Then you won't get it back at once," Oliver retorted, "not if you were the chairman of the Atlantic, Pacific, Indian, Arctic, and Antarctic air, sea, and land ways, and the Tube railways too. Not if you offered me another seventy thousand —at least, you might then. I don't know, so don't tempt me. Or rather do, so that I can say, 'Keep your dross.' Start with fifty thousand, and go up by fives."

"By God," Sheldrake said, "I'll have you all in prison for this."

"Don't be a fool," Oliver answered crossly. "Go and wake up Job Ricketts and tell him to arrest old Mrs. Ferguson for stealing your stone. I should like to see you explaining."

The quarrel raged in this manner until Mrs. Ferguson, cloak and bonnet on, came to the door to start. "Is it the gentleman's stone, sir?" she asked anxiously.

"He doesn't know, I don't know," Oliver told her. "Get you along, Mrs. Ferguson, but don't let it go out of your possession. I call everybody to witness," he said loudly, addressing Mrs. Ferguson, Mrs. Pentridge, Sheldrake, the chauffeur, and the villagers who were beginning to collect, "that Mrs. Ruth Ferguson retains the property in question—namely, a stone—on my instructions until I am satisfied of the bonafides of the claimant, one Angus M. Sheldrake on his own confession. There," he added to Sheldrake.

"What the devil do you suppose is the good of that?" Sheldrake said furiously.

"I don't really know," Oliver said comfortably, "but it creates a right impression, don't you think?"

"But do you expect me to prove the whole bally thing to any fool who stops me in the street or any pickpocket who sneaks it?" Sheldrake raged.

"To be accurate, it was you who stopped me and wanted to pick my pocket—in effect," Oliver said. "And we might as well spend the next two or three hours proving your bona-fides as not, don't you think?"

"I'm not going to let that woman out of my sight," Sheldrake said. "Where she goes I go."

"Her people shall be thy people and her gods thy gods," Oliver murmured. "Sudden conversion of a millionaire. The call of the old home. Way down on the Swanee River. O Dixie, my Dixie, our fearful trip is done."

"O go to the devil," Sheldrake said, leaping back to his car. "Barnes, follow that damned old woman in the black bonnet."

"Yes, sir," the chauffeur said obediently, and the procession started—Mrs. Ferguson and Mrs. Pentridge in front, Oliver strolling a few paces behind, the car rolling along in the road, parallel to him, and an increasing crowd of villagers, dissolving, reforming, chattering and exclaiming as the astonishing news spread. Rather owing to this tumultuous concourse than to any weakness on Mrs. Ferguson's part it took them an hour to reach the mile-distant town of Rich-by-the-Mere, commonly called Rich, where Mrs. Ferguson's asthmatic sister lived. By the time they reached her street the crowd was a mob, the car was doing the best it could among the excited groups, and Oliver had been pushed forward on to Mrs. Ferguson's heels. The old lady knocked at the door, which was opened in a minute, and there followed immediately a loud scream.

"Ruth!" cried a voice.

"All right, Annie," Mrs. Ferguson was heard to protest and the excitement in the crowd grew louder.

Sheldrake felt almost off his head with anger, despair, and doubt. He had realized during the slow crawl that to go to the police would be to broadcast the rumours of the Stone, but what was to happen he could not guess. That he would recover it he had no real doubt, but he wanted to recover it quietly and get out of England with it at the earliest possible moment. He peered out of the car to see Oliver, his back against the door of the house, giving a dramatic description of Mrs. Ferguson's recovery to as many of the crowd as could hear him; he saw, remotely, the helmets of one or two policemen approaching slowly; he saw windows and doors open all round and new conversations leaping up every moment; he even discerned one or two members of the crowd scribbling in small note books, and dropped back with an oath. But he sat up again in a moment and managed to attract Oliver's attention, who slid through the crowd to the car.

"Look here," he said, "this is past a joke. I apologize if I was rude. I can prove anything you want me to. But as a matter of fact the stone does belong to me, and I must rely on you to get it back. You believe me, don't you?"

"I do really," Oliver said. "You were a bit uppish, you know, but I don't understand what's happened. Of course, it's all nonsense about the stone healing her, but as things have turned out we shall have to go gently. We can't have the poor old thing pushed back into bed because we take it away brutally. Leave it to me and I'll get it back for you to-night. Where do you live?"

Angus told him. Oliver grimaced. "A bit of a way," he said, "but I suppose it was my fault. Well, I'll try and collect it gently to-night or to-morrow morning."

"Excuse me, sir," a voice beside him said, "but can you tell me whether it's true that an old lady has been cured of cancer

by a piece of magnetic iron? Does it belong to you or to this
other gentleman? And is it true that she——"

Oliver and Sheldrake stared at each other. Suddenly Oliver
looked round. Out of the window of the house Mrs. Pentridge
was leaning.

"O Mr. Doncaster," she called, "do please come. Auntie's
asthma's gone. It went in the middle of a cough. O do come."

The noise broke out deafeningly. Mr. Sheldrake flung himself down in the car, and the small reporter fought his way
beside Oliver to the door.

The next morning they all read it. Chloe at Highgate in a
paper purchased when she saw the placards, Lord Arglay at
Lancaster Gate in the *Observer*, Sir Giles at Ealing in his
housekeeper's *Sunday Pictorial*, Professor Palliser at Birmingham
in the *Sunday Times*, Reginald at Brighton (though this was
purely by accident, in a paper he picked up in the smoking-
room of his hotel). It was even stated long afterwards, in a
volume of memoirs, that at Sandringham the Majesty of
England, augustly chatting with Lord Birlesmere (the Minister
in attendance), the Persian Ambassador, and the author of the
memoirs, had graciously deigned to remark that it was a very
extraordinary affair. In the papers, Lourdes, the King's Evil,
the Early Christians, Mrs. Eddy, Mesmer, and other famous
healers were introduced and, almost, invoked. For the scenes
in Rich all night had been such "as to baffle description."
Once it had been understood that this impossible thing was
happening, that health was being restored, and that so simply,
so immediately, the house was almost rushed before the police
could guard it. The two old ladies—Mrs. Ferguson and her
sister—with Mrs. Pentridge were rushed up the stairs by Oliver,
who, with one policeman by him, stationed himself near the
top, exhorting, arguing, fighting. The crowd in the street
was, with usual and immediate sympathy, continually dividing
to let cripples through or the blind and the deaf. Many came
rushing to borrow the Stone for the sick who could not come.

Sheldrake's car, opposite the front-door, was turned into a
kind of Grand Stand. By midnight the whole place was in a
tumult. The loss of the Stone itself became an imminent
danger. Sheldrake was continually telling the police that it
belonged to him; the police were concerned with more difficult
matters. But the reporters had it. "The Stone," they all declared, "was said to belong to Mr. Angus M. Sheldrake, the
well-known . . ." and so on. It was known all over England on
that Sunday morning that Mr. Angus M. Sheldrake owned—
whether at the moment he actually possessed was a little
doubtful—a miraculous Stone which healed all illnesses at a
mere wish.

"Well, really," Lord Arglay said to himself, "Reginald
seems to have done it this time."

Reginald was much of the same opinion. But neither he nor
anyone else of those concerned had any idea what to do next.
The Persian Ambassador took advantage of the afternoon
quiet at Sandringham to point out to Lord Birlesmere that if
this were true, and if it were due to the relic of which he had
spoken, and if the news were telegraphed abroad the most
serious consequences might ensue. Lord Birlesmere took note
of his Excellency's communication, and, later on, got through
to Rivington Court on the telephone. He had met Sheldrake
two or three times and Angus came to speak. But when he
understood that the Foreign Secretary was hinting at a personal interview he gave a little laugh.

"My dear Lord Birlesmere," he said, "I couldn't if I would.
Not without a couple of thousand soldiers and machine guns.
They're all round the place, camping in the grounds, knocking
at the doors. Every town in the district has discharged its halt
and maimed here, and they all want me to heal them."

"And do you?" Lord Birlesmere asked, fascinated by the idea.

"What?" said Mr. Sheldrake.

"But aren't," Lord Birlesmere went on, changing the subject,
"aren't the County Authorities doing anything?"

"They've drafted all the police that they have to spare," Sheldrake told him, "and they're communicating with London. But it doesn't look as if that would help me till to-morrow."

"I'll talk to the Home Office people," Birlesmere said. "You won't mind promising not to leave England or get rid of the Stone till I've seen you?"

Sheldrake hesitated. His chief wish was to get out of England with the Stone; on the other hand his chances of doing so in the face of an antagonistic Foreign Office were small, and he was conscious that there were certain crises in which the Foreign Office would offer no strings for him to pull—the ends would all discreetly disappear. He did not completely understand why the Foreign Office was interfering at all; the Stone hardly seemed to be their pigeon. He had gathered from Cecilia when she returned the night before, or rather when he had himself returned that morning, that the Government was mixed up with it; and of course the Stone was said to have come from abroad. Still——

"Well," he said, "if you'll get me out of this at once I don't mind promising to see you before I leave."

"But can't you really get away?" Lord Birlesmere asked.

It seemed to him inconceivable that any crowd could really prison a man in his own country house, but that was because he had never seen it happen. The concourse round Mr. Sheldrake's front-door, between that and the garage, trying to look in, and even to get in, at the windows, continually flowing in through the gates, occupying the lawns, the terraces, and the gardens, consisted of more people than Lord Birlesmere had seen in all his life. They were quiet while they were not interfered with, in an uncertain quiet. They doubted whether it was much good their coming. They might, before evening, disperse from sheer discouragement and hunger; but the one or two attempts made by an insufficient band of police to shift them had merely produced irritation and, once or twice, something like serious trouble.

Lord Birlesmere, discovering all this by gentle questioning, at last, with some sort of qualified promise, put the receiver back and stared at it. Soldiers were all very well, but the Government was shaky enough, and what would the Opposition papers say if he used the Army to hold back a crowd of suffering English men and women from their chance of healing, and to ensure the escape of an American millionaire with the source of healing in his possession? The Opposition would know, as well as Mr. Sheldrake, as well as Lord Birlesmere himself, that the idea of the Stone doing anything was rubbish. He wished the Prime Minister was in London, but he wasn't; he was in Aberdeen. The best thing was obviously to get Sheldrake quietly to London—perhaps later the crowd would disperse a bit—and then there was this Sir Giles Tumulty the Persian Ambassador had mentioned—an interview there. What on earth had Bruce Cumberland been doing, if anything? The thought of the Ambassador suggested to Lord Birlesmere that it might be just as well if he did not learn too much from the Persian; he didn't want to be put too clearly in possession of the views of a friendly Government. Sheldrake had certainly better be removed quietly. He took such measures as suggested themselves.

On the same Sunday evening the Hajji came round to Lord Arglay's house. The Chief Justice threw down the latest edition of a special evening paper and greeted him with a certain pretended cynicism. "This, I suppose," he said, "is the evil you prophesied for the world—all this healing, I mean?"

"There is not a great deal of healing so far; there is a great deal of desire for healing," Ibrahim answered. "That may be an evil."

"If Sheldrake gets off to America with it, there'll be an evil all right," Lord Arglay said. "I wouldn't be a bit surprised if they passed a special act to prevent him."

"Can your Parliament do such things?" the Hajji asked.

"O rather," Lord Arglay said. "Prevention of Removal of

Art Treasures, I should think. It'll take Sheldrake as long as we like to prove the Stone isn't an Art Treasure. Or they may claim that the sale is invalid because it never was Reginald's; only then you'd want a real claimant. And who could that be? Not me, obviously; not Giles—he wouldn't; not the Ambassador—they'd have to give it back to him."

"You think they would not?" said the Hajji.

"I am absolutely and perfectly sure they would not," Lord Arglay said. "And really, Hajji, I don't know that I blame them. After all, it's not the kind of thing that any one man or family or country even ought to keep. I'm not at all sure it ought to be in existence at all, but after what I've seen I can't think how to destroy it. If you dropped it into the Atlantic I should be afraid of it floating to the Esquimaux or some such people. And it can't be left loose. Look at what happens when it is."

"What then," the Hajji said, "do you think should be done with it?"

"I can't think," Lord Arglay said. "Unless the League of Nations? With a special international guard? No? I was afraid you wouldn't agree."

"You are mocking at it and me," the Hajji said.

"No, I'm not," the Chief Justice assured him. "I'm a little de-normally-mented about it. But I take it very seriously. When the English take anything very seriously they always become a trifle delirious. People tell you that we aren't logical, but it isn't true. Only our logic is a logic of poetry. We are the Tom o' Bedlam of the nations, the sceptics of the world, and we have no hope at all, or none to speak of—that is why we are always so good at adopting new ideas. Look at the way Reginald adopted the Stone."

The Hajji went on looking at him gravely. "And what are you going to do now?" he said.

"I'm in several minds," Lord Arglay said. "And one is to take the Stone and will myself wherever what you call its

Types are and collect them all one by one, whether their present possessors agree or not, and then will myself inside Vesuvius with them all. And one is to go and look for this Pondon fellow. And another is to go and knock Giles on the head. That's three—and the fourth? The fourth is to take the Stone and will it to do what it will with me."

"And that is the most dangerous of all," the Hajji said.

"After all," Arglay argued, "if Miss Burnett seems to think she can get wisdom from it, why shouldn't I?"

"Does she?" the Hajji asked.

"No, of course she doesn't," Lord Arglay said irritably. "It was I who asked her that. Hajji, I'm just rambling. But what in God's name can we *do*?"

The Hajji brooded. "I think that it only knows," he said. "But I dare not use it at all, because it is so great and terrible, and I do not think you believe in it enough for it to reveal its will. What of this friend of yours?"

"Who?" Lord Arglay said blankly.

"This Miss Burnett," Ibrahim answered. "Does she believe?"

Lord Arglay stared at him. "What if she does? What can she believe *in*?" he said. "Are you proposing to play some such trick on her as Giles did on Pondon? Because if so, Hajji, I may as well tell you I shall stop it. Besides, why do you think she'd find out?"

"If—no, it is impossible," the Hajji said. "But I dreamed that I saw the Name of Allah written on her forehead as it is written on the Stone. And it is certain that the way to the Stone is in the Stone."

"Then," Lord Arglay said, not unreasonably, "why don't you take it?"

"Those of my house," the Hajji answered reluctantly, "who were of the Keepers have sworn always to guard and never to use the Relics they keep. Neither this nor a yet more sacred thing."

"What else is there then?" Arglay asked.

"There is that which is in the Innermost," the Hajji answered, "that which controls all things. And I fear lest by the knowledge of the Stone any shall come to find this other thing. For it is said that even Asmodeus when he wore it sat on the throne of Suleiman ben Daood in Jerusalem, and if your Giles Tumulty——"

"I expect even Asmodeus was a gentleman compared with Giles," Lord Arglay said. "But seriously, Hajji, do you mean that there is something else behind? And if so what is it?"

"I must not tell you," Ibrahim said.

"Quite," Lord Arglay answered, half as a gibe, half as a submission. "It's all very useful, isn't it? Well, Hajji, will you help me to find this Pondon man? Is there any particular formula?"

"I think you had need be careful," Ibrahim answered. "For if you will to return to the worlds that were you will not have the Stone with you."

"Giles's idea seemed to be," Lord Arglay said, "that one could will to return to the past for ten minutes or so."

"I do not see how you can bring this man back from the past without the Stone, and if you return to the past you will not have the Stone," the Hajji said doubtfully. "Besides, though you can return to your own past, I do not know whether you can return to his."

"But why can't I go to him *now*," Lord Arglay said, "wherever he is *now*? Damn it, man, he must be somewhere *now*."

"If you are right, he is nowhere at all *now*," the Hajji said. "He has not yet reached *now*. He is in yesterday."

"O Lord!" the Chief Justice said. "But he must be somewhere in space."

"O in space he is no doubt here or there or anywhere," Ibrahim answered. "For yesterday's space is exactly where to-day's space is."

"And to-morrow's also?" Lord Arglay said.

"I think that is true," the Hajji told him. "But to-morrow's exists only in a greater knowledge than ours and it can only be experienced in that diviner knowledge. Therefore to experience the future, though not perhaps to foresee the future, it is necessary to enter the soul of the world with the inward being."

"Then Giles did not miss that half-hour?" Lord Arglay said, and explained the situation. The Hajji shook his head. "I think," he answered, "that he has known, in an infinitely small fraction of time, all his future until he enters the End of Desire."

"He has foreknown that which he is now experiencing?" Lord Arglay asked.

"I think so," Ibrahim answered. "But though he knew it I do not think it is now within his memory, nor will be until he reaches the end. For to remember the future he must have foreknown his memory of that future, and yet that he could not do without first foreknowing it without memory. So I think he is spared that evil. Exalted for ever be the Mercy of the Compassionate!"

Chapter Eight

THE CONFERENCE

The room at the Foreign Office was large enough not to be crowded. Lord Birlesmere sat in a chair dexterously arranged at the corner of a table, thus allowing him to control without compelling him to preside. Next to him sat Lord Arglay with Chloe by his side; opposite was Mr. Sheldrake in a state of very bitter irritation. Reginald Montague was in an equal state of nervousness next to Chloe. Mr. Doncaster was next to Sheldrake, and a little apart were Professor Palliser and Sir Giles Tumulty. At the bottom of the table were Mr. Bruce Cumberland and a high police official. The Persian Embassy was not represented. It was about 11 o'clock on Monday.

Lord Birlesmere leant a little forward. "Gentlemen," he began, "you know, I think, why we have troubled you and why you have consented to come here. The very surprising demonstrations at Rich during the week-end are a matter which do not concern this particular Office, but—as most of you at any rate know—those demonstrations are said to be connected with a substance, reputedly a relic, in the existence and preservation of which a foreign Power has declared itself to be interested. I need not detain you now to explain to what extent that Power's representatives have taken official action. But I may say, in passing, that I myself have reason to believe that certain agitations and disturbances in the Near East during the last two months have the same cause. . . ."

"What cause?" Mr. Sheldrake interrupted irritably.

"A concern," Lord Birlesmere flowed on, "with the existence and disposal of this hypothetical relic. I am anxious to discover, on behalf of the Government, of what nature this is, whether it is one or many, to whom it now belongs, and in whose possession it now is, and how far the claims of any foreign Power can be justified. I need not say that I and any other representatives of the authorities here will treat every communication made as confidential, or that if any of you wish to make a private statement we shall be pleased to give you immediate opportunities."

Nobody leapt at the opportunity.. Lord Birlesmere said across the table: "I believe, Mr. Sheldrake, you claim that this supposed relic belongs to you?"

"I know nothing whatever about relics," Sheldrake answered. "I know that only last Friday I bought from Mr. Montague a kind of stone which he assured me could produce certain remarkable results. I tested his claims and they seemed justified; and as a result of these tests I gave him my cheque for seventy-three thousand guineas."

"Did you understand," Lord Birlesmere asked, "that this was the only stone of its kind in existence?"

"No," Sheldrake admitted rather reluctantly, "I understood there were three or four."

"And by a series of events this Stone came into the hands of Mr. Doncaster and thence to the police, performing apparently some remarkable cures on its way—yes," Lord Birlesmere said, "we needn't go into that now. Except, Mr. Doncaster, that you think these cures may really have been produced by the Stone? Or anyhow," he added, seeing that Oliver was prepared to discuss this for a long time, "you see nothing against that hypothesis?"

"Well, nothing except——" Oliver began.

"Practically nothing at the moment," Lord Birlesmere substituted. "Quite. Well now, Mr. Montague, would you mind telling us where *you* got the Stone?"

"My uncle gave it me," Reginald said very quickly. "Sir Giles." He met Sir Giles's eyes and shivered a little.

The Conference

Lord Birlesmere, having reached the desired point by a more gentle method than by mere attack, looked at Sir Giles with an engaging smile. "I wonder whether you would mind telling us exactly what you know about the Stone, Sir Giles," he said.

"I don't *mind* telling you," Sir Giles said, "but I'm damned if I see why I should. Why on earth should I tell this private detective agency everything about my personal affairs, because an auriferous Yankee loses his purse?"

Lord Arglay observed round the table a slight perplexity, except where Mr. Sheldrake jerked upright and Reginald stared downwards. In an undertone to Chloe he said: "I don't really know why he should, do you?" But Chloe was looking, rather inimically for her, at Sir Giles.

Lord Birlesmere glanced at Bruce Cumberland, who said: "Merely as a friendly act, Sir Giles, you might be willing to assist the inquiry."

"But in the first place," Sir Giles answered, "I don't see any friends here—except perhaps the Professor, and secondly, I don't know what I've got to do with the inquiry. Whoever's been curing the village idiots of England it isn't me. I've got something else to do than to cure old women of paralytic delirium."

"The properties of the Stone . . ." Mr. Cumberland began again.

"The properties of the Stone," Sir Giles interrupted, "are for scientists to determine—not politicians, policemen, and prostitutes."

Mr. Sheldrake jerked again, and kept his eyes away from Chloe with an effort. So did everyone else, except Lord Arglay who smiled at her and then looked at Lord Birlesmere. The Foreign Secretary, caught between ignoring the word and thus appearing to allow it and protesting and thus permitting the whole conversation to wander off on to a useless path, said in a perfectly audible voice to Mr. Sheldrake: "Sir Giles, like other great men, is a little eccentric in his phrases sometimes," but Sir Giles refused to be excused.

"Well, I suppose the Foreign Secretary *is* a politician," he said, "and a Scotland Yard Commissioner *is* a policeman. Eh? Very well then——!"

Bruce Cumberland leaned across towards the Chief Justice. "Perhaps," he said in a hoarse whisper, "Miss Burnett would like to withdraw. I mean, you see . . ."

Chloe's hand touched Lord Arglay's arm. "Don't make me go," she breathed to him.

"Ah," Lord Birlesmere said, delighted at the suggestion, "now if in the unusual circumstances Miss Burnett would oblige me personally by rendering the inquiry easier . . . We want," he went on rather vaguely, "to have no restraints imposed, though if the matter were less urgent . . ."

"My dear Birlesmere," Arglay said patiently, "neither Miss Burnett nor I have the least objection to Sir Giles using any language he finds congenial. We haven't even a police-court acquittal against us, and any apology seems to me to be chiefly due to the English language which is being wildly misused. Pray consider our feelings unruffled."

"Very good of you," Lord Birlesmere, rather perplexed, murmured, and returned to Sir Giles who was feeling in a waistcoat pocket and snarling at the Chief Justice. "The point is, Sir Giles," he said, "that it is necessary for the Government to know, first, what justification there is for foreign claims to the Stone; secondly, what properties the Stone possesses; and thirdly, how many there are in existence."

"The answers," Tumulty said, "are that no foreign claim to the Stone has any validity, that Professor Palliser and I are at work on an investigation of its qualities, and that I cannot tell you how many stones exist for a reason I can show you." He felt in his pocket again.

"The qualities," Lord Birlesmere said, "are said to include rapid transit through space and singular curative powers."

The Conference

"Transit through *time* and space," Sir Giles corrected him. "Two hundred miles or two hundred hours." He pushed his chair a little away from the table and set another—his own—Stone on his knee. "Don't crowd me, gentlemen," he went on, "or I shall have to remove myself at once. This is not the Stone Mr. Sheldrake flung away."

"Like the poor Indian," Oliver Doncaster put in, being a little tired of having no chance to say anything, but no one took any notice except the Chief Justice who, glancing at Sheldrake, altered Shakespeare into Pope by murmuring "whose untutored mind."

"If the Government," Sir Giles went on, "wish to conduct an inquiry into the nature of the Stone I shall be happy to assist them by supplying examples." He covered the Stone on his knee with both hands and apparently in some intense effort shut his eyes for a minute or two. The inquiry looked perplexed and doubtful, and it was Chloe who suddenly broke the silence by jumping to her feet and running round the table. Sir Giles, hearing the movement, opened his eyes just as Palliser thrust his chair back in Chloe's path, and leapt up in his turn, throwing as he did so about a dozen Stones, all exactly similar, on to the table. Everybody jumped up in confusion, as Chloe, still silent, caught Palliser's chair with a vicious jerk that unbalanced and overthrew the Professor, and sprang towards Tumulty. Sir Giles, the Stone clasped in one hand and his open knife still in the other, met her with a snarl. "Go to hell," he said, and slashed out with the knife as she çaught at his wrist.

"Miss Burnett! Miss Burnett!" half the table cried. "Miss Burnett! Sir Giles!" Lord Birlesmere exclaimed. Mr. Sheldrake, his mouth open in dismay, caught up two or three of the Stones and looked at them. Lord Arglay, leaning over the table, struck Doncaster's shoulder sharply: "Get that knife away from him," he said, and himself ran round after Chloe. Palliser, scrambling to his feet, thrust himself in Doncaster's way. "Lord Birlesmere," he called. "I protest! I demand that you shall stop this attack."

"Get out, you——" Sir Giles yelled at Chloe. The knife had shut on her fingers and blood was on her hand. But her other had already caught Tumulty's wrist and was struggling with his for the Stone. Lord Arglay's arrival did not seem materially to help her; it was Tumulty, who, as everyone rushed to do something to end the scuffle, let go of the Stone, slipped to one side, reached the table, and caught up one or two of the Types which, to the Chief Justice's hasty glance, seemed to cover it. There were by now half a dozen bodies between Chloe and Sir Giles, who however had only distanced a foe to meet a fidget. Sheldrake clutched at him. "What are you doing?" he shrieked. "What are you doing with my stone?"

"Lord Birlesmere," Sir Giles said, "unless you stop that hell-cat of Arglay's I'll ruin everything. I'll go off and flood the country with Stones. I can and I will."

Lord Birlesmere said passionately, "Miss Burnett, please be quiet. You'd better go; you'd really better go."

The Chief Justice gave Chloe a handkerchief. "You attend to Tumulty, Birlesmere," he said. "The real proceedings are only just beginning. All mankind has been searching for this Stone, and now the English Government has got it."

Lord Birlesmere came back to the table and stood by Sir Giles. "What does it *mean*?" he said.

"I will tell you now," Tumulty answered. "Anyone who has this Stone can heal himself of all illnesses, and can move at once through space and time, and can multiply it by dividing it as much as he wishes. There will be no need of doctors or nurses or railways or tubes or trams or taxis or airships or any transport—except for heavy luggage, and I'm not sure about that—*if* I scatter this Stone through the country. How do you like the idea? Look," he said, "I'll show you. Will to be some-where—in Westminster Abbey." He thrust one of the Types into the Foreign Secretary's hand, who took it, looked at it,

looked at Sir Giles, hesitated, then seemed to concentrate—
and suddenly neither he nor Tumulty were there.

As the others jumped and gaped Arglay said to Chloe, "You
can't do any more. They have it here. Go back home and wait
for me."

"I suppose I was a fool," Chloe said in a low tone. "But I
did so hate to see him sitting there, and *know* what he was
doing. And if I'd screamed at them no one would have done
anything."

Arglay nodded. "It is clear," he began, "that here—no,
never mind. I'll tell you presently. Wait." He stepped to the
table and picked up one of the Types. Mr. Bruce Cumberland
began to say something. Lord Arglay looked at him and went
back to Chloe. "Take this," he said. "No, take it. Thrice is he
armed, of course, but I would rather you could come to me."

"I don't like to touch it," Chloe looked at it in a kind of
awe.

"To the pure all things are pure, even purity," Lord Arglay
said. "Take it, child. And keep it near you, for I do not think
we know what may happen, but I think the Stone is on your
side."

"What do you mean?" Chloe asked. "On our side?"

"I haven't an idea," Lord Arglay answered. "But I think so.
Now go. Go to Lancaster Gate and wait for me. Go before the
Foreign Secretary and that Gadarene swine return." He took
her to the door, and as he returned was met by Mr. Bruce
Cumberland.

"Has Miss Burnett gone?" the secretary said. "I don't
know whether Lord Birlesmere might not want her not to go
before——"

"My dear Mr. Cumberland," the Chief Justice said, "your
certainties are as mixed as your negatives. Hasn't Lord Birlesmere been asking her to go in every kind of voice? And now
I've urged her to, just to please him. And you're still not happy.
How difficult you diplomats are!"

"But she took one of the Stones," Bruce Cumberland protested.

"Well," Lord Arglay said, sitting down leisurely, "I can easily make you another—ten, twenty more. At least, I can't, because I don't want to annoy Suleiman ben Daood—on whom be the Peace! as my friend the Hajji would say. If it belongs to him. But you can make them for yourself. What a time Giles is, showing Birlesmere the tombs in Westminster Abbey!"

Bruce Cumberland gave up the argument and they waited in silence for the return of the others. When this took place Sir Giles, with a glance round the room and a triumphant grin at Arglay, flung himself into a chair. Lord Birlesmere stood leaning on the table for some time. Then he said: "I think, gentlemen, there is nothing more that can profitably be done now. I am very much obliged to all of you." He paused, bowed, added something in a low voice to Mr. Sheldrake, and sat down. The American did the same thing. Lord Arglay watched thoughtfully till the others had withdrawn, and Lord Birlesmere was looking at him restlessly. He considered for a moment the three opposite him, and said quietly. "No, Birlesmere; you're like Salisbury, you're backing the wrong horse. And if Mr. Sheldrake wants to get his seventy thousand pounds restored I think that he's riding the wrong way. As for you, Tumulty, I don't think you know where you're riding." He got up and strolled slowly to the door.

The important conference now began. That Sir Giles was a member of it was due largely to the importance he seemed to have as the origin and scientific investigator of the Stone rather than to any actual need of him. But his impatience prevented a good deal of time being lost in an international wrangle, since neither Birlesmere nor Sheldrake wished more Types to exist than could be helped, while Tumulty was entirely reckless. All that he wanted was opportunity to investigate the qualities of the Stone, without exposing himself to any serious risk of unexpected results; and this he saw a chance of obtaining by an understanding with the Government. But to both of the others the monopoly of the Stone was rapidly becoming a matter of the first importance, and under pressure from Sir Giles something very like the first draft of a new Anglo-American treaty was reached in half an hour or so. Sheldrake had vague personal and semi-official relations with the President, and promised to bring the whole thing privately to his notice. With instruments of this nature at their disposal, and a judicious use of them, he and the Foreign Secretary saw infinite possibilities of developing power. Only one thing stood in their way, and it was this hindrance they were anxious for Sir Giles to remove. At present the successful use of the Stone depended entirely on the individual will. But for purposes of national control, it was necessary that the controllers should be able to move masses of men without the masses having a choice. It was clear that no army which had been supplied with Types of the Stone could be relied on. Mutiny might be dangerous but transit of this sort would be safe and easy. For the first time in history the weakest thing was on a level, was indeed better off, than the strongest. Besides, as Sir Giles with a certain glee pointed out, in war nothing but mortal wounds would be any use; others could be healed at once, and wars would become interminable. It was Lord Birlesmere who asked whether, if the Stone could heal so easily, it could also repair wastage; that is, prove a substitute for food. "But then," he added, startled, "it would practically confer immortality. The world would in time become over-crowded; you would be adding without taking away."

"You might," Sir Giles said, "use it as the perfect contraceptive."

Mr. Sheldrake looked down his nose. The conversation seemed to him to be becoming obscene.

"Under control," Lord Birlesmere said thoughtfully, "always, always under control. We *must* find out what it can do; you must, Sir Giles."

"I ask nothing better," Sir Giles said. "But you Puritans have always made such a fuss about vivisection, let alone human vivisection."

"No one," Lord Birlesmere exclaimed, "is suggesting vivisection. There is a difference between harmless experiments and vivisection."

"I can have living bodies?" Sir Giles asked.

"Well, there are prisons—and workhouses—and hospitals—and barracks," Birlesmere answered slowly. "Judiciously, of course. I mean, a careful investigation of the possibilities." He was distracted by Mr. Sheldrake's clamour for a licensed monopoly of the Stone for use in transit.

It took longer to satisfy the American than the scientist. Lord Birlesmere was perfectly willing to give up bodies to experiment, so far as he could, but he was very reluctant to interfere with the right of any citizen into whose possession the Stone might come, to use it as he chose. Yet nothing else, it was clear, would be of any use.

The possession of the Stone would have to be made illegal. And therefore the Types would have to be recovered. Of such Types, besides those on the table, there were at least four—Professor Palliser had one ("I'll answer for him," Sir Giles said), Reginald Montague ("and you can deal with him," he added, "frightening him will do it"), Lord Arglay, and Miss Burnett.

They looked at each other. It might be rather a difficult thing to persuade the Chief Justice to give up anything he had a right to possess and an interest in keeping.

"What about a secret Order in Council?" Sheldrake soared to new heights of romanticism.

"I don't know the legal aspect," Birlesmere muttered. "And he probably would. The English law is a difficult study, my dear Mr. Sheldrake, and Lord Arglay would probably know a good deal about it. I might consult the Law Officers—but even then—and Miss Burnett too. Being his secretary makes it so awkward. . . ."

The Conference

There was a prolonged silence. Then Sir Giles said suddenly: "What about this foreign Power of yours?"

"What about it?" Birlesmere asked in surprise.

"Persia, wasn't it?" Sir Giles said. "I had some carpet-weaver of theirs to dinner to find out about the Stone. And if they burgled me—and I'm almost sure they did—what about a neat little burglary at Lancaster Gate? And at—where does that girl live?"

Birlesmere shook his head. "It means them getting the Stone," he objected, "and I'd much rather Arglay had it. Well, I'll think about it. Perhaps a friendly appeal——"

Sir Giles made a peculiar noise and rather reluctantly abandoned the subject. He disliked any Types being in Arglay's and Chloe's possession, but his dislike was not strong enough to urge him to extreme action. But as, a little later, a temporary agreement having been arrived at, he left the Foreign Office, it occurred to him that if the Stone had shown his own action to the Chief Justice, it could be used also to discover what was in Arglay's mind, and to suggest other modes of action. With this idea possessing him he rejoined Palliser, who was staying at Ealing.

Chapter Nine

THE ACTION OF LORD ARGLAY

Lord Arglay, insisting on writing some business letters after lunch, insisted also that Chloe should wait his convenience and rest until he was ready for her. It was consequently not until after tea that he lit one of his very occasional cigars, and standing in front of the fireplace said: "And now, Miss Burnett, what do you make of it?"

"I feel an awful ass," Chloe told him, "going for Sir Giles like that. But I couldn't think of anything sane to do—I was so angry."

"The wrath of the Lamb," Arglay said. "But I didn't mean about yourself; you saved the Lord Chief Justice throwing an inkstand at Giles, which would have been more scandalous, but perhaps more effective, if I had hit him. It might even have killed him. I really meant—about the situation. Suppress, if you can, your righteous supernatural anger with him, and tell me why you hate him so."

"I *don't* hate him," Chloe said. "I only want to stop him doing anything at all with the Stone. He oughtn't to have it."

"So far as we know, he bought it," Lord Arglay pointed out.

"But it isn't *his*," Chloe pleaded, "not really."

"Mrs. Sheldrake used much the same argument to convince me that *all* the Types ought to be her husband's," Arglay answered. "Only she said, they *are* his, really. Try and be masculine and rational. *Why* isn't it his?"

Chloe made an obviously intense effort. "I think I hate the way he looks at it," she said. "He doesn't care about *it*, only about the way it works. He doesn't care about Suleiman—or Charlemagne—or . . . He only wants to see what it will do."

"And being an incurable romantic," Arglay said, "you hate him being merely utilitarian. Well, I don't suppose anyone else, for a thousand years or so, has barked their knuckles for the sake of Suleiman the King. I should think you were the first of the English to do it. Still—it's hardly reason enough for your disliking Giles quite so much."

Chloe went on looking for reasons. "He doesn't *care* about it a bit," she protested. "He throws it about as if it were of no importance at all. And he doesn't care how much he cuts it up."

"And why do we care?" Lord Arglay asked.

Chloe smiled. "I don't know," she said, "I don't know a bit, but I do. Don't you know?"

The Chief Justice frowned at his cigar. "I will offer you two alternatives," he said. "First, we are both disgracefully sentimental. We wallow in tradition. And when a traditional thing appears to produce unusual results we can't help being affected. Giles is stronger-minded. Suleiman and our lord the Prophet leave him unmoved. *J'y suis, j'y reste*, and so on. I hate being less efficient than Giles, but I fear it, I promise you I fear it." He shook his head despairingly.

"And the other alternative?" Chloe said.

"The other? O the other is that we're right in being affected," Lord Arglay answered, "that amid all this mess of myths and tangle of traditions and . . . and . . . febrifuge of fables, there is something extreme and terrible. And if so, Giles had better be careful."

"Which do you believe?" Chloe asked.

"My dear girl, I haven't a notion," the Chief Justice told her. "I don't see a little bit how we can decide. It's a question —let's be perfectly frank—of which we want to believe."

"Which do you then?" Chloe persisted.

"I don't want to believe either. I hate being foolish and I dislike being pious," Arglay said. "Do you choose first. How will you know and receive the Stone?"

"He said it was the End of Desire," Chloe murmured.

"And shall that be romance or truth for you?" Arglay asked. "Make up your mind and tell me, child; what will you have the Stone to be?"

"I would have it to be the End of Desire indeed," Chloe said. "I would have it to be something very strong and—satisfying. I am afraid of it but I—don't laugh—I love it."

Lord Arglay looked at her thoughtfully. Then, "Do you believe in God?" he asked.

"I suppose so," Chloe said. "I think I do when I look at the Stone. But otherwise—I don't know."

"Well," said Lord Arglay, "I will make you a fair proposal —I will if you will. It's all perfectly ridiculous, but since I saw those people this morning I feel I must be with them or against them. So I suppose I'm against them. Not, mind you, on the evidence. But I refuse to let you believe in God all by yourself."

Chloe looked up at him, her eyes shining. "But dare I believe that the Stone is of God?" she said. "And what do I mean by God—except . . ." she half added and stopped.

"Except——?" Arglay asked, but she silently refused to go on and he said: "If you will believe this way, then I also will believe. And we will set ourselves against the world, the flesh, and the devil, and not sit in the seat of Giles Tumulty. But I would have you be careful there for I think he hates you."

"But what can he do?" Chloe asked in astonishment.

"If I have seen his mind, as I believe I did," Lord Arglay said, "he may also see yours. Unless the Stone has varying powers. I would have you consider very closely in what way you may work with the Stone for God. Also I would have you keep it on you day and night that you may escape by it if need be."

"But what need can there be?" Chloe asked.

"Child," Lord Arglay answered, "it is clear that these men cannot stop where they are. They must either abandon the

Stone to chance and itself or they must seek to possess it. Now I do not think it is well that they should wholly possess it, and I think that you and I should keep our Types while we can. I do not know whether the Types can be united, but if I were Birlesmere I would strive for that, and the united Stone would give sole power. If this is what he does they may attempt anything within or without the Law. Fortunately," he added pensively, "the interpretation of the law so often depends on the Courts. To-morrow I will talk to the Hajji."

"But what will you do with it in the end?" Chloe asked.

"Why, that we shall see," Lord Arglay said. "For the Law is greater than the Courts, and in the end the Courts shall submit to the Law. But meanwhile you shall consider how you will follow this God that we have decided to believe in, who, it seems, may give wisdom through the Stone. And then we will free Giles's prisoner in the past." He paused and considered Chloe with an anxious protectiveness. "But if you need me," he said, "come to me at any hour of the day or night."

Chloe met his eyes gravely. "I will remember," she said, "and—and I do believe in God."

"In spite of the fact that Giles Tumulty exists, so do I," Lord Arglay said, "though in a man of past fifty it's either an imbecility or a heroism."

"And what for a girl of twenty-five?" Chloe asked.

"O in her it's either a duty or a generosity," Lord Arglay said, "but for a secretary it's a safeguard. One must have something to explain or counter-balance one's employer!" . . .

At Ealing Sir Giles got up in a rage. "Why the hell can't I find out?" he asked, throwing one of the Types on the table.

The question seemed reasonable enough. For in their preliminary investigations that afternoon both he and the Professor had found out all they wanted. Having worked out what seemed a moderately safe formula they had experimented first on such minds as Sir Giles's housekeeper, the Professor's old

aunt, Lord Birlesmere, and others. After something of the same
experiences which Lord Arglay had undergone, the results had
been satisfactory enough. Sir Giles, rather to his annoyance,
had been conscious of a strongly marked, if muddled, desire
that some malignant old beast should go to China, mingled
with an anxiety whether a girl called Lizzie should be getting
into trouble. The process was similar in each case. There
opened before the eyes of the holder of the Stone the scene
then before the eyes of the subject of the investigation, there
arose within his mind the occupation of the subject's mind, but
in words rather than in ill-defined vision. The presence of the
Stone in the hand remained throughout as a kind of anchor,
so that the connexion with the actual world was never entirely
lost, and could at will be wholly re-established.

But when Sir Giles, rather pleased at being able apparently
to get his own back on the Chief Justice, attempted the most
important experiment, he found the result negligible. He
framed the formula; he called up the consciousness of Arglay;
he intensified his will. There appeared gradually before him
the familiar study as seen from in front of the fire-place; Chloe
was sitting in front of him. Sir Giles was aware of thinking
that Arglay had an admirable taste in women, that though of
course this girl was not really intelligent she could probably
take the Chief Justice in. This consciousness went on repeating
itself again and again. He tried to empty his mind, but it was
no good. The image of Chloe occupied it, with a sort of detached irritation, until he recalled himself in a fit of anger.

"You try, Palliser," he said shortly. "Arglay can't be so de-
mented on that girl that he can think of nothing else. But I'm
damned if he seems to, unless the Stone's gone wrong."

The Professor tried, with a little more success. "The Chief
Justice," he said, "seems to be thinking of protecting God."

"Of what?" Sir Giles shrieked.

"That was the impression I got," Palliser said. "A strong
wish to protect and a sense that protection was valueless,

and the idea—the word God recurring. All aimed at the girl."

"I know Arglay's a legal hurdy-gurdy," Sir Giles said, "but even he wouldn't play that tune. But why can't I get any result?"

"You don't think," Palliser asked rather nervously, "that it's because you'd already decided what he was thinking?"

"Don't be a damned fool," said Sir Giles. "I hadn't decided. I know his feeling about the girl, of course. She's a presentable bitch and there's only one thing an unmarried senility like Arglay *could* be thinking. You don't mean to tell me he's merely altruistic? But he can't be thinking of lechery the whole time. He must be talking to her about something—even God."

The Professor continued persistent. "You don't think you're imposing your view on him?" he said. "After all, these others —your housekeeper and the rest—we didn t know or care what they were thinking about. But Arglay and this girl—you do or you say you do."

"Well, you don't seem to be much nearer," Sir Giles snapped. "What's this blithering imbecility about protecting God?"

"I may not have got it quite right," Palliser admitted. "But I certainly had the idea of protection, and of God. It may have been the girl he wanted to protect."

"A damn good word, protection," Tumulty sneered, and for a minute or two seethed up and down the room. Then he broke out: "Do you mean to tell me Arglay can read my mind and I can't read his?"

"You know best," Palliser answered. "You know how far he knew what you were doing, and how far you know what he was."

"He knew something about that Boy Scout of yours," Sir Giles said, "so he must have *seen* something. By the way, I suppose he—what was his filthy name? Pondon?—is going on his merry-go-round just the same? I'd like to have a look at him. I suppose we can?"

"Only take care you don't get caught up in the past too," Palliser said. "But I should think you could see him if you wanted to. As I understand it, all the past still exists and it's merely a matter of choosing your point of view."

"I don't see," Sir Giles said thoughtfully, "I really don't see how he's ever going to get back. Birlesmere's quite right—what we want is to control the damned thing. If I could do that I'd —I'd make Arglay an infant in arms and his girl an . . . an embryo again. Friday—Saturday—Sunday—Monday. It'll very soon be four days to the minute since your fellow willed. I suppose he just goes on willing when he reaches the top point?"

"The Stone being there too?" Palliser asked.

"I suppose so," Sir Giles meditatively answered. "If the past is continually scaled off the present, the Stone is scaled off too. And he goes on willing and dropping it. Let's have a look at him, Palliser!" Palliser hesitated a little. "We want to be careful only to look," he said. "Don't forget that half-hour."

Sir Giles looked black. "I don't," he said harshly. "But we can't do anything about that now. And we only want to see the past from the present. Come along, Palliser, let's try it. I desire—I will—to see—what was his name? Hezekiah? O, Elijah—I will without passing into the past to see Elijah Pondon—something like that, eh? What was the exact time—a quarter to seven, wasn't it? It's almost that now."

"Suppose," Lord Arglay said to Chloe, "two persons, each holding the Stone or its Type, wished opposite things at once, what would happen then?"

"Nothing probably," Chloe said.

"I wonder." Lord Arglay looked at the Type before them. "Nothing—or would the stronger will . . .? The point is this— you know the wretched fellow Giles trapped? Well, he willed of course; they must have persuaded him so far. But he must have willed merely in obedience, in anxiety to please, in a kind of good-feeling—you see——? And *at* the moment he held a Type." He paused.

"Yes?" Chloe asked.

"It's all very difficult," Lord Arglay sighed. "But if the Stone is—what the Hajji says—indivisible and that sort of thing, mustn't all the Types be, so to speak, *one*? It sounds raving lunacy—but otherwise I don't see . . . And if they are, and if a fellow had one of the Types for a moment, could we enlarge that moment by some other Type so that he saw— and did or didn't do what he did before? Do you see?"

"Not very well," Chloe said frankly. "Wouldn't you be altering the past?"

"Not really," Lord Arglay went on arguing. "If the Types are one then at his moment of holding *his* this fellow in Bir- mingham held this one, and there his present touches our present."

"But then—you mean that Time is in the Stone, not the Stone in Time?" Chloe asked.

"Eh?" said Lord Arglay, "do I? I believe I do. Lucid mind! But keep your lucidity on the practical aspect. Eschew the higher metaphysics for a moment, and tell me—don't you think we might offer him other ways *at* that moment?"

"Why are we to be so anxious to help this poor man?" Chloe asked. "You do dislike Sir Giles almost as much as I do, don't you, Lord Arglay?"

"I dislike tyranny, treachery, and cruelty," the Chief Justice said. "And I think that this fellow has been betrayed and tyrannized over. Whether it's cruelty depends on what his past was like. Besides, it's got to be a kind of symbol for me—an omen. I can't believe the Stone likes it."

"I don't suppose it does," Chloe said seriously.

A little startled, Lord Arglay looked at her. "My dear child," he said, "do you really think——?" But as she looked up at him it was so clear that she did think exactly that, and that it seemed quite natural to her, that he abandoned his protest.

"We are," he thought to himself, "becoming anthropomorphic a little rapidly. We shall be asking the Stone what it would like for breakfast next." He played privately with the fancy of the Stone absorbing sausages and coffee, and then decided to postpone any protest for the moment. "After all, I don't know any more than she does," he meditated, "perhaps it *would* like sausages and coffee. Shall I end with a tribal deity? Well then, God help us all, it shall be at least *our* deity and not Giles's and Sheldrake's and Birlesmere's. Much nicer for everyone, I should think. Now that we know we create gods, do not let us hesitate in the work." He blinked inwardly at the phrase and proceeded. "But I have promised to believe in God, and here is a temptation to infidelity already, since I know that any god in whom I can believe will be consonant with my mind. So if I believe it must be in a god consonant with me. This would seem to limit God very considerably."

"Do I really think what?" Chloe asked.

For a moment he did not answer. He considered her as she sat before him, leaning a little forward, gravity closed over fire, waiting for his answer, and "Yet it is very certain," Lord Arglay thought, "that things beyond my conscious invention exist and are to be believed. Also that if I choose to attribute such an admirable creation to God I am thereby enlarging my own ideas of Him, which by themselves would never have reached it. So that in some sense I do believe outside myself."

"Nothing, nothing," he said to Chloe. "Return we to our sheep, our ewe lamb. If his will worked merely in courtesy, might it not be swept by a stronger will?" He began to walk up and down the room. "You know, Chloe, I've a good mind to try it."

"Do be careful," Chloe said, with considerable restraint.

"I shall be extremely careful," Lord Arglay told her. "But don't forget we are rather relying on the Stone to assist us. I admit that it's purely logical and won't go against our wills, but perhaps it might even elucidate the will. Anyhow," he added suddenly, "I'm going to try. But what the devil do I say to it?"

He took up a pencil and a sheet of paper and sat down, remaining for some minutes engrossed. When he had at last, in deep concentration, made several marks on the paper he threw it to Chloe. "There," he said.

It looked almost like a magical diagram. There was a rectangle in the centre, with two or three small sketches within it which might have been meant for human figures. Above it was written "6.45 or thereabouts", and next to it "Pondon". Underneath "I will that in the unity of the Stone I may know that moment and show this present moment to him who is in the past, and that I may return therefrom."

"The last phrase," Lord Arglay said, "sounds singularly unlike a courageous English gentleman. But I shall do no good at all by being stuck in last Friday. Otherwise it's almost as good as the Hajji."

"I think the Hajji would have added one thing," Chloe answered, and blushing a little wrote at the end "Under the Protection"; then she said hastily, "What is the drawing meant to be?"

"That is the room where Giles's experiment took place," Lord Arglay explained. "The squizzle on the right is Pondon, the Greek decoration on the left is Palliser, and the thousand-legged Hindu god underneath is Giles himself. It's to help the mind. With the greatest respect to the informing spirit of the Stone I don't want to leave more to it than I can help." He looked at his watch. "Six-thirty-three," he said. "Ought one to give the Stone a little rope?"

"You think the exact time necessary?" Chloe asked.

"Not logically, no," Arglay said. "It's merely to help my own mind again. Strictly one could reach six-forty-five on Friday from any time now. But the nearer we are the sharper the crisis seems to me to be. Silly, but true."

"And what do I do?" Chloe asked.

The Action of Lord Arglay

Arglay looked at her a little wryly. "I think you'd better just sit still," he said. "You might pray a little if you feel sufficiently accustomed to believing in God." He picked up the Stone and settled himself in his armchair. But before he could begin to concentrate Chloe had moved her own chair to face him, and leaning forward, laid her right hand over his that held the Stone. With her left she picked up the diagram.

"Let me try too," she said. "I'd rather not be left here alone."

"Be warned," Lord Arglay answered. "You may find yourself merely taking down the history of Organic Law. Or even continually knocking Palliser's chair away from him and getting your fingers cut infinitely often."

"Let me try," she urged again. "Or do you think I might spoil it?"

"No," Arglay said. "I think you may save it. For I am sure you are the only one of all of us who is heartily devoted to the Stone. Well, come along then. Are you comfortable?"

Chloe nodded. "Under the Protection," she said softly and suddenly, and Lord Arglay, smiling a little but not at all in scorn, gravely assented: "Under the Protection." And silence fell on the room.

Chloe was later on very indistinct in her own mind on what had actually happened or seemed to happen. She was even shy of explaining it to Lord Arglay, though she did manage to give him a general idea, encouraged by the fact that he seemed to accept it as a perfectly normal incident. For after some few minutes while she gallantly strove to keep her mind fixed on the diagram at which she was gazing, and the unfortunate Mr. Pondon, and Lord Arglay's almost unintelligibly fixed passion for restoring him, and such difficult and remote things, it seemed to her as if an inner voice very like Arglay's said firmly: "My dear child, don't blether. You know perfectly well you don't care about this at all. Do let us be accurate. Now."

She made, or so she thought, a general vague protest that

she was anxious to do what he wanted, but Arglay, or the
Stone, or whatever it was that was dominating her, swept this
aside; she forgot it in the sudden rush of her consciousness to
its next point of rest. And this point seemed to be the memory
of Mr. Frank Lindsay. She found herself remembering with
a double poignancy at once how satisfactory and how unsatisfactory he was. The poor dear did and was everything he
could be; he held her hand pleasantly, he kissed well, he displayed becoming zeal, and if his talk was a little dull . . . yes,
but his talk was not dull but alien. Talk, they all—and two
or three other young men arose in Chloe's mind—they all
failed to be memorable in talk. There came to her almost a
cloud of phrases and sentences in different voices—preceding,
accompanying, following, incidents that had certainly not
been talk. They had been extremely delightful—incidents and
companions alike—she was an ungrateful creature. But her
palm rested on something that was warmer and closer and
steadier than any kiss on that palm had been, and the ends of
her fingers touched a hand that was warm and intimate and
serene. And again the voice that was Arglay's or the Stone's
said within her: "Go on, child." In a sudden reaction it seemed
to her that she hated that intimate but austere government.
She hung suspended between it and Frank Lindsay. Times
upon times seemed to pass as she waited, without the power of
choice between this and that, hating to lose and fearing to
gain either because of the loss of the other that such gain must
bring. She must, she thought vaguely, be getting very old, too
old to be loved or desired, too old to desire. Her memories were
spectral now; her companions and peers very faint and circling
round her in an unnoticing procession. And besides them what
else had there been in her life? There came to her a phrase—
the *Survey of Organic Law.*—*Organic Law* had never meant very
much to her, and this increasing loneliness and age was law,
organic law. But again there pierced through that loneliness
the double strength upon which her hand rested. The words

grew sacramental; they had not existed by themselves but as the communication—little enough understood—of a stored and illuminated mind. Who was it, long before, had used those words? And suddenly at a great distance she saw the figure of Lord Arglay as he stood in Sir Giles's room holding the Stone —the Justice of England, direct in the line of the makers and expositors of law. Other names arose, Suleiman and Charlemagne and Augustus, the Khalifs and Caesars of the world, of a world in which a kiss was for a moment but their work for a longer time, and though they grew old their work was final, each in its degree, and endured. Between those figures and her young lovers, now, in her increasing age, she could not stop to choose; immediately and infinitesimally her mind shifted and she forgot her throbbing past. It avenged itself at once; the names grew cold and the figures vague as she dwelled in them. She seemed to meet the eyes of the ghostly Arglay, and he smiled and shook his head. No longer strong but very faint the same voice said to her: "Go on, child." But where and how was she to go? A cold darkness was about her and within her, and at the end of that darkness the high vision of instruction and fair companionship was fading also in the night. Despairingly she called to it; despairingly with all her soul she answered: "I will go on, I will, but tell me how." The phantom did not linger gently to mock or comfort her; it was gone, and around her was an absolute desolation which she supposed must be death. All the pain of heart-ache she had ever known, all negligences, desertions, and betrayals, were gathered here, and were shutting themselves up with her alone. Beyond any memory of a hurt and lonely youth, beyond any imagination of an unwanted and miserable age, this pain fed on itself and abolished time. She lay stupefied in anguish.

From somewhere a voice spoke to her, an outer voice, increasing in clearness; she heard it through the night. "Child," Lord Arglay was saying with a restrained anxiety, and then, still carefully, "Chloe! Chloe, child!" She made a small effort towards him, and suddenly the pain passed from her and the outer world began to appear. But in the less than second in which that change took place she saw, away beyond her, glowing between the darkness and the returning day, the mild radiance of the Stone. Away where the apparition of Lord Arglay had seemed to be, it shone, white interspersed with gold, dilating and lucid from within. Only in the general alteration of her knowledge she was aware of that perfection, and catching up her breath at the vision she loosed it again in the study and found the Chief Justice watching her.

Lord Arglay's own experience had been much more definable. He shaped in his mind the image of the room in which he had seen the three men, formulated as clearly as he could his desire to offer Pondon a way of return, and made an effort towards submitting the whole thing to whatever Power reposed in the Stone. He took all possible care to avoid any desire towards an active imposition of his will, since it appeared to him that such a desire involved not only danger to himself, but probable failure in his attempt. Less moved, in spite of his protestations, by the mere romanticism of the thing than Chloe, unaffected by titles and traditions and half-ceremonial fables, he yet arrived at something of the same attitude by a process of rationalism. He did not know how far the Stone was capable of action—perhaps not at all; but until he did know a great deal more about its potentialities than he did at the moment, he refused to do more than make an attempt to provide Pondon with a way of return. How far, and in what manner, such a return would present itself to the consciousness of Sir Giles's victim, he could not tell; the endeavour was bound to be experimental only. But he did not primarily wish to move himself to the building at Birmingham; he wanted to bring that complex of minds and place and time again into the presence of the Stone. He resolved his thoughts into lucidity and sat waiting.

For what seemed a long while nothing happened. Concentrated on his thought he remained unconscious of the look of

strain that gradually occupied Chloe's face; at first he was
vaguely conscious of her, then he lost her altogether. For though
there was at first no change either in his surroundings or in his
thought yet change there was. Something was pressing against
his eyes from within; he felt unnaturally detached, floating, as
it were, in his chair. A slight nausea attacked him and passed;
his brain was swimming in a sudden faintness. The room about
him was the same and yet not the same. The table at his right
hand seemed to be multiplied; a number of identical tables
appeared beyond it in a long line stretching out to a vague
infinity, and all around him the furniture multiplied itself so.
Walls that were and yet were not transparent sometimes ob-
scured it and sometimes dissolved and vanished. He saw himself in different positions, now here, now there, and seemed to
recognize them. Whenever his mind paused on any one of
these eidola of himself it seemed to be fixed, and all the rest to
fade, and then his mind would relax and again the phantas-
magoria would close in, shifting, vanishing, reappearing. He
became astonishingly aware of himself sitting there, much more
acutely so than in any normal action; a hand was still on his,
but it was not Chloe's or was it Chloe's? No, it was another
hand, masculine, more aged; it was . . . it was the Hajji's.
Lord Arglay began to think: "But this is Friday then,"—with
an effort abolished the thought, and went on keeping the
problem in his mind clear. The myriad images of himself that
vacillated about him were vastly disconcerting—and there
were other people too, his servant, the Hajji, Chloe. He was
doing or saying something with each of them. It was like a
dream, yet it was not like a dream for distinct memory hovered
round him, and he found that only by a strong inhibition could
he prevent himself submitting to it and being conscious only
of some precise moment. The apprehensions began to deepen
downwards and outwards but not by the mere inclusion of
neighbouring space. An entirely new plane of things thrust
itself in and across various of the appearances; in an acute

angle almost like a wedge a different room thrust itself down over a picture of himself talking to the Hajji, but within this wedge itself were infinite appearances, swelling like a huge balloon with a painted cover and loosing fresh balloons and new thrusting wedges in all directions. In one group of superimposed layers he was aware of Giles doing a thousand things, and then suddenly, as if in a streak of white light driving right across the whole mirage he was aware of Giles watching. In a new resolution he turned from Giles to Pondon, but he couldn't see Pondon, or not at all clearly; it seemed to him certainly that Pondon now and again was walking about, was walking towards him, down a floor that ran level with his eyes, straight towards the bridge of his nose. The physical discomfort of the sensation was almost unbearable, but Lord Arglay held on. Pondon now like a tiny speck was right up against him, and then the discomfort vanished. A hand—not Chloe's, not the Hajji's, was closing round the Stone in his own hand. Lord Arglay made another act of submission to the Stone; all times were here and equal—if the captive of the past could understand. The Stone seemed to melt, and almost before he had realized it to reharden; the intruding hand was gone. There was a faint crash somewhere, a sensation of rushing violence. Lord Arglay found himself on his feet and gasping for breath while before him Chloe lay pallid and silent and with shut eyes in her chair.

He stood still for a few seconds till he was breathing more normally and had become more conscious of his surroundings; then, feeling slightly uncertain of his balance, he sat down again. He became aware that his hand and Chloe's were now closely interlocked; in the hollow between the two he felt the Stone. He looked more carefully at his secretary; he put out his other hand and felt the table near him; then he sighed a little. "And I wonder," he said to himself, "if anything has happened. Heavens, how tired I am! And what on earth is happening to this child? She looks as if she were going through it too. Dare one do anything? . . . I wonder why Giles shot across like that. *He* didn't seem to do anything. I wonder—I wonder about it all. Where is Pondon? Where is Giles? Where am I? And above all where is my admirable secretary? "

Very gently he disengaged their hands, but not entirely, restoring them to the position they were in at the beginning of the experiment. He looked at his watch; it marked six forty-seven. "I wonder," Lord Arglay said, still staring at it, "if Pondon caught the connexion. It's all very difficult. . . . I seem," he added, "to remember saying that before. Well . . ." He leant forward a little and said, softly, but clearly, "Chloe . . . Chloe . . . Chloe, child!"

Chapter Ten

THE APPEAL OF THE
MAYOR OF RICH

Oliver Doncaster, having been suddenly thrown over
both by Mr. Sheldrake and Lord Birlesmere, and
finding himself in London with nobody wanting him,
determined to return to his holiday village. As he walked to
the station he found himself considerably irritated by the treat-
ment he had received. He had been asked by the police to be
good enough to attend this conference, and now he was flung
into the street with the other less important people. No one
had explained anything to him. He didn't even know who
half the people he had seen were. He had heard Lord Arglay's
name and recognized it; he had a vague recollection of having
once read an extremely outspoken book by Sir Giles on the
religious aspect of the marriage customs of a tribe of cannibals
in Polynesia. But who Palliser was or the girl who had landed
Palliser on the floor he had no idea, nor why she had done it.
Why had she rushed round and flown at Sir Giles's throat?
"I almost wish," he thought, "she'd flown at mine. Or Sheldrake's. I should have liked to help her wring Sheldrake's
neck. I wonder if she hurt herself much. Anyhow it won't
matter if she's got one of the Stones. Why the devil didn't I
take one? Why does no one tell me what it's all about? Why
did Sir Giles cut the Stone to bits? And why did that girl want
to stop him?" As far as Rich he entertained himself with such
questions.

Rich itself, when he arrived there, seemed to be similarly,
but rather more angrily, engaged. There were groups in the
streets and at the doors; there were dialogues and conversations

proceeding everywhere. There were policemen—a number of policemen—moving as unnoticeably as possible through the slightly uncivil population. In fact it was, Doncaster thought, as much like the morning after the night before on a generous scale as need be. It occurred to him that he would go round and see Mrs. Ferguson's sister on his way; it would be interesting to know whether she remained in her recovered health —if he could reach her, of course, because as he wandered towards her street the groups seemed, in spite of the continually pacing police, to be larger and more numerous. The street itself however was passable, though not much more, and he had just turned into it, when he was startled into a pause by a high shrill voice some distance off which called over the street, "Where's the Stone? Take me to the Stone."

Oliver looked at the people near him. One man shook his head placidly and said, "Ah there he is again." But the rest were listening, he thought, almost sullenly, and one or two muttered something, and another gave a short laugh. Conversations ceased; a policeman, wandering by, caught Oliver's eye, and seemed to meet it dubiously as if he were not quite certain what to do.

"Where's the Stone?" the voice shrilled again. "I want to see. Won't some kind friend take a poor old blind man to the Stone?"

"What is it?" Oliver said to his nearest neighbour, the man who had laughed.

"That's old Sam Mutton," the man said in a surly scorn. "Stone-blind and half-dotty. He's heard of this Stone and he's made his grand-daughter take him about the town all day to look for it." He lifted his own voice suddenly and called back, "No use, Sam, the police have got it. It's not for you and me to get well with it."

The cry went over the silent street like a threat. But in answer the old man's voice came back. "I can't see. I want to see. Take me to the Stone." Each sentence ended in what was nearly a prolonged shriek, and as Oliver took a pace or two forward he saw the speaker in front of him. It was a very old man, bald and wizened, approaching slowly, leaning on the one side on a stick, on the other on the arm of a girl of about twenty, who, as they moved, seemed to be trying to persuade him to return. She was whispering hurriedly to him; her other hand lay on his arm. Even at a little distance Oliver noticed how pale she was and how the hand trembled. But the old man shook it off and began again calling out in that dreadful agonized voice, "I want to se-ee; take me to the Sto-one."

On the moment the girl gave way. She collapsed on the ground, her arm slipping from the old man's grasp so that he nearly fell, and broke into a violent fit of hysterics. Two or three women ran to her, but above her rending sobs and laughter her grandfather's voice went up in a more intense refrain. "Where's the Stone? I can't see. Nancy, I can't see, take me to the Stone." The policeman had come back and was saying something to Oliver's neighbour who listened sullenly. "—get him home," Oliver heard, and heard the answer, "You get him home—if you can." The policeman—he looked young and unhappy enough—went up to the old man, saying something in a voice that tried to be comfortable and cheering. But old Sam, if that were his name, turned and clutched at him, and broke out in a shrill senile wail of passion that appalled Oliver, "I'm dying, I'm dying. I want to see before I die. I'm dying. I want to see. O kind, kind friends, will no one bring me to the Stone?"

"The police have got the Stone," Oliver's neighbour called. "Who cares if you want to see? The police have got the Stone."

"God blast the police," said someone the other side of Oliver, and a young working man, of about his own age, thrust himself violently forward opposite the constable. "You, damn you, you've killed my wife. My wife's dead, she died this morning, and the baby's dead—and they'd have lived if I'd got the Stone." He made sudden gestures and the policeman, letting go of the old man, stepped back. Oliver saw two or three more helmets moving forward in support, and a voice behind him said sharply, "Now then, now then, what's all this?"

He looked round. A group of men were pushing past him. One was a short fierce-looking man, with an aggressive moustache; beside him was an older and larger man, with a grave set face. Behind these two were a police-inspector and two or three constables.

"What's all this?" said the little man angrily. "Constable, why aren't you keeping the street clear? Don't you know your orders? Who's this man? Why are you letting him make all this noise? What's he got to do with it? Don't you know we can hear him all over the town? Gross incapacity. You'll hear more of this."

The young constable opened his mouth to speak and shut it again. The tall man laid his hand on his companion's arm. "One man can't do everything, Chief Constable," he said in a low voice. "And Sam's a difficult person to deal with. I think we'd better leave it to the inspector here to deal with things quietly."

"Quietly?" the Chief Constable snapped. "Quietly! Look here, Mr. Mayor, you've been at me all day to do things quietly, and I've given in here and given in there, and this is the end of it." He looked over his shoulder. "Clear the street at once, inspector," he said. "And tell that old dodderer that if he makes another sound I'll have him in prison for brawling."

The Mayor said firmly, "You can't arrest him; he's a well-known character here, and everyone's sorry for him and his grand-daughter. Besides, it's natural enough that he should be crying out like this."

"I don't care whether it's natural or not," the Chief Constable answered. "'He's not going to do it here. Now, inspector, I'm waiting."

The inspector signed to his men, who began to make separate and gentle movements forward. But after a step or two the advance flickered and ceased. The general murmur, "Now then, now then, you can't hang about here," died in and into the silence with which it was received. The crowd remained sullenly fixed.

"Inspector!" the Chief Constable said impatiently.

The inspector looked at Oliver who was close to him, recognized his kind, and said in a low almost plaintive voice, "Now, sir, if you'd start some of them would get away."

"And why the devil," Oliver asked very loudly, "should we get away?"

There was a stiffening in the crowd near him, a quick murmur, almost the beginning of a cheer. The Mayor and the Chief Constable both looked at Oliver.

"Say that again, my man," the latter said, "and I'll have you in prison for resisting the police."

"The Lord Chief Justice," Oliver said, more loudly still, "is entirely opposed to the action of the Government." He had hardly meant to say that, but as soon as it was said he thought hastily that in the morning's conference the Chief Justice *hadn't* seemed to be exactly one with the Government. But he realized in a minute that his sentence, meaning one thing, had meant to his hearers quite another. A more definite noise broke out around him. "This," he thought, "is almost a roar."

The Chief Constable began to say something, but the Mayor checked him with a lifted hand. "Do I understand you, sir," he asked, "to say that the Chief Justice considers the action of the Government illegal? Do you speak from your own certain knowledge?"

Oliver thought of saying, "Well, I don't know about *illegal*," but the phrase was so deplorably weak that he abandoned it. Besides, in that large room at the Foreign Office—Lord Birlesmere, Sir Giles, Chloe's bleeding fingers—"The Chief Justice's secretary," he said clearly, "was seriously injured this morning in—protesting against—the action of—certain associates of the

Government, and the Chief Justice takes the most serious view of the situation."

This might be a little compressed, he felt; Lord Arglay's actual words had seemed a trifle less official. And seriously injured? Still . . .

The inspector stood still, looking worried, and glanced gloomily at the Chief Constable, who was making half-audible noises. The Mayor considered Doncaster evenly. Somebody behind shouted, "The Government's broken the law," and Oliver felt a little cold as he heard this final reduction of his own sentences to a supposed fact. In the following silence, "I want the Stone," the old man wailed again.

"We all want the Stone," another voice called, and another, "Who cares what they say? We want the Stone." Cheers and shouts answered. A man stumbled heavily against the inspector who was thrown back upon the Chief Constable.

The incident might have become a mêlée if the Mayor had not intervened. He held up both arms, crying in a great voice, "Silence, silence! Silence for the Mayor," and went to a horse-trough near by, motioning to Oliver to follow him; by whose assistance he mounted on the edge of the trough. Holding to an electric light standard he began to address the crowd.

"Good people," he said in a stentorian voice, "you all know me. I will ask you to return to your homes and leave me to discover the truth about this matter. I am the Mayor of Rich, and if the people of Rich have been injured it is my business to remedy it and help them. If, as appears, the Stone of which we have heard is able to heal illness, and if the Government are using it, as swiftly as may be, for that purpose, it is the duty of all good citizens to accept what delay the common good of all demands. But it is equally their right to be assured that the Government is doing its utmost in the matter, day and night, so that not a single moment may be lost in freeing as many as may be from pain and suffering. I shall make it my concern to discover this at once. I know the hindrances which must, and I fear those which may, follow on what has happened. I will myself go to London." He paused a moment, then he went on. "Some of you may know that my son is dying of cancer. If it is a matter of ensuring swiftness and order he and I will be the last in all the country to claim assistance. But I tell you this that you may be very sure that he shall not suffer an hour longer than need be because of the doubts or fears or stupidities of the servants of the people. Return to your homes and to-morrow at this time you shall know all that I know." He paused again and ended with a loud cry, "God save the King."

"God save the King!" yelled Oliver in a thrill of delight, and assisted the Mayor to descend. Who turned on him at once and went on talking before the Chief Constable could interrupt. "I shall want you," he said. "I want all the information you can give me, and I may need your personal help. Are you free? But it doesn't matter whether you are or not. I demand your presence in the name of the King and by the authority of my office. We will go to the Town Hall first. Barker," he went on, to a man behind him, "see that the car is kept all ready in front of the Town Hall. Inspector, I rely on you to see that the promise I have made is published everywhere, and I warn you that the bench will examine very carefully any case of reported brawling brought before them in this connexion. Chief Constable, I am obliged for your assistance, but I think the situation is well in hand, and the chief magistrate can dispense with any outside help. Come along, young man—what is your name?"

What account exactly Oliver gave the Mayor he was never very clear. But, whatever it was, it was bound to confirm in the other's mind the importance of the Stone and the need for urging immediate action on the Government. Once in the Town Hall, Oliver found himself in a maze of action. There was a small, stout, and facetious alderman who was apparently being left in charge as deputy mayor; there was an auburn and agitated Town Clerk; there were the girl typists who are

spread all over England; there were commissionaires and
chauffeurs and telephones and councillors and a male clerk—
Oliver had had no idea so many people could accumulate in
the seat of authority of a small country town. He was rather
curious to learn what the Mayor's own name was, and at last
by dint of studying the notices on the wall discovered that it
was Clerishaw—Eustace Clerishaw. He had hardly fixed on
this when its owner was on him again.

"I shall want you to come with me," the Mayor said. "I
am going to London at once."

"But what good shall I be?" Oliver asked, as he was hurried
to the door, but without any real regret at finding himself
thus caught up again in the operations of the Stone.

"I may," the Mayor went on, "want to see Lord Arglay,
but I shall go to the Home Office first."

"If you get as much satisfaction as we did at the Foreign
Office," Oliver answered, "you'll be there for months. What
do you think they'll do?"

The Mayor, taking no notice, pushed him out of the Town
Hall and followed him. There was a large crowd at the entrance, and a cheer went up when they appeared. As they
hurried down to the car which stood in readiness a policeman
sprang to open it and Oliver recognized the young constable
he had seen before. They scrambled in; the policeman banged
the door, and put his head in.

"Good luck, sir," he said. "Good luck and give them hell."

"Heavens above," thought Oliver as he sat down, "the
Pretorian Guard's beginning to mutiny."

For the rest of the journey he was undergoing a close interrogation, and by the time they reached London the Mayor
seemed more or less satisfied. He sat back and stretched his
legs.

"The Deputy Mayor, with the help of my clerk and so on,"
he said, "is getting into touch with all the Mayors in the
affected district. During Sunday crowds from at least five

other centres came out to Rich, and returned, I fear, with very little satisfaction. I have been asked questions by all the Mayors, but until I found you I had very little information to go on."

"I shouldn't think you'd got much now," Oliver said.

The Mayor looked at his notes. "As I understand," he went on, slowly, "the matter is at present in the hands of the Foreign Office, and some kind of strain exists between that Department and the Lord Chief Justice. I heard from Mr. Sheldrake —whom I saw for a few minutes yesterday—that Lord Arglay was in some way connected with the whole thing—indeed, Mrs. Sheldrake seemed to think he was responsible for the trouble. But I have always been very much impressed by such of Lord Arglay's judgements as I have been able to read and follow, and I was greatly struck by an article of his I once read on the Nature of Law. A little abstract, perhaps, but very interesting; he defined law provisionally as 'the formal expression of increasing communal self-knowledge' and had an excursus comparing the variations in law with the variations in poetic diction from age to age, the aim being to discover the best plastic medium for expression in action. Very interesting."

"He didn't look a bit like that this morning," Oliver said. "He just surveyed everything, though he moved quickly enough when that foul Tumulty creature was slashing round with a knife—at least, he told *me* to move."

"I think the best plan," the Mayor said unheeding, "would be for you to go straight to him. He may not, in his position, be able to do anything, but he said in that article that law should be an exposition of, not an imposition on, the people— so he may be more or less in sympathy. Yes, you go there—I had the address looked up—while I go to the Home Secretary's; it's no use trying Whitehall—I'd better go to his private house first. If I can get no satisfaction. . . ."

"Do you expect to?" Oliver asked.

The Appeal of the Mayor of Rich

The Mayor was silent for a few minutes, then he said quite quietly, "No, I don't. I expect there'll be trouble before we get our way. That's why I want to know about the Chief Justice. If he's on our side it will help us amazingly."

Oliver tried to imagine the large placid form who had sat comfortably opposite him at the conference leading the crowd from Rich-by-the-Mere to attack London. But though that picture faded too quickly, he realized as he thought that the assistance of the Chief Justice would give the riot an emblem of authority which would transform it into a rebellion. Only he couldn't see Lord Arglay doing it, and he was no nearer to seeing it when the Mayor turned him out of the car at Lancaster Gate and went on, leaving him staring at the front door which concealed the Justice of England. The Justice of England, he reflected, might be out; nothing in the present state of things was more probable. A little more cheerfully he rang the bell, and his hopes were defeated. The maid would see if Lord Arglay was at home. Mr. Doncaster? Would he take a seat?

"Doncaster?" Lord Arglay said, looking at Chloe. "Doncaster? Ought I to. . . . I do, vaguely."

"I think he was there this morning," Chloe said. "Just a minute." She looked among her papers. "Yes, he was, I made a list of their names in case they should be useful."

"I sometimes think," Arglay said, glancing down the slip of paper she gave him, "that the law of cause and effect isn't really understood. Since whatever you do is bound to be justified, justification is produced. This Mr. Doncaster comes merely as a result of your having written down his name. Shall we ask him what he thinks—poor deluded wretch!—made him call here?"

They had, at the moment of Oliver's arrival, been arguing whether it was safe for Chloe to go home alone. She had wished to go as usual; the Chief Justice had offered his car, his servants ("though none of them," he put in, "would be useful") and himself to take her. Alternatively, was there no friend she could telephone to, who could call at the house and look after her. "If you won't stop here, that is."

But this, considering that the servants knew nothing of the crisis, and considering also matters of dress and convenience, Chloe declined to do. She was more uncertain about summoning Mr. Lindsay. Frank *had* been rather badly treated—and he was almost certain to be in, working—and he would love to be called on. Ought she to give him the pleasure? "But we should have to tell him," she said aloud, half-unconsciously.

"The papers," Lord Arglay said, "have already done a good deal of that. And a friend of yours——" with a gesture he opened the secret to her friend's entrance.

Duty could sometimes be pleasure, Chloe thought looking at him, and certainly pleasure sometimes looked remarkably like duty. Still . . . after all, Frank *had* had a difficult Saturday. And nothing at all of a Sunday, since she had refused to stir out for fear she might be wanted. After a brief explanation therefore she got through to Frank, offered a tepid request, and came back feeling unexpectedly gloomy. It was then that Oliver had arrived.

"Yes, O yes," Chloe said, "I should ask him. I'll go and wait for Mr. Lindsay in the hall." That, she felt, described her existence—she would always be waiting for someone in the hall. While the great people talked in studies and drawing-rooms. She rather hoped Frank wouldn't come, then she could get off by herself before the Chief Justice had finished with this Mr. Doncaster. What was the shortest time she could decently wait?

"Show Mr. Doncaster in," Lord Arglay said to the maid. "And when a Mr. Lindsay whom I'm expecting comes, show *him* in. If," he went on to Chloe, "this fellow has anything really secret I'll take him away, while you tell your friend as much as you choose of the story. If you can remember it, which is more than I shall be able to do soon. I do wish I knew what, if anything, had happened at Birmingham. If that fellow Pondon has come back what a difficulty he'll have explaining to the police! Mr. Doncaster? Why yes, I remember you this morning now—Miss Burnett, if you remember Miss Burnett, remembered you before. Do sit down."

"Thank you very much, Lord Arglay," Oliver said, obeying.

"An extraordinary business, isn't it?" the Chief Justice went on. "How goes your end?—whichever *is* your end. For I'm ashamed to say I am not quite clear what party you are of, so to speak. Mr. Sheldrake's, wasn't it?"

Oliver crossed his legs. "I represent," he said gravely, "the people. I am the autos of their autocratic mouth. I am the sovereign will. I am. . . ." The solemn tone of his mock proclamation faded, and he ended, lamely and seriously, "the people."

Lord Arglay observed the change of tone and looked at him carefully. "And how do the people come in?" he asked.

Oliver, as best he could, explained. As he began he felt a fool, but his eyes lit on the strip of black silk across Chloe's hand—she had declined to attempt to heal it by the Stone—and he derived therefrom a certain strength. After all, this girl had knocked the Professor over and attacked Sir Giles; she had thrust herself across the will of that unpleasant little beast. And Sir Giles had been left with Sheldrake at the Foreign Office when the rest of them were turned out. And the people were clamouring for life and health from that Mystery which the police, on behalf of the American, had pouched.

"I don't quite see," Lord Arglay said when he had done, "on what grounds you asserted so strongly that I disapproved of the Government."

"Well, sir," Oliver said, "I thought you approved of Miss Burnett."

"I always approve of Miss Burnett," Arglay answered. "It would be temperamentally impossible to me to have a secretary of whom I disapproved. But approving of Miss Burnett has not, from the beginning, been necessarily equivalent to disapproving of the Government."

"But in this case, sir . . .?" Oliver suggested.

The Chief Justice shook his head. "No, no," he said. "In the first place I don't know what they are doing; in the second, I neither approve nor disapprove of governments, but of men, and that only according to the order and decision of the laws. I am a chair, Mr. Doncaster, not a horse—not even Rosinante."

"But if Don Quixote came before the chair?" Oliver asked.

"I should think he is very likely to, if he goes on as he is at present," Arglay said drily. "But even then—Don Quixote or Don Juan or the Cid Ruy Diaz the Campeador—it is all one. I have not eyes to see nor mouth to speak but as the laws shall direct me."

"But if it is a case beyond any law?" Oliver said.

"There is no case beyond law," the Chief Justice answered. "We may mistake in the ruling, we may be deceived by outward things and cunning talk, but there is no dispute between men which cannot be resolved in equity. And in its nature equity is from those between whom it exists: it is passion acting in lucidity."

"Mr. Lindsay," the maid said, opening the door. Chloe stood up swiftly and went forward to meet him, and as she did so it seemed to Oliver as if Arglay's last phrase took on a sudden human meaning. A vivid presence passed him, and he found himself gravely reconstructing the meaning of those words. On a sudden impulse he turned to Lord Arglay. "Is that what you would call Miss Burnett's action this morning?" he asked.

For a moment the Chief Justice frowned; it appeared to him unnecessary that this Mr. Doncaster should remark on anything Chloe had chosen to do. But the neatness of the phrase placated him; he looked at Oliver with cautious but appreciative eyes. "I will admit, at least," he said, "that, entirely as a private man, I regard Giles Tumulty as something very nearly without the law." He stepped forward to meet Frank.

The half-hour which followed was not one on which Chloe looked back, for some time, without growing hot. It was largely she felt, Mr. Doncaster's fault for arriving so late; it was largely Frank's for arriving so soon. He had been dragged from his surveyor's studies to take her home, and she didn't want to go—not until she knew whether this Mayor was coming. But if she didn't go at once she must explain, and how could she explain in front of Mr. Doncaster? And why did Frank look so *dull*? And why, in an effort to be conversational, must he ask her at once if she had hurt her hand? And why was the Chief Justice displaying a remote intention of leaving her to talk to Frank while he went back to Mr. Doncaster? She managed to introduce them, in order (by the exercise of a certain dexterity which she was uneasily conscious Lord Arglay patiently humoured), to move the conversation—it was no more lightly done—on to the common subject of Mr. Sheldrake. But it continually showed signs of breaking into two halves, and at the end of about a quarter of an hour she began wretchedly to make the first preparations for departure. She put one or two papers together, she opened her handbag, and saw within it the white silk handkerchief in which her Type of the Stone had been wrapped. Under cover of a monologue of Lord Arglay's she pushed aside the soft opaqueness and gazed at the Mystery. Nothing, she thought, had ever looked more feebly useless, more dull and dead, than that bit of white stone. The flakings were not gold, they were yellow; they were obviously merely accidental and it was only a perverse fancy that could see in the black smudges the tracing of the Divine Name. She put her hand down sharply to cover it again, and found that her fingers were unwilling to move. Dared she so, in action, deny the Stone? Thought was multitudinous but action single. A pushing aside or a ritual veiling?—one it must be. Nobody could see or know what she did, yet she felt as if an expectancy lay around, as if something waited, docile but immortal, the consequences of her choice. "Cowardly fool!" Chloe said to herself and, so protesting against her own action, drew Lord Arglay's handkerchief ceremonially over the Stone.

In spite of her delay, she had reluctantly gone, attended by Mr. Lindsay, before the Mayor of Rich arrived at Lancaster Gate. He was shown in at once and Oliver, hastily presenting him to the Chief Justice, said urgently: "Well, what happened?"

The Mayor answered slowly: "I have had to remind the Home Secretary that the office of Mayor is filled, not by the decision of the Government, but by the choice of the people."

"Have you indeed?" Oliver said.

"I had some difficulty in getting to see him," the Mayor went on, "and when I did he was bent on assuring me that the matter was being dealt with. I pressed him to tell me more. I pointed out that I was responsible for order in the town, and that the effect of maintaining secrecy would be highly damaging. We had a long discussion and in the end I was compelled to point out to him that, if no satisfactory statement were made, I should be driven to place the resources of the mayoralty at the disposal of any constitutional agitation that might arise. I was very careful to say 'constitutional.' It was then that he threatened me with removal and I reminded him that the Mayors came by vote of the Town Council who are chosen by the people."

Chapter Eleven

THE FIRST REFUSAL OF
CHLOE BURNETT

Chloe's chief regret, when she and Frank got out of her bus at Highgate, was that there was a quarter of an hour's walk before them. She made a half-hearted effort—half-hearted on his account as much as hers—to persuade him to return at once, but when this failed she resigned herself to his inevitable desire to discuss the whole matter. Saturday afternoon's experience, the Sunday papers, things said that evening, had made it impossible to keep from him the secret of the Stone. But, accustomed to him as she was, she seemed to hear in his voice a hint of anxiety which at first she attributed to his concern for her.

"It shows you things in your mind?" he said as they turned a corner.

"Apparently," Chloe assented. "At least, it showed Lord Arglay Sir Giles's mind."

He was silent for a minute or two. Then: "Tells you things?" he went on, following his own thoughts.

Chloe considered. "Tells you?" she asked at last.

"Things you mightn't know—or might have forgotten," he answered. "It would make things clear to you, wouldn't it? If it shows you thoughts."

"I suppose it might," Chloe said, rather vague about what he meant and a little irritated at her vagueness. There was another short silence.

"And it can be separated?" Frank said.

"No," said Chloe firmly, "it can't. Or only by people like Sir Giles."

The pause after this began to annoy her; the conversation was going in spasms like hiccups. "Let's talk of something else," she said. "It's only a month to the exam., isn't it? I do hope you'll get through."

"I suppose," he answered lightly, "you wouldn't like to lend me the Stone?"

"To——" Chloe stared. "The Stone? Whatever for?"

"Well," said Frank, "if it shows you things—I mean, if it helps the mind, the memory or whatever . . . well, don't you see—if one could remember at the right time——" He made a second's pause and went on "That's where an examination's so unfair; one can't remember everything just at the minute and just forgetting one single fact or formula that one knows perfectly well throws the whole thing out. It isn't even a case of wanting to be sure one would remember, because one *would* remember if one didn't forget—I mean, if one wasn't afraid of forgetting. It isn't, in that way, as if there was any unfairness. I wouldn't dream of taking an unfair advantage; it wouldn't really be doing more than taking an aspirin if one had a headache on the day. Lots of the fellows have mnemonics—it'd only be feeling that one had a pretty good system. It isn't as if——"

"Frank, do *stop*," Chloe said. "What is it you want?"

"I've just told you," Frank said. "Would you lend me the Stone just till after my exam.?"

"No, I wouldn't," Chloe answered. "I'm sorry, Frank, but I really can't."

"Well—if you don't want to part with yours—I quite understand—would you . . . make one for me?" Frank asked. "You know how important it is for me to get through, darling. I don't know what'll happen if I muff it."

"I suppose you'll go in again," Chloe said, anger growing within her. It was only, she warned herself, that Frank didn't —and, not knowing all about it, couldn't—understand. But nobody—nobody—did understand, she least of all.

"Well—perhaps," Frank said, defeated by this realism. "But it'd be much more convenient to get through at once. It might mean a great deal more than a year later on—it gives one a better chance." Chloe made a small effort. "Dear Frank," she said, "I hate to seem a pig, but I couldn't . . . I couldn't do that—not with the Stone."

"But it wouldn't be unfair," Frank urged. "Anyone who can manage any way of remembering things does—short of writing them down. It's only just to safeguard the mind against a sort of stage-fright; just a sort of . . . of . . . cooling-mixture."

"O God," Chloe said suddenly, "is there no end?"

Frank looked at her in a hurt surprise. "I shouldn't think I was asking very much," he said, "not if you really want me to pass. You might know that I wouldn't ask you to do anything unfair. It doesn't put me in a better position; it only prevents me being in a worse. They'd all do as much if they could."

"I don't care if they would or not. I don't care whether it's right or fair or whatever you call it or not," Chloe answered. "Frank, do try and see it. It's just that we can't use the Stone like that."

"But why not?" Frank asked in mere bewilderment. "If it can do all those things? Your Lord Arglay's been using it, hasn't he?"

"Not for himself," Chloe answered.

"But I'm not asking you to use it for yourself. It's really an unselfish thing you'd be doing in lending it to me, or giving me one," Frank urged. "I did think you'd like me to pass—but I suppose you don't care about that either."

"Don't be beastly, Frank," Chloe said.

"It doesn't look much like it, anyhow," the misguided Frank went on. "You don't seem to mind other people being helped—and I don't understand *why* you won't. You've always been out to make the best of your chances, and you won't do the same for me. You'd use it quick enough to save yourself being sacked, I expect."

The First Refusal of Chloe Burnett

"I wouldn't," Chloe said sharply. "I wouldn't use it to buy myself food if I was starving."

"O don't talk rubbish," Frank said and fell into sullenness.

They walked on silently. He had dropped her arm or she had dropped his; anyhow, they were disjoined. Her hands were empty but for the handbag, and in that ridiculous bag the absurd Cause. It seemed from its seclusion to taunt her. "Throw me away," it seemed to be saying, "throw me into the gutter. Am I worth all this trouble?" It wouldn't, she thought, with a touch of sanity, please Frank any better if she did—not Frank. He wouldn't appreciate the gesture. Besides, it wasn't her business to throw it away. "I am yours," the Stone gibed at her, "your own—throw me away. You're in danger of throwing him away." From somewhere her memory brought up a text—"My lovers and friends hast thou set afar from me; and hid my acquaintance out of my sight." She didn't want him to go like this.

"Darling," she breathed tentatively, "don't be cross. I'd do anything I could."

"That," said Frank coldly, "isn't true, Chloe. It's a quite simple thing and you won't do it. Very well; it's your Stone. But it's no good saying you'd do it if you could. You can and you won't."

"Do it," something said to her, "do it. Why ever not? Are you setting up to know what's right? Do it, and be a real friend to him." Friendship—after all, ought she to do for her friend what she wouldn't do for herself? Ought she to break her heart and do it? Was it only her own wish she was safeguarding?

From her own point of view it was by the mercy of the Stone that Frank said again at this moment, with a touch of superior and angry rationalism—"Yes, you can and you won't."

"Very well then," Chloe said, stopping dead. "I can and I won't. And now go away. Go away or I shall hate you. Go."

"I prefer to see you right home," Frank said formally.

The First Refusal of Chloe Burnett

"I don't want you to," Chloe said. "I can't bear it. O Frank do go."

"I don't want to be nasty," he said irresolutely, "but I can't see why you won't. I've explained to you that it wouldn't be unfair."

"I know, I know," Chloe said. "Good-night. I'll write to-morrow."

"O well, good-night," Frank answered, and found himself looking after her in a temper of which he had never imagined she could be the cause. "So ridiculous," he thought; "women never can reason clearly, but I did think she was more intelligent. It isn't very much to ask her to do for anyone she professes to like. But it's always the same; everybody wants to have their own way."

Still meditating on the insufficiency of human virtue he turned back towards the terminus at the bottom of Highgate Hill. Anxious, however, as he might be, to see Chloe's point of view, it eluded him with persistent ingenuity. As a friend, as something—well, different from a friend—she ought to have wanted to help him. Not that he found it easy to accept the Stone, but his incredulity was a good deal intimidated by the sudden arrival of Mrs. Sheldrake on the Saturday, the columns of the Sunday papers, the rather mysterious position of Lord Arglay, and Chloe's own great concern with it. He thought rather vaguely of radium, vita-glass, magnetism, and psychoanalysis, the possibility of some quickening power exercised on the brain, or some revitalization of the nervous functions. The last phrase appeared plausible enough to cover all instances of recovery to health and what—so far as he could see—was a sort of mind-reading. As for movement in space . . . perhaps it was hardly so satisfactory there. Nervous functions would have to be thoroughly vitalized in order——

A fresh voice interrupted him. He looked up to see another friend—but this time a young man.

"Hullo, Carnegie," he said gloomily.

Albert Carnegie looked at him with an irritating cheerfulness.

"What's the gloom about?" he asked. "Why the misery?"

"I'm not miserable," Lindsay said perversely. "Why should I be miserable?"

"Sorry," Carnegie answered. "I thought you were looking a bit under the weather."

"It's this damned examination, I expect," Lindsay said. "I've been sticking to it close enough, these last days."

Carnegie turned. "I'll walk back with you," he said. "How's Miss Burnett?"

"Well enough, I suppose," Miss Burnett's friend answered. "But she's got mixed up with all the business about this Stone in the papers, and she's a bit on edge about it."

"What, the Stone that makes people well?" Carnegie asked.

"Makes anyone do anything," Lindsay told him, "so far as I can understand. Makes people fly or jump or see into each other's minds, so they say."

"Fly!" the other exclaimed.

"Well, if you don't call getting from one place to another in practically no time flying, I don't know what you do call it," Lindsay said. "And I saw something like it happen myself, so I can't say it's all tripe."

"Do you mean you saw someone move through the air by using this Stone?" Carnegie asked.

"I saw a woman suddenly appear where she hadn't been—and Chloe says she's seen it done, seen Lord Arglay disappear and reappear and have been somewhere in between. It all sounds nonsensical enough, but what with what I saw and Chloe and the papers together I don't know what to think."

Carnegie walked on for some distance in silence, his mind occupied with a side of the question which had so far only occurred to Mr. Sheldrake and Reginald Montague and to them in a limited sense. But Carnegie's occupation happened to be in the headquarters of the National Transport Union, and while Lindsay was talking there came to him the idea that if—only if, because of course there couldn't—but *if* there were anything to it, then it was the sort of it that the General Secretary of the Union would think was most distinctly his own business. Any violent disturbance of transport would be, and this would be a very violent disturbance. At least if there were more than one, or perhaps a few Stones. It was against nature that there should be more.

"I suppose there are only one or two Stones in existence, so far as we know?" he said in a few minutes, as casually as possible.

"It doesn't seem to matter," Lindsay answered, still brooding over his grievance. He broke into a short explanation of his desires and was gratified by the concentration with which Carnegie listened. "So that," he ended, "I really don't think it's too much to suggest. It gives her no trouble and no one could call it unfair."

"And every single one of these things has the same power?" Carnegie asked.

"I know it's all ridiculous, but that's their story," Lindsay agreed. "So one would think that Chloe . . ."

"And who have got them now?" Carnegie interrupted.

"Well, Chloe has, and this Sheldrake man, and Arglay I suppose . . . I wish Chloe wasn't with Arglay; I think he's none too good an influence. These lawyers are such hidebound pedants very often, and Chloe's rather open to suggestion. I don't mean that she's weak exactly, but she's rather over-anxious to please, and doesn't take her own line sometimes as strongly as she ought to. Now she might have seen that in a thing like this she ought to exercise her own judgement and not be dominated by legal forms."

"Yes," said Carnegie, whom Chloe only interested at the moment as one of the holders of the Stone. "Anyhow there must be a good few knocking about at the present moment, and more to be made at any time?"

The First Refusal of Chloe Burnett

They had come out into the main road opposite a large *Evening News* placard which announced "Interview with Mrs. Ferguson." Another close by stated "Where the Stone came from," and a *Star* placard "The Stone—Government Action. Official." The *Evening Standard's* "The Situation at Rich" was comparatively out of date. Carnegie looked at them. It might be, it certainly was, a hoax somehow or other, but even as a hoax he thought the General Secretary would like to know. The only question was—now or in the, morning? At the Tube entrance he left Lindsay who went on his way meditating over Chloe's perversity.

If he had been able to press his request again at that moment he might have gained it. For Chloe was lying in bed, miserable enough, and, with her habitual disposition (as Mr. Lindsay had very nearly understood) to wonder if she had behaved unkindly to others, was almost regretting her firmness. It seemed now so small a thing that Frank had wanted, and she might have been merely selfishly one-ideaed—and her own ideaed—in refusing him. After all, Lord Arglay had made use of the Stone. Yes, but that *had* been for someone else's good. And had not she been asked only to help another's good? It wasn't her examination. And would not Lord Arglay have had her use it for her own good? had not he bidden her use it, if need were, if there were danger? Yes, danger, but Frank's desire to pass an examination could hardly be called danger. (Besides even in danger—could she?) She couldn't see Lord Arglay using it to make himself Chief Justice, though he might to ensure a right judgement and proper sentence. But had she any right to inflict on Frank her own interpretation of what the Chief Justice's will might be? Frank had no particular use for the Chief Justice. It would be, she thought, convenient if they could ask of Suleiman ben Daood himself what the proper use of the Stone was, though even Suleiman, as far as she remembered the legends she had studied a few days before, had fallen sometimes from wisdom. Asmodeus had sat on his throne, and

The First Refusal of Chloe Burnett

Pharaoh's daughter had deceived him, and he had built altars to strange gods. She remembered Lord Arglay's bargain of that evening; was she really supposed to be believing in God? And if so, who? or what? Suleiman's? Presumably. Or Octavius Caesar's or Charlemagne's or Haroun-al-Raschid's—supposing they all had one? Or the Stone's own God?

Half-unconsciously her hand felt for it where it lay under her pillow in its silken veil, and as she touched it sleep or some other healing power flowed through her. Asleep or awake, at once or after a long time—it seemed both in the dream that possessed her—she seemed to see before her a great depth of space that changed itself while she looked into it and became a hall with carved pillars and a vast crowd surging through it. Far off she heard a roaring that grew louder and by its own noise divided and ordered the crowd so that the many small scurrying figures were heaped in masses on either side. She felt herself somewhere among them, but not in any one place; she was carried through them, seeing all round her brown faces and long dark beards and bright turbans and cloaks, the roaring still in her ears. And then the crowd opened before her and she saw suddenly the great centre of the whole, but first in masses and only afterwards its own central height. For to right and left as she gazed there expanded huge gatherings of seated men: on the one side men in the same cloaks and head-dresses she had already seen, with little rolls or boxes fastened to their foreheads and wrists, and some of them held antique parchment in their hands. Their faces were Jewish, and mostly very old and lined with much thought, only here and there she saw one and another young and ardent and again one and another still older than most but astonishingly full and clear and happy. Over against them, but with a broad aisle between them were another company, in many different garbs and all unknown to her; or almost all, for among the turbans and helmets and diadems she saw suddenly a Chinese mandarin sitting gravely watchful, and another whose bearded face came to her as if she had looked on it in a gallery of high statuary among divine heads of Aphrodite and Apollo, of Theseus and Heracles and Aesclepius. But most of the rest were strange and terrible, only not so terrible as those on whom her eyes next rested. For beyond these, and again in two opposing companies, she saw figures that seemed larger or lesser than mortal man, and other figures who were of other natures and kept in them only a faint image of humanity. There a seeming fountain twisted its ascending and descending waters into such a simulacrum, and there again was one having many heads, and one again whose writhing arms encircled him round and round and sometimes leapt forth and were again retrieved till it seemed as if the ancient Kraken itself had become human. Over and among them flew many birds and by their flights her glance was drawn upward till she saw that the whole roof of that place was formed of birds, vibrating and rising and falling with persistent but unequal motion, with colours gleaming and iridescent or dull and heavy. In front there hung immovable one huge monster of a bird like the father and lord of all that are of the eagle and vulture tribe, with his eyes filmed and his head and dreadful beak a little on one side as though he listened to all he could not see. And as she shuddered and looked down she saw below him a number of huge lions' heads, and the red jaws opened in a terrific roar as the beasts seemed, some to crouch before the spring, some to be high-ramping in a wild fury. In this last astonishment all former wonder was swallowed up—and that she felt surprise and awe she knew even then, and knew also that she did not truly dream, but even while the beasts raged and roared there passed between them a note of music and a voice sang "Praise to the Eternal One; glory and honour and adoration be to the Lord God of Israel; blessed be He!" and immediately the noise of the beasts sounded in one answering roar and was still, and they also. Then Chloe saw them stand fixed, on the steps of a throne, six on the one side, six on the other; and the throne itself was above and behind them, carved as it were out of sapphire, very deep and clear; and on the throne a king sat, with a crown on his head. In the crown was the Stone, and it shone with a soft whiteness, and in it, amid the gold, in a deep blackness the letters of the Name were moving and glowing. Below the throne Chloe saw the companies assembled, the companies of the doctors of the Law and of the ambassadors from many lands, and the awful Djinn and Angels, diabolic or divine, who waited on the word of Suleiman ben Daood, king in Jerusalem. Then she looked again at the king, and saw that his right hand lay closed upon his vestmented knees, but while she looked he lifted it slowly up, the whole assemblage bowing themselves to the ground, and opened it. But what was in or on it Chloe did not see, for there leapt upon her from it a blinding light, and at once her whole being felt a sudden devastating pain and then a sense of satisfaction entire and exquisite, as if desires beyond her knowledge had been evoked and contented at once, a perfect apprehension, a longing and a fulfilment. So intense was the stress that she shrieked aloud; immediately it was gone, and she found herself standing upright by the side of the bed, trembling, open-mouthed, holding agonizedly to its framework.

She sank onto it and remained exhausted. Only it seemed in a little that the noise of the lions was still in her ears and a voice with it. Gradually she found the voice was saying: "Miss Burnett! Miss Burnett! Are you all right, Miss Burnett?" and knew it for the landlady's.

"Yes, Mrs. Webb, yes, all right, thank you," Chloe stammered. "It was just—it was—it was something in my sleep. I'm so sor—I mean, I was—please, it's quite, quite all right."

"Are you sure?" Mrs. Webb said, still doubtfully. "I thought you were being killed."

"Thank you so *very* much," Chloe said again, and then in a sudden rush of heroic virtue got to her feet, struggled across the room, unlocked the door, and spoke comfortingly to the anxious Mrs. Webb till the old lady at last went away. Chloe shut the door, with a desolating sense that she had forgotten everything, went back to bed, and as she stretched herself down into it went off immediately into a profound sleep.

So profound and effective was it that she was rather more than half an hour late the next morning in arriving at Lancaster Gate, where she found Lord Arglay in a high state of excitement. "Don't apologize," he said, "but I thought you were never coming. Nothing wrong? No, all right, that's merely my rubbing it in. Look at this and all will be forgiven." He held out to her the morning paper, directing her eyes to a remote paragraph. "Strange Incident at Birmingham," she read. "Missing Man Burgles Laboratory."

"The laboratory assistant Elijah Pondon who was supposed to have lost his memory at Birmingham was discovered this morning in curious circumstances. When the senior demonstrator visited the laboratory late last night during Professor Palliser's absence in London, whose assistant the missing man was, he found Pondon already there. His entrance is at present inexplicable as he had no key, and the laboratory had not been in use during yesterday. Efforts to obtain a statement have not so far succeeded, as he appears to be in a dazed condition. It is supposed he must have some means of entry known only to himself."

" 'Means of entry known only to himself,' " Lord Arglay said. " 'Dazed condition'! I should think he probably *was* in a dazed condition. But we've done it, child. We've given him a means of entry known . . . and so forth."

"We?" Chloe said.

"We," Lord Arglay said firmly. "By virtue of the Stone, if you like, but after all it was we who determined and tried—determined, dared, and done. Heavens, how pleased I am!" His mood changed and he began to walk up and down the room. "I wonder what Pondon makes of it," he said. "Does he know anything? does he guess anything? What did he see, feel, or do? or didn't he do, feel, or see anything? Has he just linked up with Friday night? or does his memory. . . ." His voice died as he meditated.

Chloe fingered the paper. "Do you think we ought to know?" she asked.

"I don't know about 'ought,' " Lord Arglay answered, "but I should very much like to know. Why?"

"I was wondering," Chloe said. "I could go to Birmingham if you liked and talk to him a little."

"Things are getting so frightfully complicated," the Chief Justice sighed. "There's the Government and Sheldrake and Giles and the Persians and the Mayor—all busy about it." Chloe mentally added Frank Lindsay to the list, and might (had she known in what confidences Mr. Lindsay's irritation had resulted) have added also the Secretary of the National Transport Union. But she said nothing.

"I don't really like letting you out of my sight," Arglay went on. "Yet it *might* be useful to know what this Pondon knows—if anything," he added dubiously. "Is there anyone who could go with you? What about your friend Mr. Lindsay?"

"No, O no," Chloe said, stopped, and went on. "But what do you think could possibly happen, Lord Arglay? They haven't any reason to do anything to *me*."

"I told you last night," the Chief Justice answered, "that they're bound to want to get all the Types into their possession —Sheldrake and the Government anyhow, and I suppose the Persians, only they don't stand a chance. And now there'll be the Mayor too; I don't believe he realizes yet that I have one."

"You didn't tell him?" Chloe asked.

"No," Arglay answered. "I'm becoming very shy of telling anyone anything about the Stone. But he's bound to hear, and then he'll be at me to go down to Rich on a mission of healing. Well, I won't."

This possibility was a new idea to Chloe and for a few moments she gazed at Lord Arglay in silence.

"You won't?" she asked at last, consideringly.

"I withdraw 'won't,' " he answered, "because I don't really know from moment to moment what I shall be doing. I may. I may find myself sitting in the market place or the Old Moot Hall or whatever they have there, handing the Stone to one after another, and watching the sick take up their beds and walk. Or at least get off them. O don't, don't let's go into that now. Would you like to go to Birmingham?"

"I think I should rather," Chloe said. "I should like to see the man you saved. And whether he feels anything about it."

Lord Arglay went to the telephone. With his hand on the receiver he paused. "Do you remember Mr. Doncaster?" he asked.

"Yes, of course," Chloe said. "Why?"

"Did you like Mr. Doncaster?" Lord Arglay went on.

"He seemed quite nice and intelligent, I thought," Chloe answered. "I didn't trouble about him much."

"Would you mind him coming to Birmingham with you?" Arglay said.

"It seems quite unnecessary," Chloe objected. "But no—not if you would like him to. It's nice of you to worry—" she added suddenly.

The Chief Justice, engaged in ringing up the hotel where the Mayor and Oliver had found a night's shelter, waved a hand, and then, while waiting for Oliver to be found, said: "After all, when this is over—I suppose it will be, some time—there is *Organic Law*. If you like. Not that you really care for Organic Law, do you, child?"

She answered his smile with another, flushing a little, then she said: "I do see something of it, I think. But it seems so far away from . . ."

"People," Lord Arglay said. "And yet so is the Stone. Or it looks like it. On our last night's hypothesis—Is that Mr. Doncaster? This is Lord Arglay. Mr. Doncaster, are you doing anything urgent to-day, either for yourself or for Don Quixote?

. . . I was wondering whether you could and would take Miss Burnett to Birmingham. . . . O the same story. . . . Yes, she'll tell you all about it in the train. . . . Do. Good-bye.—So that's settled."

"I don't know what use he's going to be," Chloe said.

"O—lunch," said Lord Arglay, "and tickets . . . have you any money, by the way? I'll get you some . . . and to keep an eye on your back in case a Persian attacks you with a yataghan or what not."

"And what use am I going to be?" Chloe asked.

"You will be of one chief use," Arglay answered. "You will discover all that is possible of the nature of the Stone." He put his arm over her shoulders and she reached up her hand and took his. "It may be," he went on, "that before these things are ended we shall have great need of knowing . . . and perhaps of trusting . . . the Stone."

Chapter Twelve

NATIONAL TRANSPORT

The General Secretary of the National Transport Union listened to his subordinate the next morning with considerable incredulity. It was, in fact, only the caution necessary to his official position that prevented him being openly contemptuous, and even that caution was strained.

"Do you expect me to believe that a man can fly through walls and ceilings?" he asked.

"No, sir," Carnegie said deferentially. "I don't expect you to believe anything—I don't know that I do. But I thought you'd like to know what was being said."

"But who's saying it—except some friend of yours?" the General Secretary asked. "I mean—it's not evidence, is it?"

"My friend mentioned Lord Arglay, sir," Carnegie ventured. "That's really what made me decide to tell you."

"What!" the General Secretary said, "I'd forgotten that bit. D'you mean the Chief Justice?"

"Yes, sir. This girl is his secretary."

Mr. Theophilus Merridew got up and went across to the fireplace, at which he stood staring.

"It's obviously got twisted round somehow," he said at last irritably. "But what on earth could get twisted into such a fantastic tale? I think I'd better see your friend, Carnegie."

"Yes, sir," Carnegie said. "You won't forget that he may not really have meant to tell me so much?"

"I shouldn't think he did," the General Secretary answered. "If I hadn't always found you a very reliable fellow—and if it wasn't for Lord Arglay—I met him once on a Commission

and he seemed a very level-headed sort of man. But this. . . .
No, I won't. The whole thing's too ridiculous. . . . But what
the devil can it be they've got hold of? Tell me all about it
again."

Carnegie did so, stressing his own unbelief and his anxiety
merely to bring it to his chief's notice as part of his official
duty, however wild the rumour might be, in anything that had
to do with transport.

"Can't we get hold of a bit of this precious Stone?" Merridew asked at the end. "Who's got it?"

"Well, sir, the girl's got a bit—because Lindsay wanted it,
and I understood Lord Arglay had, and of course the Government because of this affair at Rich. I don't know who else.
O! Sheldrake."

"What!" said Merridew. "What, the Atlantic Airways man?
Why didn't you say so before? I know Sheldrake well enough
—I'll go and see *him*. Whatever bit of truth there is behind this
he'll have got hold of. And if the bit of truth is anything we
ought to know about—he won't want an upset any more than
we do."

"I thought he was on the other side, sir," Carnegie said
smiling.

"Profits mean employment, employment means profits,"
said Mr. Merridew. "Didn't we agree on that at the last
Conciliation Conference? Very well then. I'll see if I can get
him at once."

It happened therefore a little later that morning that Sheldrake was asked if he could see Mr. Merridew, who for one
reason or another was a fairly frequent caller and was admitted.

"I've come on a funny business," he said cheerfully, sitting
down. "I want to know anything you can tell me about this
Stone of yours."

"Eh?" said Sheldrake, really surprised, for he could imagine
no reason why Merridew should take an interest in a medicinal

stone. And there had been nothing else in the papers. "The Stone? Why do you want to know about the Stone?"

The General Secretary, equally in fear of ridicule and negligence, went carefully.

"I want to know what truth there is in this rumour that Lord Arglay's putting about," he said, "that it's going to do something queer to transport."

"Transport?" Sheldrake asked with a pretence of renewed surprise. "Does Lord Arglay say that?"

"No, no," Mr. Merridew said. "You don't catch me committing myself to that, not with a lawyer. I don't mind letting his name drop in, so to speak, between you and me, but actually perhaps I'd better say—what truth there is in this rumour that's got about? I needn't tell you that, whatever it is, we don't want transport reduced any more than you do."

Sheldrake thought for a minute or two. On the one hand he wasn't anxious to bring anyone into the secret; on the other, to have the Union at his back would bring extra pressure to bear on the Government, of whose intentions he still remained doubtful. It had been desirable that he should recover his own Stone, but it was absolutely necessary that he should stop any ideas—still more than copies—of it from getting about. That would be, if not ruin, at least very considerable inconvenience. And it would mean very considerable inconvenience to Mr. Merridew's clients also, of that he was sure. Weighing all this in his mind, and throwing into the balance Mr. Merridew's own reputed and experienced discretion, he decided to speak. He gave, without names, a summary of how it had reached him, of the concern felt in high quarters, of its powers medicinal and expeditory. And finally he drew from his inner waistcoat pocket the absurd Thing itself, and, very carefully holding it, displayed it to Mr. Merridew, who sat staring at it.

"Well," he said at last, "that's not going to damage transport, is it? It looks like nothing on earth. What's it supposed to *do*? What . . . what *is* it?" he ended helplessly.

Sheldrake shook his head. "Tumulty says something about it being an original."

"Original enough," Mr. Merridew murmured, still staring.

"And Lord Arglay told my wife it was the centre of the derivations," Sheldrake added.

"Centre of what derivations?" Merridew asked, more bewildered than ever. "Look here, Sheldrake, can't you show me what it'll do? What *happens* when you . . . use it, if that's the word?"

Sheldrake being not unwilling to convince him, Mr. Merridew emerged from the next few minutes in a startled and very anxious condition. It seemed clear indeed that transport was going to be in a serious state of collapse if the Stone was multiplied. On the other hand he very naturally and very badly wanted it. "But what's this girl doing with it?" he asked. "Carnegie told me that his friend said she was Arglay's secretary and she had one."

"I know, I know," Sheldrake said. "Arglay and she have them, and I wish they hadn't. But I can't get Birlesmere to do anything drastic; this Chief Justice is too important to be . . . just dealt with, so he says. I don't suppose he'll do anything with it, but I wish to God we had them all under lock and key. It's not safe while they're about in the world."

Merridew got up meditatively. "Well, anyhow," he said, "we run together in this. You'll let me know of any developments?"

"I will," Sheldrake answered. "And keep it quiet. You won't want your conferences to get nervy. Tell me if you manage to get hold of Arglay's."

"I don't know about Arglay's," Merridew said, "but I wonder whether . . . All right. Good-bye for now."

He returned to his office still in profound meditation and when he had reached it sent for Carnegie.

"This friend of yours," he began, "the fellow who told you about the Stone—I've seen Sheldrake, and I'm bound to say it seems a serious business—you keep your mouth shut, Carnegie, and stand by me, and I'll look after you . . . understand? Very well. As I was saying, this friend of yours—who is he?"

Carnegie explained Frank Lindsay.

"Well off?" asked Mr. Merridew. "No, of course not. And he was a bit up in the air over it, was he? Is he a . . . sensible fellow? The kind that can see where his own interests lie?"

"I think so, sir," Carnegie said. "He always seemed to me a pretty level-headed chap. Reads a good deal, but I suppose he has to do that."

"Yes . . . umph . . . well," said the other. "Get him round here, will you, Carnegie? Ask him to look in here at lunch time; ask him to lunch—no, better not; that would look too eager. Ask him to look in and see me. You needn't let him know what you've told me. Just that I was speaking of the Stone and you mentioned you knew someone who knew this Miss Burnett who is the Chief Justice's secretary. See?"

Carnegie saw at any rate sufficiently well to lure Frank round to the offices of the Union, and there introduced him to Mr. Merridew, who was extremely interested and affable.

"Ah, Mr. Lindsay, how kind of you! Do sit down. Don't go, Carnegie, don't go. It's a shame to trouble you about this, Mr. Lindsay, but if you can help us I needn't say how grateful I should be. Of course I quite understand that this is all confidential. Now I'm in a state of great anxiety, very great anxiety indeed, and when Carnegie let out that he knew you and that you were in touch with the Lord Chief Justice and so on, I thought a little chat couldn't at any rate do any harm. It's all about this Stone of yours."

"Not of mine, I'm afraid," Frank said. His first feeling on waking that morning had been that he had been rather hard on Chloe, but as he dressed and became more clearly aware that the examination was one morning nearer this had given way to the feeling that Chloe had been very hard on him. In which opinion he still remained. "I've not even seen it properly."

"It's Miss Burnett who has it?" Mr. Merridew asked half-casually.

"It is," said Frank. "And of course Lord Arglay."

"Ah, yes, Lord Arglay," Merridew assented. "Lord Arglay —have you ever met him?"

"Once," Frank said.

"Lord Arglay is a delightful man in himself, I believe," Merridew went on, "but I'm not sure that he isn't in some ways a little narrow-minded. A lawyer is almost bound to be perhaps. However, that's neither here nor there. My own trouble is quite simple. I'm responsible, as far as any man is, for all the members of this Union getting shelter and food from their jobs. Now, I've not seen this Stone, and I can hardly believe what's said, but it's said—it is *said*—that it means there's some new method of movement. I suppose it's a kind of scientific invention."

"I really don't know," Frank said, as Mr. Merridew paused. "I only know what Miss Burnett told me. O and Mrs. Sheldrake seemed very anxious about it."

"Ah, the ladies, the ladies!" the General Secretary smiled. "A little credulous, perhaps—yes? But I do feel that, if there should be anything in it, I ought to know *what*. And as between a lady, a lawyer, and, if I may say so, a man of the world like yourself, I naturally preferred to get into touch with you. After all—I don't know what your political views may be, but after all someone ought to think of these millions of hardworking men whose livelihood is in danger."

"But I don't see quite what *I* can do," Frank said. "Miss Burnett wouldn't lend me the Stone."

"She wouldn't, you think," Merridew asked, casually looking down at his papers, "sell it?"

"Eh? sell it?" Frank exclaimed. "No, I don't—I'm almost

sure she wouldn't. Besides Mrs. Sheldrake said something about seventy thousand pounds."

"Ah, well, a poor Trades Union could hardly go to that—but then I'd be quite willing only to borrow it," Merridew said. "If for instance you by any chance had one of them—I'd willingly pay a good sum for the privilege of borrowing it for a little while. Say——" he estimated Frank for a moment and ended—"a few hundreds even. It's of such *dire* importance to my people."

Frank considered, and the more he considered the more certain he became that to offer Chloe, if she were still in her last night's mood, a few hundreds would be the same as offering a few millions or a few pence. In these silly tempers it would mean nothing to her.

"I can ask her, of course," he said reluctantly.

"If she should lend it to you for any reason——" Mr. Merridew thoughtfully said, "If, I mean, you had any need of it and —as she naturally would—she passed it on to you, perhaps you'd bear me in mind."

"I don't think she's likely to do that," Frank said.

"Or even if you could borrow it sometime—I don't mean exactly without her knowing, though if she didn't happen to want it. . . . I understand Lord Arglay has one, and I suppose if Miss Burnett works there she could always use his—if you happened across it some time. . . . I don't know whether Miss Burnett is one of those young ladies who always leave their umbrellas or their handbags or something behind them——"

"No," Frank said, "she isn't."

"Well, if she did"—Merridew went on—"or, as I say, if you borrowed it for any purpose of your own—well, if you had it in any way, and would show it me, I should be very glad to pay a fee. Better spend a few hundreds first than a few millions on unemployment pay, you know, is the way I look at it. Prevention is better than cure."

"I see," Frank answered.

He was not at all clear what he did see, moving in his mind, what kind of action half-presented itself and then withdrew, but to borrow the Stone for his examination, just for the day or two, couldn't do any harm. And if this fellow was willing to pay . . . Chloe should have it, of course; she'd only about thirty pounds at her back. Or at least they might split it—she was always very good about paying if things were rather tight, and she'd probably rather . . . only then she'd have to know. And if as a matter of fact she hadn't known, if there *were* any way of borrowing it, if. . . .

"I see," he said again, and there was a silence. Suddenly he stood up. "Well, I must be going," he said. "Yes, I see, Mr. Merridew. Well, if anything should happen———"

"Any time, day or night," the General Secretary said. "Carnegie will give you my address. And of course any expenses—taxis or anything—good-bye."

He watched Frank out and when Carnegie returned—"I wish there was a quicker way," he said. "I shall go to the Home Office after lunch, but I don't suppose they'll let one out of their hands. I wouldn't if I was them. It's up to you to keep on top of your friend, Carnegie. If he wants it himself for this examination of his we may just have tipped the balance. Though he mayn't be able to do it even so. Well, we must see. And now try and make an appointment for me with the Home Office this afternoon."

The Home Secretary was a charming politician whose methods differed from Lord Birlesmere's in that while the Foreign Secretary preferred at least to appear to direct the storm, Mr. Garterr Browne allowed it to blow itself out, after which he pointed out to it exactly what damage it had done. He got up to shake hands with Mr. Merridew and directed his attention to another visitor who was standing by the table.

"May I introduce you to Mr. Clerishaw, the Mayor of Rich-by-the-Mere?" he said. "Mr. Merridew, the General Secretary of the National Transport Union. Do sit down, both of you. I fancy this business may be a trifle long. Don't be alarmed, Mr. Merridew—I know what you want, at least I can guess. My difficulty is . . . but perhaps Mr. Clerishaw had better explain. A man always puts his own case best."

There were those who asserted that this phrase, which was a favourite with Mr. Garterr Browne, had been responsible for more quarrels in his party and crises in the Cabinet than any other formula for twenty years. After hearing it, a man was always convinced that he did, and was consequently more reluctant to abandon his case than before. The Mayor needed no convincing, but neither was he anxious to waste energy.

"I have already stated my case to you, sir, as a member of the Government," he said. "I cannot see that anything is to be gained by repeating it."

"I think, Mr. Mayor," the Home Secretary said, "that you will find it is more necessary to convince Mr. Merridew than to persuade me."

"How so?" the Mayor asked.

"Because Mr. Merridew is one of my difficulties, I fancy," the Minister answered. "Mr. Secretary, tell me how much publicity do you desire for the tale of this absurd Stone?"

"What!" Merridew exclaimed—"publicity? I don't want any publicity at all—that's the point. I want to know whether the Government are taking steps to control all of these precious Stones that are in existence . . . I mean, if there's anything in them. Or to have immediate assurances that there is nothing."

"Yes, but Mr. Clerishaw wants a great deal of publicity," Mr. Garterr Browne smiled. "O a very great deal. He objects to any kind of secrecy."

Mr. Merridew settled himself firmly in his chair. "And why?" he asked, very much as a General Secretary should.

The Mayor turned on him. "Great God, sir," he said almost fiercely, "do you want to condemn thousands of men and women to suffering?"

"I don't," Merridew said, "and because I don't I want the Stone withdrawn from . . . from circulation."

"Don't you know," the Mayor cried out, "that there are those well and happy to-day who have been in pain and grief for years—all by the healing powers of this Stone?"

"O you mean the people at Rich?" Merridew exclaimed. He had entirely forgotten, in his concern with transport, the virtues of the Stone which had caused so much disturbance in Rich during the week-end. But his phrase sounded as if he relegated the people at Rich to sickness or health indifferently, and the Mayor took a step forward.

"I speak for the people at Rich," he said, "for I am the Mayor of Rich. By what right do you speak and for whom?"

"I speak," Merridew answered, sincerely if somewhat habitually moved, "for the sons of Martha." He had found Mr. Kipling's poem of the greatest use in emotional speeches from the platform; that and some of Mr. Masefield's verses were his favourite perorations. But the Mayor, not having read much modern verse, was merely astonished.

"For what?" he asked.

" 'For the sailor, the stoker of steamers, the man with the clout,' " murmured the Home Secretary, who had heard Mr. Merridew before. "For the workers—some of them anyhow."

"And what have the workers to lose because of the Stone?" the Mayor asked. "Are not they also the people?"

"Of course they're the people," the General Secretary exclaimed, "they *are* the people. And are they to lose their livelihood because of a few cures?"

"Perhaps," the Home Secretary put in, "you haven't realized, Mr. Mayor, that this very interesting Stone has other qualities, so I am told, besides the curative. In short. . . ."

He gave a brief explanation of those qualities. The Mayor listened frowning.

"But I confess," Mr. Garterr Browne ended, "I didn't know that these facts—these apparent facts—would have reached

Mr. Merridew so soon. However, as it is——" He got courteously off the storm, and signed to it to go ahead.

"That," Merridew said, "is my case. If it's some scientific invention, as I suppose it is, it ought to be State property, and its introduction into the economic life of the country must be only brought about very, very gradually."

"While the poor die in misery," the Mayor commented.

"Damn it, sir," Mr. Merridew exclaimed, "I am speaking for the poor."

"For the sick and dying?" the Mayor asked. "For the blind and the paralytic and the agonized? Do as you will about economics—but the body is more than raiment."

"Not without raiment—not for long," Mr. Garterr Browne said. "But go on with the discussion. What were you about to say, Mr. Secretary?"

"I protest against the way my words are twisted," Merridew cried. "I've no possible objection to the medicinal use of the Stone."

"Nor I to its economic suppression," the Mayor answered and they both looked at Mr. Garterr Browne.

"Beautiful," the Minister breathed. "When democracy lies down with democracy. . . . And how, gentlemen, do you propose to use the Stone all over the country while at the same time keeping it under close guard?"

"The doctors——" Merridew began.

"Hardly," the Minister said. "For it must be in the hands and at the will of those who are to be healed. And I don't myself see what is to prevent the . . . the healee from going off by its means, once he is cured. We shan't be able to keep it quiet. And then there will be Stones everywhere. I'm not objecting. I'm only saying that we must use it either fully or not at all."

"Then in the name of God, use it!" the Mayor cried out.

"And ruin hundreds and thousands of homes!" Merridew followed him. "Suppress it, I say."

Mr. Garterr Browne waved both hands at the storm. "You

see?" he asked it courteously, and after a few moments' silence added, "If the Government heal the sick they starve the healthy. If, on the other hand, they protect the healthy they doom the sick."

Both his visitors felt a sudden touch of horror. The dilemma came at them so suddenly, and on so vast a scale, that they mentally recoiled from it. Neither of them was thinking at the moment of any others than those on whose behalf he imagined himself speaking. But to each of them the placid voice of the Home Secretary called up a vision of another hemisphere of danger and distress; and over that danger and that distress floated, ironically effective, the Stone. Of the two the Mayor suffered the more, for he had the keener sight, and at the same time the remembrance of his own son struck at his heart. He saw the silent railways and the idle workers at the same time that he heard the moans of the dying man and knew them for the moans of one among thousands. He turned sharply on the Minister.

"Is there no way of administering relief," he asked, "by the most careful vigilance?"

"There is no way to protect the Stone if we are to use the Stone," Mr. Garterr Browne said. "And now, gentlemen?"

"I cannot believe it," the Mayor cried out. "Is the mind of man incapable of dealing with this problem? Or is the Stone sent to mock us?"

"Well . . . mock?" the Minister asked, "mock? . . . But I think probably its value has been much exaggerated. We have, of course——"

"But I have seen these things happen," the Mayor said.

"No doubt, no doubt. As I was saying," the Minister went on, "we have, of course, our own scientists at work on it. Analysing, you know."

"Who are your scientists?" the Mayor asked.

"Sir Giles Tumulty primarily," the other answered. He had never heard of Sir Giles till the previous evening, but his manner implied that the name ought to settle the Mayor. "And no doubt he—they—will find some means to isolate the curative while—shall we say inhibiting?—the non-curative elements. But you must give us time."

"And am I to go back to Rich and tell the people to die?" the Mayor asked.

"You talk as if your townsfolk were all the people," Merridew muttered. "Aren't there any others to watch for the people than you? What of the Unions? Are my members to starve that your townsfolk may be more cheerful?"

"It seems," the Mayor said heavily, "that this Stone is a very subtle thing."

Mr. Garterr Browne felt that his own mind was at least as good as the Stone if it came to subtlety. It had been a difficult situation, and now everything was coming right. He looked almost gratefully at Mr. Merridew, but received no answering glance. The General Secretary was beginning to feel anxious about the future.

"At least," the Mayor said suddenly, "you will have the whole matter laid before Parliament, so that we may know what resolution is come to, and for what reason."

"I very certainly will not," Mr. Garterr Browne said, startled at this new threat of tempest. "Why, Parliament isn't even sitting. I shall let the Cabinet know. Can't you trust us to do our best?"

Neither of his visitors seemed anxious to do so. Both of them were thinking of the crowds, of voices crying out questions, of the demand of the common people for security and food and content. In the faint noise of the traffic of London that came to them in the room there seemed to be something which must either be laid hold of or itself lay hold. Merridew saw before him the massed ranks of his Conference. There was here a thing which allowed, it seemed, of no arrangement; here was no question of percentages and scales and wage-modifications over long periods—things that could be explained and defended.

If it got out, if the Stone were used publicly, the whole of his Unions would be raging round him, and all the allied trades. Yet if the Stone were refused, he seemed to see in the upright and dangerous figure of the Mayor a threat of other action, of the outbreak of the sick and the friends of the sick. He foresaw division and angry strife, and suddenly looking at the Home Secretary he cried out in answer to the plaintive appeal—"But this is civil war!"

The Mayor looked over at him. "I do not think you are wrong, Mr. Secretary," he said. "We are coming perhaps to evil days."

"But really, gentlemen," the Minister began, and then changing his intention addressed himself to the Mayor. "Do you not see," he said, "that more will suffer if the Stone is used than if it is kept secret? I am sure we all sympathize with those who are in need of one sort or another, but you cannot build up a house by pulling it down, nor do good to some by doing harm to many. Besides, so little has really been discovered about this . . . discovery that it's too soon to take a gloomy view. You, I am sure, Mr. Mayor, will explain this to the people of Rich."

"And if the people of Rich lynch me in the street I shall think it natural," the Mayor answered.

There was a knock at the door and a secretary entered. "Lord Birlesmere is very anxious to see you, sir," he said. "He telephoned from the Foreign Office just now to know if he could come across."

"Of course, of course," Mr. Garterr Browne answered, and then, as the secretary went out, turned to his visitors. "Well," he said, "I must break off the discussion. But please don't let there be any misunderstanding. The Government will take steps to find out what the truth really is. As I said before, there is always likely to be exaggeration. And then I will let you know its decision. Pray, gentlemen, exercise all your restraining influence, and do not let there be any talk of civil war. This is a civilized community. Your interests—the interests of those you represent—townsfolk or unionists—will be safe in our hands. I shall be writing to you both in a few days. No, Mr. Mayor, I can't discuss it further at present. Important things are bound to take time."

As the two were ushered out Mr. Garterr Browne shook his head thoughtfully at the still ominous storm. "What is quite certain," he said, "is that no one must be allowed to believe in this Stone any more. It simply must not be allowed."

Chapter Thirteen

THE REFUSAL OF LORD ARGLAY

"Wandsworth?" Professor Palliser said, staring at Sir Giles. "Why did you go there?"

"Can't you guess?" Sir Giles asked. "Then I suppose you won't guess what happened. Well, I don't mind telling you, Palliser, that for once neither did I. Nor the Governor, who is a beefy lump of idiocy. He got quite upset when he saw it."

"Saw what?" Palliser asked. "What have you been doing?"

"I'll tell you," Sir Giles answered. "I ought to have foreseen perhaps—but one doesn't know what the logic of the damned thing is. Well, I went to Wandsworth. You know what they have at Wandsworth?"

"Not specially," Palliser said. "A common, isn't there? And a prison?"

"And a Hottentot missionary college, and a seminary for barmaids," Sir Giles added. "What do they have at Wandsworth Prison early in the mornings?"

"Parades?" Palliser, all at sea, ventured. "Breakfast? Chapel?"

"Try all three," Sir Giles answered. "Executions, Palliser. That's what I went for. There aren't so many that I could afford to miss one, especially just after Birlesmere had given me a practically free hand. So I got a letter out of him and the Home Office scullion and down I went. After all, I argued, if this infernal Stone is a kind of rendezvous of the past and the future and every sort of place I didn't see why it shouldn't push a man over an interruption, like death. There is only one kind of death which is fixed and that's execution. Even at hospitals you can't be certain to an hour or two, and anyhow very often there people don't die intelligently; they lose themselves and drift. But the fellow who's going to be executed knows about it all right. The ape-creature who called himself the Governor wouldn't let on to me whether he usually drugged the victim, but I saw to it he didn't drug this one. I wanted all the intelligence I could find—not that there was much anyhow; he was an undersized slug who'd poisoned a woman because she'd run away with him without having any money, so far as I could understand. Not that it mattered. I got there before he'd had his breakfast, and had a little talk, asked him if he'd like to live and so on. The warder had been cleared out of the cell, so it was all right. I don't know what the wretched creature thought I was offering him, but he screamed with gratitude— quite a fascinating ten minutes, all twisting and slobbering. In fact, I began to think I shouldn't get the idea into the maggot-hole he had for a brain, but I did, and made him have a good breakfast too. Then the chaplain came in and talked about life in heaven, but my murderer was all for life on earth, and I was worth a dozen mongrel-faced chaplains to him. So he was pinioned so that he could hold one of the Stones—you ought to have seen the Governor looking like a Sunday school superintendent in a night club or something worse—and I told him to put everything he knew into choosing to live. And off we went—he and the hangman and the chaplain and the Governor and I and everyone. The funniest thing you ever saw, Palliser—if you ever did see anything funny. And there was the trap and everything. Well, do you know it was only then it occurred to me that I ought to be underneath—in the pit thing he drops into. It delayed matters a bit, but at last they grasped what I wanted: anyone except a malformed baby of two months would have understood me sooner than that Governor: and round and down I went. And down he came."

Sir Giles paused. "And now," he resumed, "what do you think happened?"

"How do I know?" Palliser exclaimed. "He was dead?"

"No," Sir Giles said thoughtfully. "No, I shouldn't say he was dead."

"He was alive!" Palliser cried. "Does it really do away with death?"

"Well, yes, I suppose in a way he was alive," Sir Giles said. "He was quite conscious and so on—one could see that. The only thing was that his neck was broken."

Palliser gaped at him. In a moment Sir Giles resumed. "There he was. Neck broken, everything as it should be, the body dead so to speak. But *he* wasn't. I can see now that it was my fault in a way. I was thinking in terms of continuation of life, so I put him on to that idea, and of course he swilled it down with his coffee. But we both forgot to arrange the conditions, so that the ordinary physical process wasn't interfered with. Yet on the other hand his consciousness just stopped there, *in* his body or wherever it lives. A damn funny result, Pallister. If you could have seen his eyes while he hung there kicking——"

Palliser interrupted. "But what did you do?" he asked.

Sir Giles shrugged. "O well, they cut him down, and stuck him in a bed somewhere privately, and the chaplain postponed any more of the resurrection and the life, and the Governor went off to get more instructions. And I hung about a bit—in fact, I've been there all day on and off; but there doesn't seem to be any change. There he lies, all broken up, and just his eyes awake. No use at all to me or anyone, damn and blast him for a verminous puppy-dog!"

Palliser moved uneasily. "I'm beginning to be afraid of it," he said. "I wish we knew what it was."

"It's the First Matter," Sir Giles said. "I told you that was what I thought it was, and I'm more sure than ever now. It's that which becomes everything else."

"But how does it work?" Palliser asked. "How does all this movement happen? How does it carry anyone about in space?"

"It doesn't," Sir Giles answered immediately. "Can't you see that it doesn't move people about like an aeroplane display. Once you are in contact and you choose and desire and will, you go into it and come out again where you have desired because everything is in it, anyhow. Do try and see further than a wax doll on a Christmas tree can."

"So that if you were set in contact you might, even if you only partly knew . . .?" Palliser began slowly and stopped.

"I expect so," Sir Giles said sweetly, "if your hearse of a mind could only get to the cemetery a bit quicker. What might you?"

"I was thinking of Pondon," Palliser went on. "That might explain how it was that he's . . . returned?"

"He's what?" Sir Giles said sharply. "What d'you mean, Palliser? He hadn't a Stone, had he?"

"Your brother-in-law must have done it," Palliser answered, feeling some pleasure at the connexion. "You know you thought you saw him when we were trying to get at Pondon the other night and failed. There seems to have been a paragraph in the paper, but I missed that. But when I got to Birmingham yesterday morning, he was there. He'd been found in the laboratory when my demonstrator went in at about ten o'clock. He was a bit bewildered then, I gathered, so I went round to see him. And who do you think I found there?"

"Arglay!" Sir Giles exclaimed. "By God, I'll tear Arglay into bits."

"Not Arglay," Palliser went on, "but that girl who was with him—his secretary. She'd told him some tale and got on his right side, for there he was talking away to her, and telling her how he couldn't make out what had happened. I was rather sorry I'd turned up at first, though he was quite all right with me—asked me if the vibrations were all right. You remember we told him some tale about testing etheric vibrations—on the lines of my *Discontinuous Integer*?"

"He was damn near being a discontinuous integer himself,"

The Refusal of Lord Arglay

Sir Giles said snappily. "And what had Arglay's woman to say about it?"

"I don't like it," Palliser answered. "O she didn't *say* much, just cooed at him now and then. But from what he said, while he was doing his job as usual, he found his hand holding this Stone—and he knew he'd been holding it, so (as far as I could understand) he took a tighter grip and said to himself, "This is where I ought to be." And then he remembers pitching right over, and there the demonstrator found him. But that girl and Arglay have had something to do with it, and if they're going to interfere continually——"

Sir Giles put up a hand as if for silence, and sat meditating for several minutes. Then he drew a deep breath and got up. "I'm going to try something," he said. "I've had enough of this young Hecate mixing herself up with my affairs because that bestial leprechaun who employs her tells her to. I'll give Miss Chloe Burnett something else to do with her mind, and perhaps with mine. If she can use the Stone so can other people. Where is it? Go away now, Palliser, and let me try."

It was perhaps the greatest mistake which Giles Tumulty had ever made to allow what had been in general a cold, if rather horrible, sincerity of investigation into remote states of mind to become violently shaken by a personal hatred of his brother-in-law. He and Arglay had always mutually despised each other, but until now they had never been in conflict. The chances of the last few days however had turned them from contemptuous acquaintances into definite enemies. Indeed at that moment, though no one of those connected with the progress of the Stone and its Types had realized it, the Chief Justice and his secretary were becoming the only single-minded adherents it possessed. Lord Arglay certainly could not be thought to feel any passionate devotion to it; but he strongly disliked all that he saw and felt of the greed by which it was surrounded. The Persian Government, the English Government, the American millionaire and his wife—these he knew;

and there were others he did not know—Merridew and Frank Lindsay; even, in some sense, though a holier, the Mayor of Rich and the Hajji Ibrahim. All for good or evil desired to recover the Stone, and use it, and most of them desired greatly to possess all its Types as well. Doncaster and Mrs. Pentridge hardly knew enough or were hardly in sufficient contact with the movements it had caused to make any demand. But Lord Arglay, at once in contact and detached, at once faithless and believing, beheld all these things in the light of that fastidious and ironical goodwill which, outside mystical experience, is the finest and noblest capacity man has developed in and against the universe. And now this itself was touched by a warmer consciousness, for as far as might be within his protection and certainly within his willing friendship, there was growing the intense secret of Chloe's devotion to the Mystery. As if a Joseph with more agnostic irony than tradition usually allows him sheltered and sustained a Mary of a more tempestuous past than the Virgin-Mother is believed to have either endured or enjoyed, so Lord Arglay considered, as far as it was clear to him, his friend's progress towards the End of Desire. To that shelter and sustenance she had eagerly returned from her absence on the Birmingham errand, and she and her companion were now telling him and the Hajji, who had been summoned, of the occurrences of that errand.

Of one thing however Chloe did not speak. She might have gradually revealed it to Lord Arglay, but she certainly was not going to mention it before the Hajji, and as in a way Mr. Doncaster was it or the occasion of it she could not before him. Chloe had usually found a fairly long train journey—especially in the first class compartment Lord Arglay had naturally assumed she would take—in the company of an intelligent and personable young man who rather obviously admired her, a very pleasant, and even exciting, method of spending the time. There was so happy a mixture of the known and the unknown; there was all the possibility of advance and yet all the surety of withdrawal—there was in short such admirable country for campaigning that she could not very clearly understand why she had today looked at it without any thought of a campaign. She had thrown out a squadron or so to check Mr. Doncaster's early moves, and had with small expenditure of effort immobilized him. The journeys were ended and there was no regret. She must, Chloe thought when she became conscious of this, be terribly excited. But she was not excited. She only wanted to serve the Stone—and Lord Arglay—as much as Lord Arglay—and the Stone—wanted. There was a slight doubt in her mind which of them, if it came to a crisis, was the more important, but it hadn't come to a crisis and very likely never would. Once or twice her experience in the operation which she and the Chief Justice had directed occurred to her; with the suggestion of a possibility that there indeed a choice beyond her knowledge had been made and a first separation from mortality dutifully and sadly undergone. It would have seemed to her silly and pretentious to put it like that, but when she said to herself: "I don't think perhaps I shall care about it so much," it might have meant much the same thing, at least to any of the Types of the Stone or to the wisdom of Suleiman ben Daood, king in Jerusalem.

"We went to the University first," Doncaster was saying, "but he wasn't there, and they didn't or wouldn't know anything, so we went to his house."

"How did you find it?" the Chief Justice put in.

"Telephone Directory," Doncaster said. "That was my idea —I thought in his position he'd almost *have* to be on, and he was. But it was Miss Burnett got us into the house—the usual kind of house; just the thing you'd expect of him. He lived with his mother, and I thought we could swear we were journalists; but before I could say anything——" He paused and looked at Chloe.

"And what did Miss Burnett swear you were?" Lord Arglay asked.

"I said we were his friends," Chloe answered, with a simplicity and a certainty in her voice which—Arglay thought—would have opened any doors. Some new completeness seemed to be growing in her. He permitted himself to test it with another question.

"And did you also think it was the kind of house you would expect of him?" he asked, throwing a side glance of humorous apology at Doncaster.

Chloe frowned a little. "I don't think I know," she said. "I mean, I didn't expect anything. It was—it was a house, and he and his mother lived in it. I don't see what more one could say."

"It didn't," Arglay asked again, "seem to you of any particular kind?"

"It was a very nice house," Chloe said, "but—no, I didn't notice anything else."

"It had an aspidistra in the window," Doncaster put in.

"It certainly had," Chloe agreed, "and a very good aspidistra too. I admired it."

Lord Arglay signed to Doncaster to go on—after a slightly perplexed glance at Chloe, he obeyed.

"So Miss Burnett said, 'We are his friends,' and his mother let us in and took us to the aspidistra, and presently he came in. So we—at least Miss Burnett—told him she knew all about it. . . ."

"Did you?" Arglay interrupted.

"Well, in a way," Chloe answered. "It seemed as if he thought he had seen me before; he looked at me so hesitatingly at first. And I said I knew something of what had happened, and was anxious to know if we could do anything more to help him. So we . . . we stammered a little at one another, and then he broke out. He said he didn't know what had happened. He remembered Professor Palliser talking to him about etheric vibrations, and asking him to test them by wishing—he said wishing—to be at an earlier point of time, and then he wondered if he had been."

"He was very muddled about it all," Doncaster added. "And about what happened afterwards: he was doing his job in his usual manner and suddenly he felt as if he were holding on to a post and something was saying to him, 'This is the Way.' He couldn't get nearer than that. And he saw a kind of photograph in the air."

"A what?" Lord Arglay exclaimed.

"He didn't say a photograph," Chloe cried out. "He said a picture."

"He said, to be exact, 'a picture just like a photograph'," Doncaster insisted, "of the same room. And it got bigger. But go on, Miss Burnett."

"I think he saw them in the Unity," Chloe said. "He said he felt as if he were standing between them, and he didn't know which he ought to be in, but it was frightfully important for him to choose rightly. And he wondered which the Professor and his friends wanted. But then he thought he saw . . ." she hesitated . . ."me in one of them, and moved to ask whether I wanted to see the Professor!"

"And then crashed," Doncaster ended. "And knew nothing more. It was at that point that the Professor arrived. He looked a trifle embarrassed when the mother brought him in and he saw Miss Burnett—embarrassed first and then rather annoyed. So there was general conversation for awhile, and I chatted to the Professor—at least, I asked him what he thought of it all, while Miss Burnett and Pondon talked. And then we came away."

"I like the notion that he thought you wanted Palliser," Lord Arglay said contentedly. "The Stone seems to have a subtle irony of its own. But why *you*? Very much pleasanter for him, of course; but I had an idea, from what you said, that I was doing most of the work. Why didn't he see me?"

"It may be," the Hajji said, "that it was by your work that this man beheld her. For all that you showed him was the Stone, and it may be that Miss Burnett's work was in the Stone, and that he beheld her there. It was in its degree, redemption which you offered him, and if she was toiling also at redemption—the Way to the Stone is in the Stone."

"And yet his desire was to do what Palliser wished," Arglay demurred.

"His desire was to fulfil good as he knew it," the Hajji said. "Therefore he was capable of receiving within those conditions the End of Desire, which is eternally good."

"All times are within it and all places, it seems," Arglay said. "Are not therefore its own Types within itself?"

"I think that is true," the Hajji answered. "Certainly therefore this Thing contains its own Unity; it is for us to find the path by which that Unity may be manifested."

"It seems to me," Doncaster began. . . .

For some time Chloe had been conscious of a restlessness which she had been trying in vain to subdue. She was tired or something, she supposed, but things looked different somehow. What a lot of bother everyone was making! after all, there were other things in the world. And all this talk about redemption and the End of Desire. The end of desire was to get what you wanted. The Hajji was rather a silly little old man, she thought with his Compassionates and his Muhammeds and his Peace be upon him and his under the Protection—what protection and from what? A little intelligent watchfulness was all the protection she needed, and she could supply that herself. As for Lord Arglay—Lord Arglay, it occurred to her, was unmarried, and if not rich—he could hardly be that—still he must have. . . . And no-one but Reginald Montague to leave it to! Old men sometimes . . . after all he wasn't repulsive. If he married Chloe Burnett, Chloe Burnett would have a more comfortable life. And if he didn't marry still he was the kind of man who would probably treat his mistress very fairly. Suppose he had one already? That must be seen to. Chloe Burnett might not be exactly beautiful, but she had (so she had been told) a genius for making the most of herself and her art. There wouldn't be many mistresses who could outdo her if it really came to a tussle.

The Hajji stopped speaking, Lord Arglay stirred, and Chloe woke to sudden anxiety. What on earth had she been thinking? Thoughts had passed through her mind in their usual way, but not—surely not!—usual thoughts. Had she really been guessing how much money Lord Arglay had, and whether she could get it? Had she really been planning to use the hands clasped beneath her chin to trap him? Now if it had been this young Doncaster man . . . his hair would be rather pleasant to pull rather hard, he had thick hair; and well-made wrists, better than Frank's. Not that there would be any need to give up Frank, or anyhow not entirely. Chloe Burnett could deal with them as Sir Giles dealt with Arglay and the Hajji or the fellow at Birmingham, a silly fellow as she remembered him. Useful no doubt in a way, and amusing to think of him lost in the past. But very, very dull and only meant to be made use of by other people much more intelligent—Sir Giles for instance.

"Bloody fool!" Chloe said aloud.

As Oliver Doncaster had just begun "It seems to me——" her words caused, even in that company, a moment's attention . Oliver stopped speaking with a shock and found himself faced with the unbelievable. The Hajji turned on her a look of sudden alarm. Lord Arglay, taking her in with a side glance, said casually—"Not you, Mr. Doncaster; I think probably Palliser. But in any case we have for the moment done what we can. Would it be too much to ask you to call in the morning?"

Oliver had had earlier some general expectation of seeing Chloe home. But he wasn't as clear as the Chief Justice that the words hadn't been meant for him, and of course if that was what she thought the sooner he got away the better. Dare he risk shaking hands? He offered her his as charmingly as possible. "Very well, Lord Arglay," he said. "Good-night, Miss Burnett. Thank you for letting me come to Birmingham."

Chloe gave him her hand and looked at him. Oliver who

had been all day conscious of being held at an emotional distance discovered, with the second shock in two minutes, that he was being deliberately invited to be—understanding. Her fingers caressed for a moment the back of his hand; her mouth shaped itself for the kiss the circumstances forbade; her eyes mourned rebukingly over his departure. "Good-night, Mr. Doncaster," said a voice full of suggestions of intimacies that, so far as he could remember, hadn't happened, "We may meet —again—in the morning then?"

"She can't have meant him," the Chief Justice thought to himself. "But it certainly sounded as if she did. 'Bloody fool'— it's the way these modern young creatures talk. Yes, but not here, not—with other people about—to me. I shouldn't have thought she'd have done that. Still—she did. No," he thought suddenly. "I don't believe it. She never talked like that—except for amusement or from bitterness. And never *so*. She is civilized; she is in obedience to the Law."

He had been taking Oliver to the door while he was thinking and once that was closed he hastened back to the study. Chloe was standing by the fireplace, looking round the room. Lord Arglay had seen her standing just there often enough, but in her eyes now there was a difference. They surveyed, they considered, they calculated; so much he saw before she brought them back to meet his with a smile. But even that had something unnatural about it, a determination of quite another kind from that which had on other occasions once or twice appeared in the depths of her look, a hardness alien to the secretary the Chief Justice knew. For a moment, as their glances met, this gave place to a sudden bewilderment, but before he could say a word she had turned aside and was looking towards the window. Lord Arglay looked round for the Hajji, who had apparently withdrawn into some corner, and found him at last by his elbow. In that room they were far enough from Chloe not to be heard if they spoke softly, and in a such a tone the Hajji said: "Something has frightened you?"

"No," Arglay answered, "not frightened. I was a little startled, but I expect it's all right. No doubt Miss Burnett is a little overtired."

"I do not know Miss Burnett," the Hajji said, "except that I saw the Name upon her forehead. But I have watched her eyes, and I think you are right to be anxious."

"Why?" Arglay said abruptly.

"Her eyes and her mouth have changed," the Hajji answered. "They are curious and greedy—and even malicious. And if, as I think, she is not by nature greedy or malicious...."

He paused, but Arglay only said, "Well?"

"Then," the Hajji concluded, "something or someone is making her so."

In case Chloe should catch his eyes again Lord Arglay looked at the Hajji and said, "It seems a damn silly thing to try to do. What good would it be?"

"It might be a good deal of good," the Hajji said, "if indeed they desire to obtain the Types which you have. But even if not, have you never known men act from hate and anger alone?"

"And is this also, if it is so," Lord Arglay said, ironically, "part of the miracle of the Stone?"

"I warned you that there might be much evil," the Hajji answered, and fell silent.

Lord Arglay glanced again at Chloe. "You think they may be playing tricks on her?" he asked, but more as if in courteous conversation than in inquiry, and the other did not trouble to answer. At last, "Well," he went on, "if this is so I will do what can be done."

"Will you try and find her in the Stone?" the Hajji asked.

"No," Arglay answered, "no, I do not think I will take up the Stone. Between her and me I will not have any even of these things."

"You love her?" the Hajji said, half in statement, half in interrogation.

The Refusal of Lord Arglay

"Why, I do not very well know what love may be," Lord Arglay said, "but so far as is possible to men I think that there is Justice between her and me, and if that Justice cannot help us now I do not think that any miracles will."

"This is a very rare thing," the Hajji said doubtfully.

"My secretary," Lord Arglay said, half-lightly, half-seriously, "is a very rare young lady." His voice became entirely serious, as he added, "And if it is Giles, I will perhaps kill him tomorrow. But now I will see what is at work here."

"Cannot I help you?" the other asked.

"No," Arglay said. "I will do this alone. Good-night."

He shook hands and opened the door. The Hajji, without going nearer, bowed to Chloe and walked out. Lord Arglay shut the door and strolled across the room.

"I thought he was never going," Chloe said.

The remark was so perfectly normal that for a moment the Chief Justice felt almost idiotically defeated. But something reminded him that Chloe had never been the kind of secretary who remarked in that way on her employer's visitors. She would have thought it presumptuous and rude, and the affection that had grown between them had never made her more careless of her behaviour as a subordinate or as a friend. In both capacities the remark was inadmissible, and Lord Arglay knew it as he took the last three steps that brought him level with her. He smiled at her and for a moment considered.

"Do you feel very tired?" he asked.

"Well, it was a hell of a journey," Chloe said, "but no—not if you want me, I mean."

"Too tired," Lord Arglay said, "to do a little *Organic Law*?"

Chloe looked at him blankly for a moment. "O!" she exclaimed, and before she could add any more the Chief Justice went on easily, "I want you to consider it in connexion with our last night's resolution. I want you to *think*." His voice on the last word became suddenly authoritative.

Chloe laid a hand on his arm. "I am *rather* tired," she said, "but of course if you must have it done——" The hand slid down his arm to his hand and lingered there. Lord Arglay took it and held it. "Yes, *think*," he said. "Think, very carefully, yourself."

Chloe pouted. "What about?" she said. "Isn't there anything better to do? It's you that ought to think, not me."

"Good God!" Lord Arglay said, really annoyed, "don't talk such rubbish, child."

A quick tremor shook Chloe, she released his hand, and slid round to face him. "Am I a child?" she said, and suddenly anger contended with cunning in her eyes. She paused uncertainly, as if something within her, unaccustomed to the instrument it was using, was fumbling with it; she half put out her hand again and withdrew it; she leaned forward but whether in desire or hate Arglay could not tell. He kept his eyes on her now, saying nothing for a moment that the remembrance of the Chloe Burnett he knew might gather more mightily within him. For the change that had come upon her was provoked by no natural alteration of mood, and for a moment he wondered whether indeed he had been wise in this extremity to refuse the mysterious capacities of the Stone. If he could use it to rescue Pondon might he not with a thousand times more reason use it here? Might it not be a wise and proper thing to do? But however wise or proper it might be he knew he could not; to do so would be already to confess defeat—there was something else on which he relied and it was the mere fact that they two were what they were and had been what they had been.

He said, with a certain slowness, "Child, I would have you think of what we chose to do."

"I do not want to think of anything that is past," she answered sullenly, and to that he said in a growing passion of authority, "But I will have you do this, and therefore you shall do it now. I will have you do it."

She moved her head from side to side as if to avoid the charge he laid upon her; then, abandoning a direct refusal, she said in almost a whisper, "But first let us think of other things."

"Child," he answered, "the things of which you would think are neither here nor there, nor do you think of them. You think and you shall think of all that we have done together, and of how we determined to believe in God."

"I will believe in you instead," Chloe said and took a small step forward in the small distance that separated them.

The sentence was so unexpected, she was herself so close, that Arglay for a moment hesitated. It was not so much desire for her that filled him as a willingness to accept himself on those terms, to take this offered substitution. To play deity to an attractive young girl—there was, for a moment he felt, a certain point to the idea. But even as the point pricked him ever so slightly he smiled to think of it, and the consciousness of the prick passed from him. His own belief in God was still small, but his feeling for Organic Law was very strong, and his dislike of any human being pretending to be above that Law was stronger still. The temptation rose and was lost in its absurdity. And yet . . . She looked up with an inviting smile. He took her suddenly by one shoulder with his hand.

"You will not believe in me," he answered, "as more than a servant of that which you serve. Answer me—what is that?"

"It is nothing with which you have anything to do," she said, "unless you will do also what I will."

He smiled at her in a sudden serenity. "Now I know that I shall have my way," he said, either to her or to that which was within her, and added to her alone, "since it is impossible that we should be so separated for ever."

"You!" she said harshly. "Will you govern me with your bit of filthy pebble?"

"I have no need of the Stone," he answered, still smiling at her, "for all that is in the Stone, except the accidents of time, is here between us and perhaps more than is in the Stone. And in that you will answer me. Tell me, child, what is it you serve."

She wrenched her shoulder away from him. "Keep your beastly hands away," she cried. "I am my own to keep and command."

"And if that shall be true to-morrow," Lord Arglay said, "it is not true now." His voice took on a sternness and he looked on her with a high disdain. "Answer," he said; "will you make me wait? Answer—what is it that you serve?"

She moved back a step or two, and suddenly he put out his hand, caught her wrist, and pulled her back close to him; then, his eyes on hers, he said: "Child, you know me and I know you among the deceptions. What is it, what is it that you serve?"

She gave a stifled cry, and slipped forward so that he caught her—"I know," she said, "I know. Hold me; I know."

When at last he moved she stood up and did something to her hair; then she looked at him with a faint smile. "I do know," she said.

"Then I think it is more than I do," Lord Arglay said. "But that is very possible."

"Have I been saying anything—very silly?" she asked, picking up her handbag and looking for her powder-puff.

The Chief Justice considered her. "How do you feel?" he asked. "Well enough to talk a little about it?"

"Quite," Chloe answered, sitting down, and adding after a moment's pause, "Have I been a nuisance?"

"Don't you remember?" Lord Arglay asked. "Suppose you tell me first—whatever seemed to happen."

"I don't know that anything exactly happened," Chloe said. "I just began to think about . . . began to think in a different way."

"In *quite* a different way?" Arglay interrupted. "I mean, in a way you had never thought before?"

The Refusal of Lord Arglay

The colour flamed in Chloe's cheeks. But she met his eyes and answered, "Partly. I don't think I ever *calculated* before—not so much anyhow. Or not at the same time that I felt . . ." she struggled bravely on and ended . . . "desirous."

The Chief Justice considered again. He had seen the farewell she had taken of Doncaster; he had observed, when he had returned to the study, the valuation to which she was bringing its furniture; he had remarked the cold intention in her eyes when the two of them were talking; and he decided that in this case desire and calculation were two different things. But by what means, if by any outside herself, had they been loosed?

"It came on you suddenly?" he asked.

"It came," she answered, "as if I thought I was walking down one road and found I was walking down another. It didn't even come; it was there. I lived into the midst of it."

"And it?" Arglay said, "it seemed like some other self of yours? Did you know yourself in it?"

"In a way," she answered, "all the things that I have sometimes hated most in myself. But not altogether. Never—no, in all my life, I never wanted so utterly to grab without giving anything at all, never before." In her agitation she stood up. "I'm not like that," she said, "O indeed I'm not."

"No," Lord Arglay said, "but I think I could guess who is, and whose mind was thrust upon yours then. But even he, even in the Stone, could only affect you through your own habits and emotions. So that both he and you troubled and hid your heart." He paused for a moment and went on. "Child, in those past times that you speak of, how have you governed yourself?"

"By this and that," Chloe said. "By trying to think clearly and by trying to be as nice as I could to people."

"It is very well said," Lord Arglay answered. "I do not think Giles or anyone else will easily overcome that guard of yours."

"I will take care of that," Chloe said in quite a different voice. "I shan't be caught twice."

"Well," Lord Arglay answered comfortably, looking round the room, "I mayn't be what Reginald's unfortunate American would call rich, but I should think I am quite the most well-to-do person you know. So if you are going to make an attempt on anyone it will probably be on me again. Which won't matter, will it?"

"No," said Chloe, "though it seems funny that it shouldn't. And in a way it does."

"O la la! in a way——" Lord Arglay said. "But only in a way conformable to the Stone. Now it *is* funny, if you like, how determined I was not to use the Stone. One might have thought I didn't care *what* happened to you. I might have been the Hajji; indeed I was worse than the Hajji, for he at least thought about using it."

"Why—if I may—why didn't you?" Chloe asked shyly, but her eyes were glad as she looked at him.

"I couldn't see that it was going to be of the slightest use," he answered. "It just wasn't there. Or else—since we have decided to believe in it—it was there anyhow, and to have it materially wouldn't have helped."

"Is there then something greater than the Stone?" she asked. "I dreamed last night that the King lifted up his hand and there was a great light."

"Also the Hajji spoke of a greater secret," he answered. "I do not think Giles quite knows what he is doing."

"Do you think it is dangerous to him?" Chloe said.

"Anything that one uses is apt to become one's master," Arglay answered. "And if the Stone should become Giles's master—what would he find it to be?"

Chloe looked at her fingers. "Do you think," she said doubtfully, "we ought to try and . . . warn him or . . . help him . . . or anything?"

"Help him—help Giles?" Lord Arglay exclaimed. "My dear

child, don't be absurd! After he . . . O you're tired out; I shall take you home. Unless—I ask you again—unless you'll stop here?"

"Not to-night, please," she said. "I shall be quite safe now. If he tries it again, I shall just *think*."

"Do," Lord Arglay approved. "My present problem in *Organic Law* is this—Good heavens, you want to know! O come along, you're merely making altruism into a habit."

Chapter Fourteen

THE SECOND REFUSAL OF
CHLOE BURNETT

Lord Arglay asserted later that whenever Chloe declared that she would be quite safe something perilous was certain to be approaching. But since he knew that she was in possession of one of the Types and therefore had at her disposal a means of escape from any crisis and a place of refuge in his own house it did not seem to him that she was likely to be in any unavoidable danger. For alternatively if any one of those who were bound to regard them as enemies should seize on the Type she had, then his object would be achieved. The Stone possessed, there would be no point in harming Chloe; it would indeed be a stupid and risky thing to do, arousing that very attention which it was important to avoid. It appeared therefore to the Chief Justice that though she might be inconvenienced she could not be seriously endangered.

This argument, though sound within its limits, suffered from the same trouble that invalidates all human argument and makes all human conclusion erroneous, namely, that no reasoning can ever start from the possession of all the facts. The two facts which Lord Arglay's reasoning left out of account were, first, the inclusion of the Prince Ali among the pursuers of the Stone, and second Chloe's increasing determination not to use her Type for her own safety. It was this omission which proved his conclusion wrong and did actually put her in peril.

For whatever the Persian Ambassador might diplomatically desire, and whatever the Hajji Ibrahim might religiously assert, Ali had no intention at all of relinquishing his efforts—if necessary, his militant efforts—to recover all the Types if possible, and if not at least one; by the possession of which he hoped to procure the rest. His first objective had been Sir Giles. But Sir Giles had made it clear that any attempt to recover the Type in his possession would mean a multiplication of Stones which from Ali's point of view would be not only sacrilegious but extremely troublesome. He had not for some days been at all clear where the rest of the Types were. Reginald Montague had apparently had one, but then—he gathered from the papers—so had Sheldrake; were they one or two? Ali could not, in his position, afford to make a number of violent and unsuccessful efforts to recover it or them; the Ambassador's modernity and the Hajji's piety might agree in removing him to Moscow or having him recalled to Tehran before he achieved what he wanted, should either of them suspect what was happening. He had not dared so far to make any effort to excite the temper of the East. But he had, with the greatest caution, sounded the mind of one of his friends in the Embassy; he intended to gather about himself a small group of similar spirits in order that when a convenient time came he might, if necessary, strike in several directions at once.

Nothing however was further from his mind than that he should be rung up by Sir Giles Tumulty. It was not the first telephonic conversation which had proceeded between the Embassy and the English that morning; the Hajji and Lord Arglay had been talking earlier. The Chief Justice had briefly explained that all was well with Miss Burnett, and had added that he was still in two minds about going off to Ealing and quite simply killing Sir Giles.

"What good do you think that would be . . . in the End?" the Hajji said.

"I haven't an idea what good it would be in the End," Lord Arglay assured him, "but it seems as if it might be a considerable good here and now. After all, we can't be expected to put everything off because of the End or we should just be putting off the End itself. At least it seems so to me, but I'm no metaphysician."

"What would Miss Burnett desire?" the Hajji asked.

"That's my only difficulty," Lord Arglay explained. "I don't think she'd like it—and yet I don't know. Everybody else would be pleased. I might be hanged but I should be almost certain to have a memorial statue somewhere, probably by Epstein. I like Epstein too. Well, I suppose I shan't."

He might however have been almost inclined to turn the only half-fantastic idea into an act if he had overheard Sir Giles a quarter of an hour later. The whole history of Tumulty's dealings with the Stone had roused in him a state of increasing irritation with Lord Arglay and his secretary. There had been the spying on him, as he chose to call it, at Birmingham; Arglay's refusal to investigate the half-hour's break; the affray at the Conference; his own impotence to understand Arglay's mind; the rescue of Pondon. And now . . . He was not very clear what had interfered with his domination of Chloe. He had, after the usual preliminary attention and concentration, become aware of looking through Chloe's eyes much as Arglay had looked through his own. He had been aware of a feeling for the Chief Justice which, since it certainly wasn't his own, must be Chloe's. He had attempted to turn that emotion into his own desire to use Arglay and then throw him aside. But he had not reached to the extremer places of Chloe's own manner of experience; it had been but her conscious thought that he could dominate, working inwards from without. He had so far conquered that his intention had imposed itself on her as her own, although with the changed appearance which, in their turn, her physical and mental desires had wrought in it. But at the time when Lord Arglay had called upon his friend with the authority to which she was accustomed and which she loved, Giles's will had been swept aside. A darkness fell upon him; he became aware of the Stone in his hands, it seemed to move in them and itself to thrust him back. He dropped it suddenly as if just in time to avoid its growth against him, and took, as he became again conscious of his outer surroundings, a few angry steps about the room. "I don't know if this is a damned nightmare," he grunted, "but it felt as if I was going to be swallowed by the bloody thing. I wonder if I'm letting the idea of getting back at Arglay and his whore run away with me. One does, sometimes; and that's just death to observation. I wish there was someone else who could tackle them. And by God," he exclaimed, "there is. I suggested it to Birlesmere myself—there's the Persian."

As he thought about it he decided that his, in default of a better, was the momentary solution. The Prince Ali was probably still anxious to recover the Stone, and if he happened to kill Chloe or Arglay in the process so much the better. Anyhow even to lose their Types would certainly annoy them, and if at the worst Ali or his friends failed or suffered there was no particular harm done to Sir Giles himself. "Ali and this screaming peahen can fight it out together," he said, and looked up the number of the Persian Embassy.

The Prince was considerably surprised when he was first told that Sir Giles Tumulty wanted to speak to him, but he condescended to answer.

Sir Giles was obscenely abrupt. On condition that he was left alone he would give the Persian a chance of recovering something, if Ali thought it worth while. Was he to be left alone? The Prince, as abruptly, agreed. Then at Lancaster Gate and wherever the secretary hibernated, were Types of the Stone, if they were wanted.

"But why," the Prince said curiously, "do you tell me this?"

"What in hell's name does that matter to you?" Sir Giles asked. "I gave him one when I thought you were after me, just to make you and your company of date-eaters think a bit. But he annoys me, and I'd rather you had it."

The Second Refusal of Chloe Burnett

The Prince thought, but did not say, that the Foreign Office would hardly have agreed. Sir Giles had thought of it but he was far too angry with his brother-in-law to care about all the Foreign Offices in Europe.

"Well, there you are," he said. "I suppose you can hire somebody to do the job."

"That I will see to," the Prince said. "If this is true I cannot thank you, but I will at least ignore you."

"You'll do what?" Sir Giles almost yelled, but recovered himself and slammed down the receiver. "And I hope they assault the girl and assassinate Arglay," he thought to himself as he prepared to go out again to Wandsworth.

The exact measures which the Prince took were, not unnaturally, never explained. But by the time that Chloe, after an uneventful day, returned home, they had been carried out. His friend had left London for Brighton and Reginald Montague. He himself was waiting for night.

Chloe and the Chief Justice had—quite seriously—discussed the possibility of attempting to recover all the Types and of escaping with them from England. But neither of them, especially as they grew less and less inclined to use it—or, as Chloe had said—to dictate to it, had been quite prepared to take such extreme measures. Lord Arglay viewed with a certain hesitation the annexation of Sheldrake's Type, for which after all he had paid and from which he was presumably entitled to get such satisfaction as he legally could. The Mayor of Rich had called to ask the Chief Justice to draw up a public statement and petition on behalf of all the sick, and on the first draft of this Lord Arglay, with a wry smile, had spent some time. Rich, he gathered from the papers, was still in a state of simmering discontent. Oliver Doncaster had called, very uncertain of his behaviour in Chloe's company, and rather defeated at finding that everything seemed normal. No one alluded to her remark of the previous night, and the Chief Justice being in the room all the time there was no opportunity for him to make the running on the strength of her own behaviour. As, rather gloomily, he departed, Lord Arglay looked at Chloe. "Of course he doesn't appreciate Giles," he said.

"But what must he think of *me*?" Chloe asked despairingly.

"I can't begin to imagine," Lord Arglay said. "Nor as a matter of fact can he. You can, but you needn't at the moment. For I am utterly convinced that Austin—Austin!—never said '*Attribuat igitur rex legi, quod lex attribuit ei, videlicet dominationem et potestatem. Non est enim rex ubi dominatur voluntas et non lex.*' Don't you know the sound of Bracton's voice, when you hear it? 'Therefore let the king attribute to the law that which the law attributes to him, namely, domination and power. For where the will rules and not the law is no king.' You haven't checked your references, child, and, as a result, you've got this whole page of quotations wrong."

Chloe bit her lips, crossed out the attribution, and plunged back into legal histories.

This unfortunate lapse, the more maddening that it had been a page she had written out some weeks earlier, and before the Stone had preoccupied her mind, was annoying her when she returned that night. For she had rather prided herself on her secretarial efficiency, and Lord Arglay's quite pleasant, but quite firm, criticism of it distressed almost as much as it pleased her. Almost, because she thought as she took off her hat how much worse it would have been if he had pretended that, because of their friendship, it didn't matter. "It was," he had said, "no doubt the prophetic soul of your wide world dreaming on things to come. But don't let it be dreaming too much about the law-makers who are gone, will you? Or let us be quite clear when it is." Chloe kicked herself again and made some coffee.

The incident however sent her to bed even more certain of the edge of incapacity and void upon which she dwelt than she normally was. What with Frank Lindsay being angry with her for one thing (and even now she wasn't clear that she had been right), and Lord Arglay being critical of her for another (and she was quite clear that she had been hopelessly careless), she seemed to herself a sufficiently ineffectual creature. It was true she couldn't much care whether Frank was angry or not, and didn't in a sense mind whether Lord Arglay was displeased or not; if the one didn't understand, well, she couldn't help it, and of the other she would always be secure no matter how unhappy he might, very properly and rightly, make her. Still, if this was the result of her emotional and intellectual life—merely to annoy everybody! She looked at herself in the glass and wondered as on several other occasions during the last few days what the Hajji had meant by saying that the Name was upon her forehead. The Name of the God in which she and Lord Arglay had decided to believe? What did you do if you had decided to believe in God? So far as her early training served her, she thought you gave up your will to His. *Non est enim rex ubi dominatur voluntas*—for where the will rules there is no king. But Bracton—damn her stupidity!— had been talking of feudal law, and yet . . . She wandered slowly back and lifted from her handbag the Type of the Stone that she carried, to lay it under her pillow for the night. "The End of Desire" . . . "the Stone which is between you and me." You gave up your will, did you? Your will by itself produced pretty poor results, it seemed. *Attribuat igitur*—let the king attribute to the law . . . But how to find the law? "The Way to the Stone which is in the Stone." The Stone, Lord Arglay, God— the End of Desire. Was this then what her absurd childish prayers meant? "Our Father which art in heaven," she thought, "Hallowed be Thy name, Thy kingdom come, Thy will be done on earth as it is in heaven"—and what did that mean? Of course if it all did mean something it was quite easy to believe she hadn't yet understood, but in that case she wanted, she wanted very much, to understand; and very much indeed, with her body and mind and everything else, she desired the End of Desire. Still thinking about it, still trying over to herself the first few phrases of that august ritual of intercession she got into bed, laid the Type of the Stone under her pillow, and settled herself to sleep.

Or to think. But bed, as Chloe had on other occasions discovered, is not really a good place in which to try and do both, even sequentially. When she decided that she had thought enough and ought to go to sleep, for fear the next day should find her making a muddle of more quotations, she found it was too late. Bits of her previous thoughts half imaged themselves to her, and disappeared before she could do more than recognize them. She thought of getting up and reading, but she couldn't think of any book in her rooms which she wanted to read—not even Mr. Ford Madox Ford's novels or the life of Sir Edward Marshall-Hall (which, a fortnight before, had seemed to her to unite law and interest—Chloe had never quite freed herself from the idea that she ought to read in her leisure something that had a bearing on her work). And anyhow——

She lay very still suddenly. Something, surely something, had sounded. Only the door-handle. But it had, ever so faintly, clicked. Doors did make noises in the night—but door-handles? She felt hastily round to see if she could remember a door-handle clicking. Was there somebody—had somebody come for the Stone? She thrust both hands under her pillow in a panic, and her fingers closed about it. The moonlight came half across the room, alongside her bed; surely no one at least could reach its—and her—head, and the Stone, unseen. She began to strain her eyes towards the foot; then she shut them, in case there was anyone, and that she might be thought asleep; then she partly opened them that she might see what was happening. There was a faint movement somewhere, as if of a breath being loosed, then another silence. Chloe's right hand grasped the Stone; her left held the bed-clothes tightly.

What, what, if there was anyone there, was she to do? O for Lord Arglay now!

She remembered suddenly, still desperately watching, what he had said, "Come to me"—yes, but how was she to come? O why wouldn't he come to her? "Come to me." But how— but of course the Stone. She only had to make use of the Stone and all would be safe. In the thrill of assured safety she all but made a face at the unknown, if there were an unknown. And there was; for one second on the edge of the dark an edge of a finger showed. Something was moving towards her in the night. Well, that was all right; they could go on moving. She had only to will and—— She had only to will . . . to use the Stone. In a horror of anguish she understood the choice that was presented to her.

Her thoughts went through her head like Niagara. Lord Arglay had told her but even Lord Arglay didn't feel like that about the Stone and she had said to Frank she wouldn't use it if she were starving and what was the man doing and what would he do if she screamed and even if she did perhaps Mrs. Webb wouldn't come down this time and what could she do if she did? O it wasn't fair, it wasn't fair! How could she use the Stone? yet how could she bear not to if whoever it was came nearer? He was probably trying to see if her hands were empty; well, they weren't. He won't know if I've got it in my hand or not, she thought. Could she sit up, switch on the light, and with the Stone in her hand dare him to move? No—it was too risky; he'd think of something she wasn't prepared for and per- haps snatch it from her. Then she would use it; after all she was using it to save it. She was doing for it what it could not do for itself. She was protecting it. Not being a reader of religious history Chloe was ignorant what things have been done in the strength of that plea, or with what passionate anxiety men have struggled to protect the subordination of Omnipotence. But in her despair she rejected what churches and kings and prelates have not rejected; she refused to be deceived, she refused to attempt to be helpful to the God, and being in an agony she prayed more earnestly. The God purged her as she writhed; lucidity entered into her; she turned upon her face, and with both hands beneath her pillow holding the Stone, she lay still, saying only silently in her panting breath: "Thy will, . . . do . . . do if Thou wilt; or"—she imagined the touch of the marauder on the calf of her leg and quivering in every nerve added—"or . . . not."

In the darkness the Prince Ali almost made a movement of delight. He had got into the house, by the aid of certain hangers-on of the hangers-on of the Embassy; secret service, from which even a minor Embassy is not entirely exempt, sets up connexions which are useful at times, and judicious inquiries that afternoon by a gentleman in search of lodgings had let him know which Chloe's room was. The actual seizure of the Stone he had not dared to entrust to anyone else, but he had been disturbed to find Chloe still awake. He had reckoned on sleep, darkness, and chloroform, but he had not dared cross the moonlight while she lay awake, for he had some idea of how swiftly the Stone would work and he had no wish to be confronted with an empty bed. Now that she had turned on to her face, however, his opportunity was at hand. He felt very carefully for the chloroformed pad, and at that moment a cloud began gradually to obscure the moonlight. The Prince hesitated and determined to wait for that fuller darkness; while he waited he took out his electric torch with his left hand, and rehearsed his movements. A few quiet steps to the top of the bed, the torchlight on her head, the pad over her mouth. He was practically certain that the Stone would be under her pillow—or perhaps in a bag round her neck; at any rate once she was unconscious he would be able to search at leisure, with the room light on. It would, he felt, have been more satisfactory to his outraged creed to destroy the woman who had done dishonour to the sacred thing even by possessing it, and to avenge upon her the insult offered to his God. But this relief he could hardly allow himself; Allah himself must punish. The moonlight had disappeared; the room lay in darkness, he stepped forward, his finger on the switch of the torch.

When Chloe had heaved herself round with that last movement her heart had been beating wildly, and her breath coming in quick pants. Now as she lay she felt both of them beginning to move more quietly and more largely; she drew long and deep breaths and her heart composed itself to a corresponding rhythm. She still saw before her mental vision the edge of a finger against a darkness, or rather not now the edge but the finger itself, and at its back an indeterminate shape as if it were thrust a little forward from the whole hand; and she realized that it was not the same finger which she had seen a few moments earlier. Between these two palenesses therefore she lay, the one remembered, the other beheld, yet both present, and, almost as if in the uncertainty before sleep, she was vaguely conscious that the two came together and formed one stream of pale but increasing light. From somewhere beyond her, where her hands clasped the Stone, that narrow line of light emerged; she lay within it and it passed through and about her without hindrance. The more clear it grew to her knowledge, the more clearly within she enunciated the formula she had shaped with such pain and at last unconsciously abandoned the formula itself for the meaning that lay within it.

"Do, or do not," she silently uttered, and fell even mentally into stillness in order that unhindered that action might or might not take place. The light grew suddenly around her; some encumbrance for a moment touched her mouth and would have interrupted her appeal, had it been vocal; a vibration went through her, as if a note of music had been struck along her whole frame, and far off she heard as it were a single trumpet at the gate of the house of Suleiman with a prolonged blast saluting the dawn.

The police-constable on his beat outside had come slowly

down the road, and from a few yards off saw a dark heap at the door of Mrs. Webb's house. He broke into a run, bent over it for a minute, then straightened himself, and blew his whistle. It was the body of a man that lay there; they found afterwards that it was burnt as if by lightning and broken as if cast from an immense distance. The constable's whistle sounded again as if with a prolonged blast saluting the dawn.

Chapter Fifteen

THE POSSESSIVENESS OF
MR. FRANK LINDSAY

Neither Mrs. Webb nor Miss Burnett were of much use to the police in that morning investigation. Neither of them recognized the body, and though it had lain huddled against the front door of the house, there was nothing to show that, alive or dead, it had ever been inside the door. Besides which, burning and breaking, as that body was burnt and broken, are not injuries which the two women seemed very capable of inflicting, and the inspector in charge leaned to the idea that it had been brought from a distance and dropped at this spot. The usual inquiries were set on foot, with a casual jest or two about the possibility of the Rich Stone being responsible. But Miss Burnett was not prevented from departing to her employment, though some care was taken to see that she actually went to Lord Arglay's as she had professed to intend; since with these modern girls, as someone remarked, you never knew. The police had cause to be glad that they had not interfered, since in quite a short time the Home Office was intimating to them that the whole incident had better be kept as quiet as possible, and the stop-press paragraph which, by the chance of a belated journalist, had appeared in one morning paper had better be left without any sequel.

The Chief Justice had listened in silence to Chloe's account of the night.

"And that blast of sound went on," she ended, "and it seemed to be a long time before I understood it was just a police whistle, and all that light was just the moon. And then

I knew that whatever it was had gone away; so I got up and looked out of the window. And there they were."

"The police?"

"The police. They saw me and I asked a question or two, and they asked more—of Mrs. Webb too. But they couldn't do anything to us. I don't even know whether . . . what they had was what I saw."

"It may not have been," Arglay said. "But I think it is likely. Did you see the . . . the result?"

"Yes," Chloe said, her face white but rather with awe than horror or fear, "it was as if it had been struck by lightning."

"It wasn't Giles?"

"It was someone I have never seen before," Chloe answered. "A dark man, a foreigner I think. Not a negro but someone Eastern."

"As a Persian, for instance?" Lord Arglay asked. "Though how they knew of you I don't understand. Well, we can ask the Hajji if he knows anything—I don't think he'd be in it. He seems to have too low an opinion of violence and too high an opinion of you."

Chloe looked at her feet and said nothing, and in a moment the Chief Justice went on. "Yes, we will talk to him, and also I will speak to Bruce Cumberland. He won't want the thing broadcast, if it is the Persians, and it may save you some trouble. At any rate, you will sleep here now."

"Yes," Chloe said simply, "I will. Shall I send a note to Mrs. Webb explaining?"

"Do," Arglay said, "while I telephone."

Mr. Bruce Cumberland, when he heard the news, took the steps he was expected to take. The police were warned to be careful in their inquiries, and to turn those inquiries to discovering whether any member of the Persian Embassy was missing. But before Lord Arglay had finished talking to the Hajji a caller arrived at Lancaster Gate.

The Possessiveness of Mr. Frank Lindsay

Mr. Frank Lindsay had seen the newspaper paragraph, and alone among its readers had known the street for Chloe's. He did not seriously connect her with "the dead body of a man found early that morning," but there flashed through his mind the notion that here was an opportunity for an anxious inquiry. Within that opportunity another possibility lay curled, vivid with a delectable poison. Sometimes with, sometimes without, his own consent, Merridew's proposal had demanded consideration, each time more urgently, each time more plausibly. But however reasonable it had begun to seem, since after all it would do Chloe no harm and himself a great deal of good, he could not discover how to carry it out without a depressing sacrifice of his own proper pride. She had refused his suggestion almost—no, quite—rudely; she had dismissed him; she had promised to write and had not written. Even for the sake of his examination and (what of course did not weigh with him) the fee Merridew had spoken of—for a fee, nothing more, was what it was—even for these things Lindsay could not see how to make any movement towards a reconciliation. But every day made the need of that reconciliation more urgent, if it was to be in time to be any use, if (he said to himself) they were to be on their old terms again, and hardly knew that by the phrase he meant very new terms indeed. It was not that Chloe would bear any malice, but that swift willingness of hers to hurry all occasion of mischief into oblivion at times rather annoyed him; it seemed a little undignified, and was one of the things in which he suspected the influence of Lord Arglay encouraged her in lessening herself. Of course, it was different when he was concerned, though even then it was difficult for him to be gracious when she so speedily abolished the opportunity for grace. She ran where he walked, and he thought walking the more handsome movement. But now—with a dead body in the street—yes, a real concern was permissible. And if that concern repaid its possessor in other ways—but he was not thinking of that, he was thinking of a dead body. He was perfectly correct, but a more accurate vision would have told him that he was thinking also of a dying soul, and that his own.

She would be at Lancaster Gate, and to Lancaster Gate, rather nervously, he went. The telephone seemed inadequate to his anxiety; an actual meeting, a clasping hand, a reassuring embrace, if possible, if the Chief Justice was out of the way, seemed to be demanded. From every point of view he hoped that Lord Arglay would be out of the way.

Lord Arglay, seeing the maid speak to Chloe and seeing also Chloe's glance at himself, cut short his conversation with the Hajji, and, hearing that Mr. Lindsay had called, took immediate steps to be out of the way. "You can call me for a minute when he's going," he said, "if you think it would look more courteous. But do as you like about that. The Hajji won't be here just yet."

"But I don't know that I want you to go," Chloe said uncertainly. "No, I'm sorry, I didn't mean to put it like that. I didn't mean to talk as if I had a right. . . ."

"I feel," Lord Arglay said, "that God—it's curious how easily one accepts the idea; atavism, I suppose—would rather I went; at least, the God in your friend. There is courtesy everywhere, and this, so to speak, is that. Besides, now I know you're safe, I should like him to."

Chloe did her amiable best to reassure Mr. Lindsay, but she felt all the time that she couldn't much mind whether he were reassured or not. Unless indeed he had undergone a conversion of which she would not look for the signs for fear they should not be there. She said nothing about the invasion of the night and at first took great care not to mention the Stone. Yet since it was so much in her thoughts she did find herself wishing that he, so young, so ignorant, so well-intentioned, as he seemed to her, could feel as she felt about it, or could at least see what she felt, and when after about a quarter of an hour she felt that he might as well go, she said hesitatingly: "You do understand, Frank, about the other night, don't you?"

Frank, whose inner thoughts had also been occupied with the Stone, said brightly: "O of course, of course. Don't worry; that's quite all right. I see what you meant," and wondered, for the fifteenth time, whether she had brought it with her or left it at Highgate. It wasn't on any of the tables, but her handbag lay by the typewriter; could it be——

"Would you like just to speak to Lord Arglay?" Chloe said.

That meant that she was expecting him to go, he thought very swiftly; if he said yes would she leave the room? or would she send a maid? It was growing urgent, this need of the Stone, though, of course, he could perhaps take her home. But where did she keep it? Suppose she had it round her neck in a bag? Girls did; and then—— Even his mind refused to contemplate what measures, and in them what treachery, might be necessary: after all, they had been friends. "Yes" then, and pray heaven she went to tell Lord Arglay herself.

"Perhaps it would be better," he said.

She kissed him—persevering upon the Way—pressed his hand, went to the door, threw him a last smile, and disappeared. And he, swiftly and quietly, his eyes on the closed door, moved to her work-table, opened the bag, felt the Stone, withdrew it, stared at it, slipped it into his trouser pocket, where he thought among his keys and money it would be least noticeable, re-fastened the bag, and almost ran to the window. And even then there were two or three minutes given him for repentance, before Chloe opened the door for the Chief Justice, and stepped softly aside, as a secretary should, that her employer might enter. This careful subordination had always pleased Lord Arglay, and after the occurrences of the last few days gave him an increasing joy, as if it were part of the habitual ritual that surrounded his office, but much more delightful, more dear, and in some way more important than the rest.

Lord Arglay shook hands. Mr. Lindsay, a trifle awkwardly

apologized for disturbing Miss Burnett at her work. Lord Arglay said that any friend of Miss Burnett's was free at all times to disturb her in her work, which owing to her sense of form was rapidly becoming a great deal more her work than it was his. Mr. Lindsay said that the paragraph in the paper had alarmed him; he had been afraid there might have been some disturbance in the street, or even that some attack. . . . Lord Arglay said that he had feared the same thing and had been very anxious until Miss Burnett arrived. Mr. Lindsay was greatly indebted to Lord Arglay. Lord Arglay hoped that Mr. Lindsay would believe that their common friendship with Miss Burnett put his own house at Mr. Lindsay's disposal at such— or any—times. The maid announced Mr. Ibrahim. Mr. Lindsay was again obliged and must go. Lord Arglay regretted, understood, and parted. The maid showed Mr. Lindsay out.

With his departure the three in the study seemed to enter into a common concern. The Hajji, as the sound of the front door closing was heard, said quite simply: "It was Ali."

"That is your nephew?" Lord Arglay said.

"He was my nephew," the Hajji answered, "but more than death has separated us. For he also has wished to lay violent hands upon the Stone."

Lord Arglay said, as he motioned to them to be seated, "Hajji, the whole world seems to agree with him there."

"It is the worse for all of us," the Hajji answered sadly.

"You are sure of this?" Arglay asked, as he too sat down.

"As sure as I can be without seeing him," Ibrahim said. "He is not at the Embassy this morning, none knows where he has gone, and I know what he unwisely desired."

"I am very sorry for your house," Lord Arglay said, "for this is becoming a very terrible thing. But because of others will you tell us what you think happened last night? Why did this man die?"

The Hajji looked at Chloe. "Tell me," he said, "what you did when you knew that someone was in your room."

Chloe tried to express it. "I didn't think I ought to use the Stone for myself," she said, "and I didn't think I knew what it willed for itself, so I—I did nothing except hope that it would —deal with things."

"Of itself?" the Hajji asked softly.

"I suppose so," Chloe admitted. "I didn't know what I ought to do."

The Hajji nodded slowly, and looked at Lord Arglay. "It should be clear to you what has come about," he said. "A thing has happened which has not been possible for a thousand years."

"I can quite believe that," Lord Arglay said. "A thousand years seem to be considerably less than a day in this case. But I am not at all clear what this thing is."

"This Holy Thing has been kept in seclusion," Ibrahim answered, "through many centuries, and in all that time none of its keepers have approached or touched it. And since Giles Tumulty stole it men have grasped at it in their own wisdom. But this woman has put her will at its disposal, and between it and her the union may be achieved by which the other Hiddenness is made manifest."

"What is the other Hiddenness?" Lord Arglay asked.

The Hajji hesitated, then he turned his eyes back to Chloe and seemed to ask a question of her. What answer he saw on the forehead at which he gazed she could not guess, but he spoke then in a low and careful voice.

"In the Crown of Suleiman the Wise—the Peace be upon him!—" he said, "there was a Stone, and this Stone was that which is the First Matter of Creation, holy and terrible. But on the hand of the King there was a Ring and in the Ring another secret, more holy and terrible than the Stone. For within the Ring there was a point of that Light which is the Spirit of Creation, the Adornment of the Unity, the Knowledge of the Loveliness, the Divine Image in the mirror of the worlds just and true. This was the Justice and the Wisdom of

227

Suleiman, by which all souls were made manifest to him and all causes rightly determined. Also when within the Holy of Holies in the Temple that the King made he laid his crown upon the Ark and between the wings of the Cherubim, and held his hand over it, the Light of the Ring shone upon the Stone and all things had peace. But when the King erred, building altars to strange gods, he dared no longer let the Light fall upon the Stone; also he put aside the Ring and it is told that Asmodeus sat upon his throne seven years. But I think that perhaps the King himself had not all that time parted from his throne, how closely soever Asmodeus dwelt within his soul. And of the hiding place of the Ring I do not know, nor any of my house; if it is on earth it is very secret. But the Light of it is in the Stone and all the Types of the Stone—and the Power of it is in the soul and body of any who have sought the union with the Stone, so that whoever touches them in anger or hatred or evil desire is subjected to the Light and Power of the Adornment of the Unity. And this I think my nephew did, and this is the cause of his blasting and hurling out."

He looked straight at Chloe. "But woe, woe, woe to you," he said, "if from this time forth for ever you forget that you gave your will to the Will of That which is behind the Stone."

Chloe started to her feet with a cry. "It isn't true," she broke out, "it isn't true! What have I done to bring all this on me? I can't bear it; it isn't, it mustn't be true."

Lord Arglay's voice answered her. "All is well," he said, "all is well, child. You shall do nothing that you cannot do and bear nothing that you cannot bear. I will see to that." He held out his hand towards her, and, shaken and terrified, she caught it. "Sit down," he went on, smiling at her, "and we will know what all this is."

"What are you," the Hajji asked, more astonished than indignant, "to promise to govern the Stone?"

"Why, in some sense," Lord Arglay said, smiling again, "I

am at the moment, as you say, the Light that is in the Stone. Not that I ever meant or wanted to be."

"I do not understand you," the Hajji exclaimed in bewilderment. "You act as if you believed in the Stone, yet you talk like an infidel. Are you for or against this Sanctity?"

"That it may decide for itself," Lord Arglay said. "I am no light to my own mind, I promise you. But if what you say is true, and the Stone is a thing of goodness, and has saved this child last night, then we may agree yet."

The Hajji shook his head. "I do not understand," he said almost pitifully. "Why will you always mock?"

"I do not mock," Arglay answered, "or if I do I would have you consider whether this may not be part of your Mystery. But we will not now talk of the place of mockery among the gifts of the King Suleiman, although if he never smiled at himself the Court of the King must have been a very sombre place. I have known other Courts which were so, but they were, often, without any kind of light. Let us talk quietly of this."

He drew from his pocket a small jewel case and laid it on the table, then he released his hand from Chloe's and touched her shoulder as she sat. "Is everything well?" he said.

She looked at him, in a returning serenity. "Everything," she said, "I was afraid."

"Do not be afraid," he said. "Consider that we, if anything at all can be, are in the knowledge of the illuminated Stone."

He opened the case, and his Type lay before them, but in it there was a change. The Stone was glowing with a stronger colour than before; its size was no greater but its depth seemed, as in some great jewel, to be infinitely increased, and in that depth the markings which had seemed like letters arose in a new and richer darkness. It expanded within; and the eyes of those who gazed were drawn down the shapes of the Tetragrammaton into its midst where the intervolutions of cream

and gold mingled themselves in what was more like cloud than
Stone. The Hajji looked and covered his eyes with his hand,
pronouncing in a low voice the formula of the Unity. Lord
Arglay looked and there came' upon his face a half-smile of
such affectionate irony as that with which he had glanced at
Chloe—"this thing," he seemed to say, "cannot be and yet
it is." Chloe looked, and unconsciously put out her hand
towards the Stone, not as if to take hold, but naturally as if it
were on the point of clasping that of some sufficient lover. It
moved forward and then sank and rested on the table close
to the Stone, and Lord Arglay, including it also in his gaze,
wondered suddenly at the kinship between the two. For the
hand and the Stone were to his eyes both softly translucent;
though the shapes were different, the matter of both was the
same, and if the one was to be raised the other was capable of
raising it. He permitted for a moment the fancy that that hand
was but pausing before it lifted up, not the Stone, but the
whole round world, playing with it as a ball upon its palm.
He remembered the Hand thrust out from a cloud in many an
early painting to image the Power behind creation, and the
hand that lay open before him seemed meant to receive that
creation as it came into being. He saw—even while, rightly
wise in his own proper generation among these things, he
refused to believe too easily—that the Stone no longer rested
on the table but that it threw out of itself colour shaped into
the table: the walls and furniture were in themselves reflections
of that Centre in which they secretly existed; they were
separations, forms, and clouded visibilities of its elements, and
he also and other mortals who moved among them. The Stone
quivered with its own intense and hidden life, and through the
unknown hand that appeared close beside it there passed an
answering quiver. Arglay saw it and held his breath for what
might ensue. But nothing more ensued, or nothing that could
be apprehended by his critical mind. The hand which had
been for a moment a mystery of the same nature as the Stone

resolved itself again into the hand of Chloe Burnett. The Stone, parted to his vision again from the world, lay on the table where he had set it. He looked up suddenly and as Chloe also moved their eyes met.

"And still," he said, "even so, you *did* muddle up those quotations."

She smiled across at him. "Am I not forgiven?" she asked.

"No," Lord Arglay said thoughtfully, "no, I do not think you are *forgiven*." He considered the Stone again. "Lay your Type here," he went on, "and let us see if they agree."

She went across the room to her typewriting table, picked up and opened her bag, looked into it, felt in it, looked again, and turned to him with an exclamation. "It isn't here," she cried.

The Hajji looked round with a start of attention; Lord Arglay went swiftly over to her. "Was it there?" he asked.

"Certainly it was," Chloe cried. "I looked at it this morning just before Frank came in."

Arglay turned back towards the table where the Type lay. "Can the two already have become one?" he said. "Are all the Types of the Stone restored?"

Ibrahim joined them, asking, "What is the matter?"

"I had a Stone here," Chloe said, agitation growing in her— "not an hour ago it was here, and now it is gone."

The Hajji gazed, and shook his head. "I do not think they are yet all one," he said, "for no soul has yet made itself a way for the Stone to be what it will in itself. I think it is more likely that you have been robbed of it."

Lord Arglay frowned, but before he could speak Chloe broke out in an exclamation of horror. "O no," she cried, "no," and looked at him with troubled eyes.

"Who has been here since you saw it?" the Hajji asked, and the girl, still staring at Arglay, answered, "It couldn't be," but more in fear than doubt.

"Why, all of us are capable of all misfortunes at all times,"
the Chief Justice answered. "Are you very certain that it was
here?"

"I am quite certain," Chloe answered, "for I . . . I adored it
while you were telephoning."

"And are you certain," Arglay said to Ibrahim, "that the
Types of the Stone are not yet made one?"

"I am not certain," he answered, "who can be certain of the
movement of Justice? But I think that a further devotion is
needed."

Lord Arglay turned back to Chloe, "Well," he said, "there
is no need for us to decide, for there is nothing that we could
do. If it has been taken, let us desire that goodwill may go with
it, and that I will very gladly do."

"But I must go after him," Chloe said, "I must make him
give it back. It is my fault—perhaps I ought to have given it
to him. Only . . . O what have I done?"

"Nothing but what was wise," Arglay said. "Let us forget
it. You and I are here, and also a Type of the Stone. Let it rest
at that, and we are where we were before."

"Not quite," the Hajji said, "for as there is but one End, so
there is now but one Stone with you, and it may be one path
for the Stone. It may be that the path and the Stone and the
End are shown you that they may be one."

Lord Arglay had turned to go to the Type that remained
when he was interrupted by the entrance of the maid with a
telegram. He took it from her, opened and read it, and gave a
low exclamation. Then, "There is no immediate answer," he
said, and as the maid went out he went back to the other
two.

"They have dealt with Reginald," he said. "Your friends
again, I expect, Hajji."

Chloe said, "What has happened to Mr. Montague?"

"They have killed him," Arglay answered, and for once
negligent of an absurdity read the telegram aloud.

The Possessiveness of Mr. Frank Lindsay

"From the Hotel Montespan, Brighton. Gentleman serious-ly injured by burglars and afterwards died here registered as Reginald Montague Rowland Street West gave your name as that of relation burglar unfortunately escaped but no apparent trace of theft would like to confer Gregson manager."

After a moment's silence Arglay said, "I am sorry for Reginald. He was a fool but he wasn't malevolent. . . . And now there is only us—and the others."

"Shall you go to Brighton?" the Hajji asked.

"Certainly I shall go," Lord Arglay said, "for if by chance it was not a thing done to gain the stone then any that he had may still be there. I do not think that I shall find one, but I will take no risks. Besides, as things are, I would not have even Reginald's death quite unnoticed, whatever catastrophe awaits us."

"And this Type that you have?" Ibrahim asked, pointing to it.

"That I will leave here," Lord Arglay said, "and Miss Burnett shall guard it for the few hours that I shall be gone. They will not attack the house of the Chief Justice in full daylight, and if any come to take it in the name of the Law then Miss Burnett shall do what she chooses. And you, Hajji?"

"If this is true," Ibrahim answered, "I will not go back to those who are already shedding blood."

"Then you also shall be here," Lord Arglay said, "and you two shall talk together and see if there is anything to be done. For so far," he added in an unwonted outbreak of anger, "I have done nothing at all. Nothing. I have been only a useless loquacity."

"It isn't true," Chloe said.

"Well—if you can think of anything, excepting trying to bring a laboratory assistant out of yesterday . . ." the Chief Justice answered, still bitterly.

233

"You may have been more than you know," the Hajji put in.

"O I may . . ." Lord Arglay said. "They also serve who only sit about and chat. But after believing in God——"

"Ah but you do!" Chloe cried, "and is that doing nothing?"

Lord Arglay looked at her. "It is giving a new name to old things," he said. "Or perhaps an old name to new things. Don't worry, child. I will go to Brighton, and do you consider the doctrine that is within the Stone."

Chapter Sixteen

THE DISCOVERY OF SIR GILES TUMULTY

The same afternoon while Lord Arglay was hearing at Brighton of the extraordinary events (so the manager called them) of the previous night—how someone, so far untraced, must have got into Mr. Montague's room, and how Mr. Montague's mutilated body had been discovered there in the morning; while he himself was finding that there was no trace of any Type of the Stone among Reginald's belongings— while this separation of a single Type from the rest was proceeding, Lord Birlesmere and Mr. Garterr Browne sat in a room at the Home Office and talked. Lord Birlesmere was agitated; Mr. Garterr Browne was calm and bright.

"Tumulty tells me nothing," the Foreign Secretary was saying. "I tried to get hold of him yesterday, but I couldn't. That fellow Palliser who was with him would only say that he hoped in time to find some way of control."

"It might be awfully useful if he did," Mr. Garterr Browne said, "I see that. But it's going to take time, and I don't think at present either of us can afford the time."

"That's quite true. I don't know what's happened," Birlesmere answered, "but there was an unpleasant note in the Persian man's voice. I've just seen him, and they're more sure of themselves. He even began to hint at Geneva and perhaps something more."

"Well," Mr. Garterr Browne went on, "I think I may say that, as soon as I heard of it, I saw what would have to be done.

One thing, anyhow, I don't know about Persia, but I think it'll quiet things here."

"And what's that?" Birlesmere asked.

Mr. Garterr Browne smiled slyly. "Ask yourself," he said, "why people—this Mayor, for instance—are making such a fuss about the Stone. Why, because they think it *does* things."

"So it does," Lord Birlesmere said.

"Never mind whether it does or not," Garterr Browne said sharply. "The point is that they believe it does. Very well. What do we want to do then? Stop them believing it. How do we do that? Tell them, and show them, that it doesn't."

"But it does," Lord Birlesmere said again.

"The first thing I said to myself," Mr. Garterr Browne went on, "when I realized it, was—people must simply not be allowed to believe in it. The second thing was—thank God it's stone."

Lord Birlesmere sat and stared. Mr. Garterr Browne sat and smiled, then he resumed.

"How can one stop them believing in it? As I've just said— tell them it doesn't work; show them it doesn't work. And if it does, show them something that doesn't."

"Good God!" Lord Birlesmere exclaimed.

"Stone," the other said, still smiling, "isn't rare. Marked stone isn't rare. Of course, to a shade the markings. . . . I don't say that the tints are exactly. . . . But near enough. I got hold of a man, and I went over his place, and I found bits. I've known him rather well for years—he was a contractor for the new Government buildings—and I found a bit of what I wanted."

He pulled out a drawer and extracted something from it which he threw across to Lord Birlesmere. It was a fragment of square stone, having a black streak or two in it. But it was a poor imitation of the Stone of Suleiman, and so Lord Birlesmere, having considered it, felt compelled to say.

"No one would take it for the same thing," he said.

"No one who hasn't got the original is likely to be able to compare," Garterr Browne said. "And who's got it? Sheldrake —well, he must keep his for the present; the Persians—well, if they know we'll keep it quiet they won't want to make a fuss; Tumulty and Palliser—well, they must be careful in their experiments, but they're not likely to act in public; you—that's all right; Arglay—that is a little awkward, but he's a sensible fellow and we'll talk to him. I fancy Merridew's trying to get a bit but I don't think he has yet—and anyhow he'll want it kept quiet; he was here saying so."

"But, good God," Lord Birlesmere said, "people won't believe that these cures and so on didn't happen."

"We shan't ask them to," Garterr Browne explained. "They may *have* happened; they don't happen now. Something has changed—the Stone has been exposed to the air or something. Rays . . . rays might have been exhausted. Tumulty and I'll manage a convincing statement. Just keep it firmly in your mind that people must not be allowed to believe in it."

"But then why worry about having this thing?" Birlesmere asked. "You can tell them all that anyhow."

Mr. Garterr Browne almost winked. "You wait," he said. "That Mayor's coming round here agian, and it'll sound more convincing if I produce this. Besides—I'm not certain, but I *may* decide to get a few scientific opinions on the virtue and age of the thing, a few doctors or something."

"They certainly won't believe that *that* did anything," Lord Birlesmere said.

"Nor very likely did the other," Garterr Browne answered. "Think of the number of people who *don't* believe in it now, and those who don't want to. All we need for public opinion is a focus." He got up in great glee and pointed to the bit of stone. "This is the focus." He made gestures with both hands. "We concentrate," he said, "by a semi-official statement. Now how many people, in face of that, and their neighbours, are going on believing in an obviously absurd Stone? Ask yourself, Birlesmere, would you?"

"If, I'd *seen* it . . ." Lord Birlesmere began.

"Pooh! coincidence," said the other. "Pure coincidence."

"And suppose one of the original Stones gets about somehow?" Birlesmere asked. "How will the Government look then? It's a damned risky business, Browne, and I don't half like it."

"Nor you mayn't," Mr. Garterr Browne, a little huffed, answered. "But you don't like simplicity. Look here—this *is* the Stone, don't you see? It is ; just is. And it doesn't do anything at all. Of course, we shall try and get hold of all the others. Tumulty ought to do that."

"Tumulty won't do anything but what he wants." Birlesmere said. "And I don't like the way the Persians are talking. Suppose it *does* come up at Geneva?"

"Well, give them this," the Home Secretary suggested. "Who's to know? They only want it for a temple or something, I suppose, so this would be just as good. It isn't as if it was a matter of practical importance. And would even they know the difference? Why, I can hardly believe there is any."

"O I think there is," Birlesmere protested. "The marking looks different."

"O the marking, the marking," said Mr. Garterr Browne impatiently. "God's truth, man, what does the marking matter? Here am I faced with a riot or a strike and you with a war, and there you sit bleating about the marking. If you get to rock-bottom, if you come down to actual facts, it is that or this. Which will you have?"

"O this of course," Lord Birlesmere said.

"Do you agree to my telling this Mayor, when he comes in a few minutes, that this is it?" the other pressed again.

"Yes, O yes," Birlesmere assented. "Only you must back me up too with the Persian."

"United we stand, divided we fall," Mr. Garterr Browne

almost sang. "It's quite simple, Birlesmere, so long as you keep firmly in mind that people *must not* be allowed to believe in it. In fact, of course, they don't believe in it; nobody could. So we're only making their real minds clear to them."

"But——" the Foreign Secretary began.

"I know, I know," the other interrupted. "You used it, didn't you? You and Tumulty. Yes, but, my dear fellow, are you sure you did? Looking back now, are you sure it wasn't a kind of illusion? You may know it wasn't because you have the Stone, but will those who haven't it know?"

The telephone rang and he bent to it. "O bring him in," he said. "Now here is the Mayor; now you see."

The Mayor came in heavily. His meeting with Merridew had shaken his determination far more than he had known at the time, for since then he had become gradually aware of how strong, within his public feeling and his desire for the good of the common folk, had been the hope to save that son who lay cancer-stricken at home, and also of what a strong case Merridew might present for the suppression of the Stone. He had supposed good to be single, and it was divided; to be clear, and it was very clouded; to be inevitable, and it was remotely receding. With dull eyes, and a heart almost broken by public and private pain, he faced the Home Secretary.

"I have come to know if you have any news for me," he said.

Mr. Garterr Browne shook a sympathetic head. "I am afraid," he said, "that what I have is, in a sense, worse even than you might fear. In fact, we have discovered that the matter has settled itself." He paused and the Mayor stared at him; then he resumed. "Yes, settled itself. You see," he picked up the stone that lay on the table, "you see apparently this thing changes; at least, I mean a change comes in it. It doesn't *retain* its powers. Lord Birlesmere here will bear me out that we have been very much startled and shocked to find that after a while the qualities of the Stone, the special qualities both of transport and medicine, disappear. It becomes apparently just an ordinary piece of . . . mineral. We are, as I told you, having it investigated, but our advisers report to the worst effect, and I am bound to say that what Lord Birlesmere and I myself have been able to see has confirmed us in accepting that report. It may be that the air has a . . . a modifying effect or that some inherent virtue becomes exhausted—like radium, I mean like radium doesn't if you follow me. It may be that some central ray-diffusing nucleus disperses itself gradually. I couldn't say. But as a result—well, there we are. Nothing happens. I chanced," Mr. Garterr Browne went on suddenly, apparently resolving to do the whole business well, while he was about it—"I happened to have neuralgia early this morning rather badly, and so of course I thought . . . But there it is, my neuralgia didn't stop. I'm very sorry to have to tell you this, for I know what you must be feeling, what indeed I'm feeling myself. But there it is. Truth will out."

With this sudden peroration Mr. Garterr Browne put the stone back on his table and looked at the Mayor. The Mayor, without invitation, sat down suddenly. He stared at the stone which, up to now, he had not seen.

"This is it?" he asked.

"This is it," Mr. Garterr Browne said regretfullly, while Lord Birlesmere inhaled audibly and thought of that earlier moment when Lord Arglay's secretary had made a scene in a Government office on behalf of the Stone of Suleiman. How much quieter things were, he considered, round Browne's stone! If only it could be kept up, and after all there was no reason why it shouldn't be. No one could tell, except by the general growth of peace and quiet, which stone had really better exist. Strong measures perhaps, but difficult times required strong measures.

The Mayor said slowly: "Do your scientific men, your doctors, assure you that this is quite useless?"

"Alas, yes," Mr. Garterr Browne said reluctantly.

"And what of the other Stones?" the Mayor asked. "Have they also become useless?"

"Well, so far as we can test them," the Home Secretary answered, with an air of complete frankness. "There are one or two we haven't got, of course. There's Sir Giles Tumulty's; he's working on it, so no doubt we shall hear."

There was a short silence. Then the Mayor said, "It is certain that this Stone can do nothing?"

"It is perfectly certain," Mr. Garterr Browne answered, tasting the words as if he were enjoying the savour of the truth that they contained, "that this stone can do nothing."

The Mayor stretched out his hand, picked up the stone, looked at it, turned it over in his hand, and then sat for a moment holding it. At this last moment of his hopes, when he realized that, in consequence of this new discovery of the mysterious nature of the stone, he was about to return to Rich disappointed and crushed and compelled to crush and disappoint—at this moment it was impossible for him not to make one last personal effort. It was useless, of course, but if any virtue remained, if, defeated in the State, he could still succeed in the household by some last lingering potency, if he could help his son.—He shaped the wish to himself and put all his agony and desire into it, clutching tightly the useless bit of matter meanwhile, and the two Ministers watched him with rather obvious patience. At last he stirred, put it down, and stood up.

"It seems I can do no more," he said. "I will go back to Rich and tell them that there is no hope."

"A great pity," Lord Birlesmere said, speaking for the first time; and "A very great pity," said Mr. Garterr Browne, adding, both to create a good impression and with an eye to any extremely improbable future eventualities, "Of course, if any fresh change should occur, if (for example) it should be in any way *cyclic*, I pledge you my word to let you know. But I haven't much hope. A most remarkable phenomenon—that it should have reasonably aroused such hope."

"A very common phenomenon—that the dying should hope for life," said the Mayor, and with one abrupt farewell went out.

"And now," Garterr Browne said, leaning across his table towards Birlesmere, "*now* for Tumulty."

The Foreign Secretary in turn leant a little forward, so that to observant eyes, perhaps to Lord Arglay's, the two might have seemed as they bowed towards each other across the office table and the mock stone, like two figures of cherubim bowing over another Ark than that which was in the Temple of Suleiman, and over the false treasures of an illusory world. The light of the Shekinah was hidden, but there was something of a light in Mr. Garterr Browne's eyes as he said, "Birlesmere, now we've got rid of him, now he's been worked, is there any reason why *we* shouldn't have it"—he dropped his voice a little— "and stick to it? You and I and Sheldrake if we must, and Tumulty to experiment? It may be able to do very great things. Life—for all we know; and gold—for all we know; and control."

Lord Birlesmere paled a little, but he also had felt during the last few days a small and strange desire moving in his heart, and he did not dispute with his colleague. He only said, "Can it be done?"

"Let us talk to Tumulty," Mr. Garterr Browne answered and took up the telephone.

It was, however, much later in the evening before Sir Giles could be got hold of. He had that day been again to Wandsworth considering the detestable bed where the living and broken victim of his experiment lay, sustained against all likelihood in a dreadful mortality by the rigorous operation of the Stone. He had then proceeded to a hospital where he proposed to institute a series of experiments to see how far health could be restored or abolished, and to note the effect of the Stone upon the bodies in a state of disease, and he had made arrangements to visit a madhouse on the next day, where among the merely imbecile he hoped to be able to measure the degree of personal will necessary for any working. He was consequently both tired and snappy when the Home Secretary began talking, and shut down on the conversation in a few minutes.

"It's always the same damnable chit-chat," he muttered as he went up to his bedroom and flung his Type on a table by the bed. "Always this infernal control. I'd control *them* fast enough if I could. If I could get past whatever sailor's knot the thing tied itself into the other day when I wanted to try it on that bitch of Arglay's. Can't that hog-headed paroquet of a Secretary have Arglay and her jailed for something or other? I can't get rid of a notion that she's peering over the blasted thing at me. Am I losing my nerve and beginning to see things?" He had sat down, half-undressed, on the side of the bed, and in a sudden outbreak of rage he picked up the Stone again. "Damn you," it was Chloe whom he half-unconsciously apostrophized, "are you tucked away in it as if it was Arglay's bed? I only wish I could get at you."

As he spoke the Stone seemed to open in his hand. He found himself looking into it, down coils of moving and alternated splendour and darkness. Startled, he dropped it on the table, or would have done, but that, as he loosed it, instead of falling, it hung in the air, dilating and deepening. It was no more a mere Stone, it moved before him as a living thing, riven in all its parts by a subdued but increasing light. He sprang up and took a step or two away, nor did it pursue, but he somehow found himself no farther off. He backed, cursing, to the extreme other side of the room, but there once more he found himself close to what had by now become a nucleus of movement which passed outward from it into the very walls and furniture. They, so far as the mind which was now striving to steady itself, could discern, were themselves shifting and curving. He put out his hand to the bed and found himself holding the cord of one of the pictures; he stepped aside, and one foot was on the pillows of the bed and one crashing through the glass of the wardrobe. "The damn thing'll get me down if I'm not careful," he thought, and made a great effort to hold himself firm, and see in its natural shape the room he knew so well. But whether within or without, the awful change went on; it was as if the room itself, and he with it, were being sucked into the convolutions of the Stone. Its darkness and its light were no more merely before him but expanding upwards and downwards till they rose to his head and descended to his feet; he felt himself drawn against all his efforts into some un-naturally curved posture—he knew of pain somewhere but could not keep his mind on it. For before him in arch after arch, as if veil after veil were torn swiftly aside, that which was the Stone was opening its heart to him. His eyes could not properly see, nor his brain understand, what those swift revelations held; he thought once or twice he saw himself, he was sure he caught sight of Lord Arglay moving in some ab-stracted meditation upon some serious concern. And then suddenly he saw her; he say her lying in bed asleep, far off but very clear, and felt himself beginning to be entirely drawn down the long spiral passages through which he gazed. He set, in one last gigantic effort, his whole will against this movement and for a moment seemed to stay it. So clear was the vision that he saw Chloe stir and turn a little in her sleep. In a suddenly renewed rage he felt himself cry out at her, "O go to hell," and as the words, from within or without, reached his mind, Chloe stirred again and woke. He saw her wake; his eyes met hers; he saw them but saw in them no recognition—not of horror or anger or fear; nor indeed of pity or mercy or distress. She looked at him through the distances, and as if unconsciously put a hand beneath her pillow. And as she did so the vision passed and he saw her no more.

For now, and now that sense of pain in his limbs grew stronger, he saw That which had lain beneath her pillow;

within the Stone he saw the Stone. Not in the sense of which the Hajji had spoken or Lord Arglay had talked to Chloe, but for him more agonizingly the way to the Stone lay indeed within the Stone. Its greatness was all about him, yet its smallness lay, glowing gold, at the remote centre. There was something or someone behind and partly above it, and below in a fiery circle of guardianship he saw figures that seemed each to wear it in ring or crown, in swordhilt or sceptre, and then the Stone in the centre changed and was the Stone no more.

For whatever brooded over it had moved, and at the movement the light leaped out at him, and suddenly Giles Tumulty began to scream. For at once the light and with it the pain passed through him, dividing nerve from nerve, sinew from sinew, bone from bone. Everywhere the sharp torment caught him, and still, struggling and twisting, he was dragged down the curving spirals nearer to the illumination into which he was already plunged. And he remembered—now suddenly he remembered how he had seen in a vision what was to be. He had willed to be in the future, and since that could not be, for the future as yet had lain only in the Mind to which it equally with the past was present, the Stone had revealed the future to him. He remembered; he knew what was to happen, for the merciful oblivion was withdrawn; he saw himself gathered, a living soul, into the centre of the Stone. That which he had been to men, that by which he had chosen to deal with others, by that he was to be dealt with in his turn. The wheeling and looming forms of giant powers amid whom he was drawn turned on him their terrible and curious eyes; under the gaze of everlasting dominations he was exposed in a final and utter helplessness. He was conscious also of a myriad other Giles Tumultys, of childhood and boyhood and youth and age, all that he had ever been, and all of them were screaming as that relentless and dividing light plunged into them and held them. He was doing, it seemed, innumerable things at once, all the things that he had ever done, and yet the whole time he was not doing, he was slipping, slipping down, and under and over him the Glory shone, and sometimes it withdrew a little and then pierced him again with new agony. And now he was whirling round and round, having no hold above or footing below, but being lost in an infinite depth. Above him the light was full of eyes, curious and pitiless, watching him as he had often watched others, and a subtle murmur, as of some distant words of comment or of subdued laughter came to him. From the spirals of time and place he felt himself falling, and still he fell and fell.

When they found him, but a few moments after that raucous scream had terrified the household, he was lying on the floor amid the shattered furniture twisted in every limb, and pierced and burnt all over as if by innumerable needle-points of fire.

Chapter Seventeen

THE JUDGEMENT OF LORD ARGLAY

Twenty-four hours after his theft, Frank Lindsay had begun to realize that the emotions which accompany possession are sometimes as hard to deal with as the difficulties which precede possession. Before he had had the Stone in his pocket he had seen quite clearly what he would do; he would divide it, keep one part, and pass the other on to Mr. Merridew in return for a fee. That two identical Stones would result from the division he had not understood, only that each part of a divided Stone possessed the virtues of the whole. But he found that such a proceeding was by no means easy. His irritation with Chloe had prepared the way for his desire of success in his examination, winged by the promised fee, to pass into action; but when action was for the moment over, he found the second step more difficult than the first. He had been squeezed by circumstances and a narrow chance into the first act, but time opened before him for the second, and he could not move. He continually found himself staring at the Stone; he continually fingered his pocket-knife, and even took it out and opened it. But he could not put the edge to its work.

For one thing the Stone itself surprised him. He had not understood from Chloe—and for a good reason, since at that time she had not made herself a path for the Will of the Stone, and the Light within it had not expanded in proportion—that it was so strange, so active, and even so terrible an object. He was—he had to admit—frightened of touching it; he felt as if it would bleed at a cut and pour out its life before him. He hesitated even to touch it; it looked sometimes as if it would burn him if he lifted it. On the other hand, he could not bring himself to part entirely in his mind from Chloe by passing it on to Mr. Merridew in its completeness. He thought of ringing Carnegie up and refrained; vaguely it seemed to him that Chloe might, she *might*, be willing to lend him one of them if he didn't. After all, she might take another view of his needs even now, even if she found out; but he realized that if she found out that it had passed to Merridew, his own days would be short in her land. And at that he began to realize that he was very near finding Chloe indispensable to him, or (as he called it) loving her. He didn't want her to leave him, and while he had the Stone (he thought hopefully, in the manner of lovers of the sort) he could bribe, or lure, or bully her into nearness. The idea had occurred to him in the night, and he took it with him to the offices where he worked, and his own small room.

The only difficulty in the way of re-establishing relations with Chloe while retaining the Stone was the explanation of how he had got it. He hardly saw himself saying to her, "I have stolen this from you, and I want to use it. But if you are very nice to me I will not give it to anyone else, though I might make a hundred or two by doing so. I will, that is, buy you with a hundred pounds and the preservation in my own hands of your property." The nearest he got to saying that even to himself was to recollect that she had occasionally, in times of financial stress, jested, half-mockingly, half-grimly, on the amount for which she would sell herself. But he realized that anyone who offered five pounds, or indeed five pence, would stand a better chance than he himself coming with such a bargain. Besides, of course, he didn't want her to sell herself; he wanted her to love him—in exchange for his loss of a hundred pounds and his promise only to use the Stone for his own purposes.

It was at that moment she arrived, following up an office-boy, who just had time to say, "Miss Burnett to see you," before he was dazzled out of the way by her smile as she passed.

The smile vanished as she shut the door behind her; she turned on the wretched, goggling, and gasping Frank a face which he had never seen before. Chloe laughing, Chloe irritable, Chloe impatient, Chloe affectionate, Chloe attentive, Chloe provocative, these and many another he had known—but this, this was hardly Chloe. It was not that she looked angry or harsh; there was rather in her face a largeness of comprehension, a softness of generosity and lovely haste to meet any approach, which bewildered him.

"Dear Frank," she said, tenderly, "how silly of you!"

Frank went on goggling. She added simply, "I couldn't come yesterday because Lord Arglay was away till very late, and I didn't like to leave it while he had told me to stop. Not that it mattered. So I had to come here." She smiled at him. "Darling," she added, "you were rather rash, weren't you? and a little rude?"

Frank's mind tried vainly to understand. He was being accused—it must in the circumstances surely be an accusation? what could she do except ask, or appeal, or accuse? Only this didn't sound like any of the three; it was more like sympathy. But if he were being accused, it was of a breach of manners and not of morals, which put him at a disadvantage, since the second can be defended on the grounds of some better, or at least different, morality, but the first is a matter of taste and defence is only communicable by emotion. Of her emotions at the moment he was altogether ignorant.

"Rude?" he said, "rude? What do you mean—rude?"

"Well . . ." Chloe sketched a gesture. "You might have asked me again first if you needed it so much."

Whether this subtlety was from the Stone or from her own feminine mind was hidden at the place where the Stone and her mind were finding their union. The only answer of which Frank was capable was criticism in turn.

"I did ask you," he said, "and you wouldn't . . . But anyhow, I don't know . . ."

He could not finish. Her swift and luminous eyes prevented him, passing in front of him with what shone in them, as they turned his excuses and denials aside, like a new and overwhelming mastery and knowledge. She came lightly to him and paused.

"Will you give it back to me?" she said simply and stretched out her hand.

In the stress of the moment he almost did. They had, they had been friends, great friends. They had had good times together; she had mocked and teased and helped and liked him; their hands and their mouths, their voices and their glances, were familiar. All but the sovereign union had been theirs, and if, for Chloe, that sovereign union had by now been made with other worlds, and if its image and instrument in this world lay between her and her other friend and master, yet of these things Frank was ignorant. And since assuredly that full and sovereign union permits no exclusion of any beauty, since the august virtue of its nature is to receive into itself all which partakes of its own divine benignity, since there—and there alone—is neither one nor many, neither lesser nor greater, but all is perfect and free, since even in its reflections upon earth the marvellous liberty of the children of God is to be experienced by all who devoutly and passionately desire, then even at that single moment Frank Lindsay might have entered into its sweetness and strength could he have met her as she came, and answered her in such a voice as that in which she asked. But such a voice can carry no selfish complaint, no wrangling excuse; it is a sound which, native to heaven, can on earth be vocal and audible only between spirits already disposed to heaven. So disposed, for all of clumsiness or roughness or anger or haste or folly that needed still to be cleared and enlightened, she stood and faced him. So indisposed, for all of industry and care and thought and study, he stood and looked away.

"Give what back?" he mumbled.

She sighed a little, and a faint shadow came upon her. She

dropped her hand and said gravely, "Will you give me back the Stone that you have taken?"

Between denial and excuse he hesitated; then, abandoning both, he began, "Chloe, I don't think you quite understand——"

"Need I understand more?" she asked.

"It's like this——" he began again, and again she checked him.

"There is no need," she said, and then more swiftly, "Frank, dear Frank, will you do this?"

He made another effort, letting go the pretence of ignorance. "Are *you* asking me to?" he said. "I mean, do *you* want it?"

"No," she said, and ceased.

"But if you don't want it, then why . . . I mean, mightn't it as well be here—or even——" He was a little disappointed by her negative, and yet uncertain of the wisdom of introducing Merridew.

"It does not matter much where it is, I think," she said, and again affection broke into her voice as she said, "I'm not asking for it. I'm asking you."

"You're asking me for it," he said intelligently.

"No," she answered again. "I am asking you to restore it, if you will, before——"

"Before?" he asked, really startled. Surely Arglay, surely she, couldn't be thinking of the police! Curiously enough, he had never thought of the police until now. But she wouldn't, she couldn't, not with him! And Arglay couldn't be such a cad.

"Before"—for the first time she faltered—"I don't know; perhaps before it is restored. But that doesn't matter; only I can't wait. Lord Arglay is expecting me; he let me come because he knew I wanted to, but I can't wait. Frank, if you have liked what we have had, you and I, will you give me back the Stone?"

"It isn't that I wouldn't—soon," Frank answered.

"Will you now?" she asked.

"I think we ought to talk it over a little," he said defensively. "I think you ought to try and get my point of view. I think I——"

She moved away and walked, a little sadly, to the door. There she paused and looked back. "Thank you for everything you have done for me," she said. "They were good times. Good-bye, darling."

He began to stammer some further explanation, but she was gone, and he stood alone with an emptiness and an uncertain fear invading his heart. In his haste, when she had entered, he had flung his morning paper over the Stone, which had been lying on the table, and now he moved that away, and again looked at the thing which he had denied her. He thought uncertainly of the examination, and unpleasantly of Mr. Merridew; of course, if she really wanted——It was a long while before, still disturbed, but still following the way he had begun to tread, he rang up Carnegie at the Union offices. Nor even then had he ventured to divide the Stone; he would talk to them first.

Carnegie, a cheque in his pocket, and the General Secretary's urgent instructions in his mind, arrived as quickly as possible, and as quickly as possible cut short Frank's talk, and procured the exhibition of the Stone. He agreed to every condition Frank made about having it returned—or a part of it—for the examination, passed over the cheque, picked up a spare envelope, slipped the Stone into it, put it down for a moment on the table again, and slapped Frank on the shoulder.

"Good man!" he said. "Merridew will be frightfully bucked, and you may find he can be useful to you yet. He will if he can after this. Well, I must get back at once. On the twenty-third you want it then?"

He grinned cheerfully at Frank, moved to pick up the packet, and looked vaguely at the table. "Where——" he began, picked up an empty envelope, the only one in sight, and said with some sharpness, "Where the devil is it?"

They both looked, they separated and sorted papers, they searched table and floor, they looked inside the envelope a dozen times, and still the Stone was undiscoverable.

"What's the idea?" Carnegie asked. "Is this a joke?"

"Don't talk rubbish," Frank answered sharply. "Did you put it in your pocket?"

It seemed not, though the cheque had remained in Frank's. Carnegie searched, threatened, expostulated; Frank, maddened by an implied accusation of a theft of money, snapped, and later raged. They searched and quarrelled; they hunted and denounced. And for all their effort and anger and perplexity, the Stone of the King was not to be found.

But while Frank had, after her departure, still been standing, dimly puzzled and unhappy, Chloe had been on her way back to Lancaster Gate, back to the Hajji and Lord Arglay and the Unity in the Stone. All the previous afternoon she had watched it, or—to the best of her power—prayed, or meditated, or talked or listened to that foreign doctor of the mysteries. The realization of the theft of her Type had caused that which remained to seem very precious to her; the thought of the attempt in her room and of the death of Reginald Montague had brought the sense of necessary action very close, but she did not yet see what that action was to be. The Hajji had talked as if but one stage had been reached; she had made an opportunity, he implied, for the Stone, and the Indwelling of the Stone, to operate in the external world, but there it could at best only heal and destroy and its place was not there. He would not formulate for her what more remained, and she reposed now on the hope, the more than hope, that Lord Arglay and the Stone would direct her. Her unhappiness about Frank lay rather round than in her; she saw it as a sadness rather than felt it as a sorrow, for within she was withdrawn to an intention of obedience and a purpose not yet unveiled.

She got out at the Tube station, smiled at the newspaper man, picked up an agitated old lady's umbrella, threw a glance over the Park and came after a short walk to the house. When she opened the study door she was at first unobserved, for Lord Arglay was standing with his back to the door listening to the Mayor of Rich. At least, she supposed it must be the Mayor, from what he was saying, and from Oliver Doncaster's presence a few paces distant. The Hajji was sitting close by. The Stone, infinitely precious, glowed upon the table. On another smaller table were her typewriter, her notebooks, one pile of ordered manuscript which was the first few chapters of *Organic Law*, and another pile of papers which were the notes and schemes and drafts and quotations and references for the remainder. She closed the door softly behind her and for a minute or so stood and gazed.

Her gaze took in, it seemed, the symbols and instruments of her life, but they were real things and she felt with increasing happiness that what was there had, however hidden, run through her life. The muddled, distressed, amusing thing that her life had been resolved itself into four things in that room— the manuscript, and Oliver Doncaster, and Lord Arglay, and the Stone. Whatever was coming, it was good, and she was fortunate that her work had entered into the Chief Justice's attempt to formulate once more by the intellect the actions of men; she was fortunate to have had even so small a part in the august labour. Whatever was coming, it was good that all her transitory loves should touch with so pleasant a glance as Oliver Doncaster's her renewed entrance. She remembered how she had thought of his hair, and with a secret smile she assented—not in desire but in a happy amusement. "The dear!" she thought, caught his eyes, saw the admiration in them, preened herself on it for a moment's joy, and looked on. Of the Hajji and the Mayor she felt little; they knew and did things, but they answered to no need or capacity within her except as teachers or clients. And of Lord Arglay and of the Stone she could not think, only she hoped that, whatever happened, neither of them would be lost to her for ever.

She took off her hat and coat, went and put them on her chair, and came softly back. The Mayor saw her and stopped. Lord Arglay questioned her with his eyes; she shook her head. He nodded, and considered; then he said:

"It seems then, as the Hajji said yesterday, that there remains but this Type. And three of us are agreed that there is but one End. But the Hajji declares that there is but one Path also."

"And what is that?" Chloe asked.

"It is through the Restoration of the Stone," the Hajji said, but before he could add anything Lord Arglay went on, "Only the Mayor here believes that there is another Path, for having heard"—his little finger indicated Oliver—"that we preserve the Stone he has come here to ask me to use it for all sorts of good things."

"But I thought," Chloe said, "that the Government——"

Lord Arglay allowed himself to smile. "The Government," he said, "have found that the Stone has unfortunately exhausted its powers."

"What!" Chloe exclaimed.

The Hajji got up. "It is the most horrible blasphemy," he said.

"Why, that may be so," Lord Arglay said, "though I can very well believe that the stone they have produced is an exact presentation of the feeling between Birlesmere and Garterr Browne. So that even in such a blasphemy the Justice of things is maintained."

"But exhausted——?" Chloe asked, staring at the marvel which from its place directed the movements of her heart.

"O la la!" Lord Arglay answered, "let us forget their tricks." He too looked at the Stone, and added, almost as if speaking to it, "But what can you expect, with such an Executive?" Then he went on, "So the Mayor has come to us, and he would have us do what we may with the Stone to cure all the broken and diseased men in his city."

He paused, but Chloe only waited for him to proceed as (he thought) she had so often done while he dictated the sentences of *Organic Law*. He went on.

"And here therefore we are," he said, "wondering what path to follow. For the Mayor and the Hajji disagree, and Mr. Doncaster and I have no clear idea, and though doubtless the Stone knows very well it does not give us much help. What do you think?"

She shook her head, and as she did so the Mayor broke once more into his plea for those whom he sought to serve. But after a while he stopped.

Lord Arglay said, "All this is true and dreadful enough. But even yet I am not clear what should be done."

"If you are afraid to act——" the Mayor cried out.

"No," Lord Arglay said, "I do not think I am afraid."

"Then divide the Stone," the Mayor exclaimed, "and let me have a part, and do what you will with the other."

The Hajji made a movement, but Lord Arglay checked him with a hand, and said, "No, that I will not do; for I am still the Chief Justice—though I cannot think I shall be so for very long—and it is not in my judgement to commit any violence upon the Stone."

"Then for God's sake say what you will do," the Mayor cried out in pain, "and put an end to it all."

Lord Arglay stood for a minute in silence, then he began to speak, slowly and as if he gave judgement from his seat in the Court.

"I think there are few among my predecessors," he said, "who have had such a matter to decide, and that not by the laws of England or Persia or any mortal code. But God forbid that when even such a matter is set before us we should not speak what we may. For if this is a matter of claimants then even those very terrible opposites shall abide the judgement of the Court to which chance, or it may be something more than chance, has brought them, as it was said in one of the myths of our race that a god was content to submit to the word of the Roman law. But it is not in our habit to wash our hands of these things, whatever god or people come before us. Also this is a question, it seems, between God and the people. It is a very dreadful thing to refuse health to the sick—but it is more tragic still to loose upon earth that which does not belong to the earth, or if it does only upon its own conditions and after its own mode. Therefore I would not compel the Stone to act or ask any grace from it that it did not naturally give. And it is clear to us at least since last night that this thing belongs only to itself. So that I say that it is necessary first that it may be offered again to itself, but whether or how that may be done I do not yet know. For of all of us here one has sworn an oath and will keep it, and one claims the Stone for his purposes, and two are unlearned in its way. And therefore there is but one Path for the Stone, and since she has made herself that we will determine the matter so."

He looked at Chloe, and his voice changed. "Are you to be the Path for the Stone?" he said.

"That is as you will have me," Chloe answered.

"Are you to be?" he asked, with a tender irony. "Will you sit on the throne of Suleiman, and of all those who have possessed the Stone, kings and law-givers, Nimrod and Augustus and Muhammed and Charlemagne, will you only restore it to its place?"

Chloe flushed, and looked at him in distress. "Am I being silly?" she asked. "I do not compare, I was only asking what you wanted me to do."

"Be at peace," he answered, "for no man has yet measured his own work, and it may be you shall do more than all these. They laboured in their office, and you shall work in yours. But why will you have me tell you what to do?"

"Because you said that the Stone was between us," she answered, "and if that is so how otherwise can I move in the Stone?"

"And if I tell you to do it?" he asked.

"Then I will do what I may," Chloe said.

"And if I tell you not to do it?" he asked again.

"Then I will wait till you will have it done," she said, "for without you I cannot go even by myself."

He looked at her in silence for a while, and as they stood there came through the open window the shouting of the newspaper boys. "More Rioting at Rich," they called, "Official Statement." "The Stone a Hoax." "Rumours of War in the East." "Rumours of War . . . rumours of war."

Lord Arglay listened and looked. Then, "Well," he said, "whether I believe I do not know and what I believe I most certainly do not know. But it is either that or this. And since this is in your mind I also will be with your mind and I will take upon me what you desire. So, if there is indeed a path for the Stone, in the name of God let us offer it that path, and let whatever Will moves justly in these things fulfil itself through us if that is its desire." He lifted up the Stone, kept it for a moment raised upon his hand in the full view of all of them, and held it a little out towards Chloe. "Go on, child," he said.

With the words there came to her the memory of her other experience in that room, when in dream or vision she had heard some such voice command her and struggled desperately to obey. There was no struggle or desperation in her movement or consciousness now as, so summoned, she went forward and paused in front of him, holding out her joined hands below his. He lowered his own gently till it lay in the cup of hers, and said in a voice shaken beyond his wont, "Do you know what you must do?"

She looked at him with a docile content. "I have nothing at all to do," she said, and the Hajji cried suddenly aloud, "Blessed for ever be the Resignation of the elect."

"Under the Protection," Lord Arglay said, with the smile he had for her, and, as she answered, in a voice that only he could hear, "Under the Protection," he leaned his hand very gently so that, as if almost of its own motion, the Stone rolled over into hers. She received it, moving a step or two backward till she stood a little apart from them. The Hajji broke into the Protestation of the Unity—"There is no God but God and Muhammed is the Prophet of God."

The Mayor had turned half aside and had sat down, but he looked back now at the figures before him. Oliver Doncaster gazed with the ardent worship of young love at Chloe, but he also was in the rear. Upright, attentive, providential, Lord Arglay maintained his place, and stood nearest to her of all who watched.

She turned her eyes from his at last, downwards upon the Stone. It lay there, growing every moment more dark and more bright within itself; it seemed larger than it had been, but they could not properly judge because of the movement within it. Chloe looked at it, and suddenly there came into her mind the memory of Frank Lindsay. "Poor darling," she felt with a renewed rush of pity and affection, "he didn't, he couldn't, understand." In her own understanding she offered his failure and his mischief to That which she held, and with him also (moved by a large impulse which she endured without initiating, but with which she gladly united herself) all those who for any purpose of good or evil had laid their hands or fixed their desires upon the Stone. Vague in image, but intense in appeal, her heart gathered all—from herself to Giles Tumulty—in a sudden presentation of them to the Mystery with which they had trafficked.

Opposite her the eyes of Christopher Arglay had been watching it also. But as, in the passion of her intercession, she raised her hands and bent her head as if to carry the Stone into her breast and brood above it there, his gaze slid along those arms to her form, and took in not only that but the open window and the sky beyond.

He looked out, and in the sky itself there was a change. There was movement between him and the heavens; the

chimneys and clouds and sky took on the appearance of the
Stone. He was looking into it, and the world was there, continents and cities, seas and their ships. The Stone was not these,
yet these were the Stone—only there was movement within
and beyond them, and from a point infinitely far a continual
vibration mingled itself with the myriad actions of men. And
then, in the foreground of that vastidity, he saw rising the
Types of the Stone, here and again there appearing and
through all those mingled colours rushing swiftly together.
Loosed from their cells and solitudes upon earth, living suddenly in conjoining motion, closing within themselves the
separation which men had worked on them, those images
grew into each other and were again made one. For a moment
he saw the Unity of the Stone at a great distance within the
Stone which was the world, and then the farther Mystery was
lost in the nearer. Colour and darkness were a great background for her where she stood; they concentrated themselves
upon her; through her they poured into the Stone upon her
hands, and behind her again appeared but the sky and the
houses of a London street.

The Hajji's voice called: "Blessed be the Merciful, the Compassionate! blessed!" and he got to his knees, immediately
afterwards prostrating himself towards the window, the East,
and Mecca. Moved by the action and by some memory of
churches and childhood, Oliver also knelt down; so that of all
those in the room only the figure of Lord Arglay remained
still upright and vigilant before her as the great change went
on.

The strength of the appeal within her faded; it had achieved
itself and she was hastened to what remained in her will. She
became conscious of the movement of her hands and her head,
and stayed them, for they seemed to suggest, however slightly,
a removal and possession of the Stone. Her hands went a little
from her, the Stone exposed upon them; they lifted a little
also, and her head was raised and thrown back. But still her

eyes were upon it, and her will abolished itself before its own. Where before she had prayed "Do or do not," now she did not even pray. Her thought and her feeling passed out of her knowledge; she was the Path and there was process within her, and that was enough.

It was not given to her—or to most of the others—to see the operation by which that Mystery returned to its place. For the Hajji's eyes were hidden, and the Mayor still brooded over the needs of men and was but half-attentive, and Oliver Doncaster's look was for Chloe rather than the Stone. Only the justice of Lord Arglay, in the justice of the Stone which lay between himself and the woman he watched, beheld the manifestation of that exalted Return. He had seen the Types come together and pass through her form, colouring but never confusing it, till they had entered entirely into the Type upon her hands. But scarcely had the last vestige of entwined light and dark grown into the One which remained, scarcely had he seen her in herself standing again obedient and passive, than he saw suddenly that the great process was reversing itself. As all had flowed in, so now all began to flow out, out from the Stone, out into the hands that held it, out along the arms and into the body and shape of which they were part. Through the clothes that veiled it he saw that body receiving the likeness of the Stone. Translucency entered it, and through and in the limbs the darkness which was the Tetragrammaton moved and hid and revealed. He saw the Mystery upon her hands melting into them; it was flowing away, gently but very surely; it lessened in size and intensity as he watched. And as there it grew less, so more and more exquisitely and finally it took its place within her—what the Stone had been she now was. Along that path, offered it by one soul alone, it passed on its predestined way—one single soul and yet one not solitary. For even as she was changed into its nature her eyes shone on her mortal master with an unchanged love and in the Glory that revealed itself there was nothing alien to their habitual and reciprocal joy. The Stone that had been before them was one with the Stone in which they had been; from either side its virtue proclaimed itself in her. At last the awful change was done. She stood before him; her hands, still outstretched, were empty, but within her and about her light as of a lovely and clearer day grew and expanded. No violent outbreak or dazzling splendour was there; a perfection of existence flowed from her and passed outward so that he seemed both to stand in it and to look on it with his natural eyes. With such eyes he saw also, black upon her forehead, as if the night corresponding to that new day dwelled there for a while apart, the letters of the Tetragrammaton. She stood, so withdrawn, as the Stone sank slowly through her whole presented nature to its place in the order of the universe, and that mysterious visibility of the First Matter of creation returned to the invisibility from which it had been summoned to dwell in the crown of Suleiman the King. As in the height of his glory the Vicegerent of the Merciful One had sat, terrific and compulsive over spirits and men, and the Stone had manifested above him, so now from the hands stretched to grasp it and the minds plotting to use it, from armies and conspiracies, greed and rapine, it withdrew through a secluded heart. She stood, and the light faded and the darkness vanished; she stood, one moment clothed in the beauty of the End of Desire, and then swiftly abandoned. She was before him, the hands stretched not to hold but to clasp, the eyes wide with an infinite departure; she exclaimed and swayed where she stood, and Lord Arglay, leaping to her as she fell, caught a senseless body in his arms.

Chapter Eighteen

THE PROCESS OF ORGANIC LAW

Cecilia Sheldrake was always, everybody said, extra-ordinarily kind to her husband, which may have been why he committed suicide some ten years after the vanishing of the Stone. No one quite believed, and very few people understood, what her hints to her intimate, and indeed her less intimate, friends exactly meant; that she and he had possessed some marvellous thing by which anyone could go anywhere, and that, having nearly lost it once in a motor-car, he had shortly afterwards entirely lost it in her drawing-room. She never reproached him, or not after the first year or two, and even then never with the virulence of the first week. They had, people gathered, been looking together at whatever it was—nobody remembered and nobody cared to remember, and then he had mislaid it. At least, for the first year or two he had mislaid it, and after then nobody ever understood quite what he had done with it—sat on it or swallowed it or sold or secreted it, according as it seemed to the hearer most like an egg, a bon-bon, a curiosity, or a jewel. But somehow he had got rid of it, and Cecilia's life was ruined. As, very justly, it actually was—first, by the discontent which she perpetually nursed, and secondly, by the drastic financial rearrangements which followed on her husband's suicide.

Mr. Garterr Browne, being unmarried, and having definitely himself preserved the Type which he had had, found himself in the difficult position of having nobody but himself to blame. His position therefore was so far worse than Mr. Sheldrake's, and it was for a few months made worse still by his having at odd times to deal with the doctors and scientists whom he had summoned to report on his own substitute for the Stone. Fresh reports kept arriving for quite a long time from scientific men of whom he had never heard, but who (with an indecently unselfish ardour) kept on taking an interest in the remarkable cures at Rich and their relation to the wretched fragment which Mr. Garterr Browne had handed on to his earlier advisers and they had passed to their friends who were interested. Exactly how it was that he and Lord Birlesmere could never afterwards be persuaded to take the same view on any question, not even the Prime Minister, whose Government was twice wrecked, ever properly understood.

Between those two politicians, between Sheldrake and his wife, between Carnegie and Frank Lindsay, there lay continually suspicion, anger, and hatred. Negligent of them and their desires, the Mystery had left them to their desires, and with those companions they lived. For it was not in the nature of the Stone to be forgotten, and even in her village Mrs. Ferguson entertained her friends with the tale of her recovery rather from an unappreciated love of it than because she was as talkative as she seemed.

The Persian Embassy fell silent; Professor Palliser fell silent. Only one event caused a common flicker of satisfaction to rise in the hearts of the professor, the millionaire, the thwarted General Secretary (who never understood what the trouble had been about), and the politicians. That event was the sudden resignation of his office by Lord Arglay.

For in the house at Lancaster Gate Chloe Burnett lay, uncomprehending and semi-paralysed, for a long nine months of silence. On the same day when at Wandsworth the unhappy wreckage of a man passed into death, and his bed lay empty, the wreckage of his saviour was carried to a bed in the Chief Justice's house. Her mouth was silent, her eyes were blank, and that whole side of her which was not for ever still shook every now and then with uncontrollable tremors. The doctors stated that it was a seizure, a verdict on which only once did

Lord Arglay permit himself to say that, whatever it was, it was precisely not that. All the rest of the time he maintained a silence—his secretary had been taken ill while at work, and since apparently she had no relations and no friends with a better claim, and since he felt that it was probably his fault for overworking her, and since the house was large, it was better that she should remain. This was the general interpretation which Lord Arglay allowed to arise. "For if," he said to the Hajji before the latter returned to Persia, "if we profess that this is the End of Desire, fewer people than ever will want to experience it."

"Her spirit is in the Resignation," the Hajji said.

"Quite," Lord Arglay answered. "So, you may have seen by this morning's paper, is mine. As entirely, but in another sphere."

"Did you not hold," the Hajji asked, "that your office was also of the Stone?"

"I have believed it," Lord Arglay answered, "but for one thing I will not now make that office a personal quarrel between these men and myself, though I think that otherwise even the Government would find it difficult to turn me out. But the Law is greater than the servants of the Law, and shall I make the Law a privy garden for my own pride? Also since this child has come to such an end I will have none but myself, so far as is possible, be her servant for the rest of her time."

"I do not understand your mind," Ibrahim said. "Have you known and seen these things and yet you do not believe in the Stone?"

"Who said I did not believe?" Lord Arglay asked. "I believe that certain things have emerged from illusion, and one of them I have resigned for its sake and the other I will watch for hers."

"You are a strange man," the Hajji said. "Farewell then, for I suppose you will never be in Persia."

"Do not despise us too much," Lord Arglay said. "It is our

habit here to mock at what we love and contemn what we desire, and that habit has given us poets and lawgivers and saints. Good-bye, Hajji."

"The Mercy of the Compassionate be with you," the Hajji said.

"And even in that, for a reason, I will believe," Lord Arglay answered, and so they parted.

To Frank Lindsay Arglay sent a short note, saying nothing of the Stone but only that Miss Burnett had suffered from—he paused and with a wry smile wrote—a seizure, that she remained at Lancaster Gate, and that he would at all times be very happy to see Mr. Lindsay there. Frank however did not come. For a number of days he intended to answer the note, but he could think of nothing to say that seemed adequate. If Chloe wanted to see him, he argued, she would send a special message; it was not his business to intrude. So safeguarding himself from that intrusion he safeguarded himself also from any, and all that he might have known of the conclusion of the Mystery was hidden from him. He passed however a not unsuccessful life in his profession, and the only intruder he found himself unable to cope with was death.

But every few days through months Oliver Doncaster called and saw Chloe and talked a little with Lord Arglay, and it was to him only that Arglay on a certain day sent a note which read:

"MY DEAR DONCASTER,

"Chloe died yesterday evening. The cremation will be on Thursday. If you could call here about eleven we might go together.

"Yours,

"ARGLAY."

There had been no change and no warning of that conclusion. Whatever process had been working in her body, since the day when her inner being had been caught with the Stone into the Unity, closed quietly and suddenly. The purgation of her flesh accomplished itself, and it was by apparent chance that Arglay was with her when it ceased. He had paused by the bedside before going to his own room next to hers for the night. As he looked he saw one of those recurrent tremors shake her, but this time it was not confined to one side but swept over the whole body. From head to foot a vibration passed through her; she sighed deeply, and murmured something indistinguishable. So, on the moment, she died.

Arglay saw it and knew it for the end. He made no immediate move until he touched with his fingers the place where the epiphany of the Tetragrammaton had appeared. "Earth to earth," he said, "but perhaps also justice to justice and the Stone to the Stone." His hand covered her forehead. "Under the Protection," he murmured. "Good-bye, child," and so, his work at an end, left her.

In the car, as they returned from the crematorium, Oliver Doncaster said to him, almost bitterly, "Was it a wise thing to tell her to do it?"

"Why, who can tell?" Lord Arglay answered. "But she sought for wisdom, and what otherwise should such spirits as hers do upon earth?"

"She might have had love and happiness," the young man said, "and others too. There was always a light about her."

"Why, so it seemed," Lord Arglay said, and after a moment's pause, looking out of the window of the car, he went on. "But who can tell how that light came to be? It is but a few weeks since I gave sentence upon a man before me who had murdered through some sudden jealousy the girl he was to marry. And when, as is the ritual, I asked him if he had anything to say, he cried out that though I might hang him justly, for he confessed his crime, yet that there was a Justice against which he had sinned which was greater than I and had already purged him. And though I have never made it my habit to do as

267

some of my brethren do, offering their own moral opinions
and the ethical and social rules of their own world, and con-
demning the guilty by such verbiage as well as by the law, I
answered him that this also might be possible and that such a
Justice might already be fulfilled in him. But if indeed there
be any such sovereign Justice, may not this child have found
a greater thing than either you or I could give her? Could she
do more, while she was upon the stepping stones, than smile
at the water that ran by her?"

"Must the water always run by?" Oliver said.

"It is its nature, as it was hers to pass over it," Lord Arglay
answered. "And it may be that she has come into the light
that was about her and the God in whom we determined to
believe."

At Lancaster Gate he bade Doncaster farewell, came again
into his study, and stood still to look round it. His charge
was at an end, and for all he could tell there were still before
him years of life. Something must be done, and instinctively
he looked at the MS. of the *Survey of Organic Law* which had
laid so long neglected, then he walked over and picked it up.
The type-written sheets bore in places his own alterations and
in places hers. There were sheets of annotations she had typed
and sheets of references in her writing. Lord Arglay looked at
them, and for a moment it seemed to him an offensive thing
that another handwriting should be mixed with theirs. Yet
after a moment he smiled: to accept such a ruling would indeed be to go against the whole nature of the Stone and the
work they had done together. For here was this lesser work,
and if it were worth doing—as it might be—and if without
someone to supply necessary detail it would probably not be
done—was not this also as much in the nature of organic law
as the operation of the Stone? . . .

"Besides," Lord Arglay said aloud, "in a year's time, child,
I should be finding an excuse. I think I will not find an excuse.
The way to the Stone is in the Stone, and I will choose to do

this thing rather than to leave it undone or to be driven back to it by the weariness of time."

He walked across to the telephone, looked at it distastefully, and turned the pages of the directory.

With his hand on the receiver, "Also," he said, "though the King wrote Ecclesiastes, yet the Courts gave judgement in Jerusalem. This, I suppose, is Ecclesiastes. . . . Paddington 814. . . . Is that the Lancaster Typewriting Agency?"